BEYOND THE UTMOST BOUND

A YOUNG MAN'S ADVENTURE IN SEARCH OF FREEDOM

JOSEPH CLINTON

Cup O' Joe
Press

Published in the United States by Cup O' Joe Press.

Cover: Laura Duffy Design
Cover Image: Kasa_s/Shutterstock

First Edition

ISBN: 978-1-7337113-1-9

"Version 1"

This is a work of fiction. Names, characters, places, and incidents either are the
product of the author's imagination or are used fictitiously. Any resemblance to
actual persons, living or dead, events, or locales is entirely coincidental.

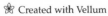 Created with Vellum

For Beth & Bodie

"...if your heart and your brain aren't connected, aren't working together harmoniously,... you're just hopping through life on one leg."
  -Tom Robbins

"All man's miseries derive from not being able to sit quietly in a room alone."
  -Blaise Pascal

"The intuitive mind is a sacred gift, and the rational mind is a faithful servant. We have created a society that honors the servant and has forgotten the gift."
  -attributed to Albert Einstein

CHAPTER ONE

September 2001

I heard silence speak.

It came from my grandmother as she sat on the couch in absolute, stunned disbelief. Her lips never moved. Her eyes never blinked. No sound. No motion. Yet anger, confusion, and sorrow all spoke with loud, clear voices. Somehow movement existed in her stillness.

As she rubbed the back of my neck with a cold, wet cloth, I was able to catch a few of the images that had so captivated her on the television, but before I could make sense of them, my lungs called for more help. I put the towel back over my head, wrapped it around the vaporizer, and took another hit of Vicks VapoRub and steam.

My mother had been out all night and hadn't come home. Again. She had inadvertently taken my special asthma inhaler with her, and she wasn't answering her phone. The occasional hits of steam were the only thing keeping my lungs open. I was sweating. I was dizzy. I heard every short, muted breath. They were getting shorter.

The universe was screaming at civilization that something was wrong. I heard that too, yet didn't know what it meant. And didn't care. I couldn't breathe. Civilization wasn't the only one who was dying.

Fortunately for me, my grandma rushed me to the emergency room in time. A shot in the butt, a blast from an inhaler, and my lungs magically reopened.

An oxygen mask covered my mouth and nose as my head lay on my grandma's lap. She caressed my hair with her soft, gentle hands. We stared into each other's eyes for a long while. I flashed her the peace sign. She flashed it back.

I slipped further into another realm, a peaceful trance brought on by exhaustion, dehydration, and a lack of self-consciousness. How beautiful. How free. All the answers sitting in front of me like a daisy waiting to be picked. That was the first time I passed through the door into the void and touched that wonderful, magical place. How simple and easy the trip seemed. I didn't know it then, but my life's journey was to become a search for a way back.

I looked at my grandmother as she sat next to me in this sea of energy. She seemed happy and at peace. I faded off to sleep.

I was six.

CHAPTER TWO

Eight Days Later

I peered out the backseat window of my mom's green Honda Civic as we drove through the Texas countryside. My suitcase sat next to me. Smoke from her Virginia Slims filled the car.

"Can I roll down the window, please?" I asked from the back seat.

"I have the air conditioning on. Let's not be wasteful," she said.

Wasteful of what, I thought. *Her smoke?* I got the feeling she didn't like me much. She wasn't mean. Just not loving. Not like my grandma. I was an inconvenience, and we both knew it.

"Where are we going?" I asked.

"To visit with your grandfather."

"I have a grandfather?"

"Yes."

"I don't know him," I said.

"Neither do I."

My grandmother had met him at a dance hall in San Antonio when she was young. He was a much older man. They danced all night, got drunk, did the deed, and along came my mom. My grandmother took full responsibility. It was her mistake. She let it happen. She would raise the child on her own. When my mother was a little older and started asking questions, my grandmother decided maybe her decision had been wrong. Her daughter had the right to know her father. And the father had a right to know he had a daughter. Unfortunately, it was too late. Grandma didn't know where to look for him. She remembered he was tall, handsome, had a great laugh, flew planes in World War II, and called himself Joseph. But that was it.

Then, about a year ago, while she was reading a story in *Texas Monthly* about Native Americans who had served and fought in the military, he resurfaced. A photo of Sergeant First Class Joseph Tewanima standing next to his fighter plane. There was no mistaking that grin. The article said he was one of the first Hopi Indians to fly and train during World War II. He talked about piloting what he described as "the flying coffins." How flawed the technology was. How the engines cut out for no apparent reason. How often they crashed because of mechanical failure. How he feared his machine more than the enemy. How many times he'd been to the hospital. How lucky he was to be alive.

The article said he had settled in the Texas Hill Country, a few hours away. When my grandmother shared this information with my mother, my mother didn't seem to care. She had enough issues and didn't need another. She had made the same mistake, and history had repeated itself. She met a man at a bar, got drunk, did the deed, and along came me. She didn't even get the guy's name. He was gone when she woke up the next morning in a cheap motel room.

She didn't want to give me up for adoption, yet wasn't ready to be a mom, either.

So, for the most part, she wasn't. Grandma was.

As I fiddled with one of the many holes in the back seat I asked, "Where's Grandma?"

"I told you. Visiting friends. She won't be back for a while," my mother said.

4

"What friends?' I asked.

She lit another Virginia Slim and turned up the radio. "Spinning Wheel" by Blood, Sweat, and Tears blared from the speakers as we cruised through the Texas Hill Country.

> *"Someone is waiting, just for you*
> *Spinnin' wheel is spinnin' true*
> *Drop all your troubles by the riverside*
> *Catch a painted pony*
> *on the spinning wheel ride."*

As it turned out, my grandfather's place was by a riverside. I soon found out I was the troubles.

I had not seen a house for miles, only rolling brown land that looked like toast, a few clusters of trees, and the occasional cow. The car slowed, and we turned onto a dirt road. My mother hit the brakes and jumped out to check the number on the faded mailbox.

"Where are we?" I asked.

She didn't reply.

"I don't see a house. Maybe he moved. Maybe he doesn't live here anymore," I said.

Again. No reply.

"Why don't you call him?" I asked.

"He doesn't have a phone," she said.

We drove up and over a large hill, and from the right side of the car, a house appeared down below. It sat in the shade among large oak trees. It was simple. A large porch protruded from the front and was host to a few chairs and a porch swing. To its left was a barn, a garden, and a small lake with a dock sitting in the middle of it. As we got closer, I saw water flowing in the river nearby. The area around the house was green and lush. It seemed to be alive, unlike the land we had driven through for the past hour.

She stopped the car in front of the house, put out her cigaret^{..} and looked over the front seat to me in the back. "Grab yo^{..}

case and go sit on the porch while I talk to your grandfather," she said.

As we walked to the porch, music eased out of the screen of the front door. Before my mother could knock, a voice from inside said, "Can I help you?"

As my mom began to talk, the voice invited us inside. I didn't budge. I sat on the steps of the porch with my back to both of them and stared at the dirt on the ground. I wanted my grandmother. I didn't want any part of this.

"It's probably best if he stays here while we talk," she said to the voice on the other side of the screen. As he opened the door to let her in, a black-and-white mutt ran out and plopped down next to my suitcase. "His name is Bodhi," the voice said as my mom disappeared inside.

Bodhi and I sat speechless next to one another for the next hour as my grandfather discovered for the first time he was not only a father but a grandfather, and how my mom was hoping to get a job in Dallas and start a new life. Surely, he could help and watch me for a few days.

I picked my head up and looked over to Bodhi. He picked his head up and put it on my suitcase. I saw in his eyes he wanted to be my friend. He saw in mine I wasn't ready. The front door finally opened. "Tag. Say hello to your grandfather," said my mom. I looked up, and my heart skipped a beat. Above me stood this tall old man with high cheekbones, big nose, dark skin, and long white hair. He was an injun. I'd seen them on TV and in old Western movies I had watched with my grandma. They scalped men and killed women and children. This was who I was going to stay with? I was paralyzed. I couldn't speak. He must have sensed my fear, because he slowly raised his right hand and in a soft yet serious voice said, "Hau."

Several moments of silence passed before his seriousness turned into uncontrollable laughter. He tried to stop but every time he looked at my shocked expression he let out another high-pitched giggle. Each giggle led to another and another. This went on for a while longer as my mom, Bodhi, and I watched this

Indian man crack himself up. He must not be a real Indian, I thought. Real Indians don't laugh. I was more than confused.

He knelt down to my level, looked deep into my eyes as though searching for something, and said, "Ah, yes. Pahana."

It was strange. His eyes smiled at mine.

He stood up. My mom apologized for the inconvenience. She bent over and kissed me on the forehead. "I love you, honey. I'll be back in a few days," she said as tears ran down her cheeks.

I knew she wouldn't.

"Be a good boy," she said as she walked away.

A few minutes later, her car vanished over the hill.

She was free.

CHAPTER THREE

The next morning, I woke up in a strange bed in a strange room. I got up and walked through the house. No one was home — not even Bodhi, who had slept at the foot of my bed. I went outside and stood on the porch and looked around. The Indian was sitting on the square dock in the middle of the lake, facing the other direction and wasn't moving.

I looked back at the dirt road heading up over the hill and stared at it for a long time, hoping if I looked long enough my grandma would appear in her car, racing to pick me up and take me back home. Despite my best efforts, the car didn't show.

I walked over to the edge of the lake and sat down next to Bodhi on a large rock. We both watched the Indian man with curiosity. What was he doing? How did he get over there? There was no boat. I guess he swam. But why? Why not sit over here? After about twenty minutes and no movement from the Indian or Bodhi, I got tired and went back inside.

I had not spoken to the Indian yet. He had asked me a few questions, but I'd kept silent. He didn't push it. "When you're ready," he would say.

For the next week, I'd get up in the morning, stare at the road, then sit next to Bodhi, and watch this strange man on the dock. Each day I tried to stay longer. It became a game. I wanted to see him move before I got tired or bored and went back inside. I never won.

On the fourth day, I started to feel alone. So, that morning, as Bodhi and I watched the sitting Indian, I put my hand on Bodhi's head and rubbed it. He picked his head up and put it on my thigh. I now had a friend.

During the day the Indian would write, read books, listen to music, paint, work in the garden, fish the river, run barefoot in the hills, or go inside the barn and work on a motor of some sort. I watched him closely. He seemed at peace with whatever he was doing. He melded into the scenery of which he was a part. At times, I swore he disappeared. He would occasionally say something strange to me while never taking his eyes off the task at hand. "Pahana. Still not talking? Good. Talking interferes with listening, and listening is the key to knowing."

He didn't talk like an Indian either. In fact, he didn't have any accent at all. My fear of being scalped or killed lessened as the days passed. Yet I still wasn't talking. I guess I was mad. Mad at my mom for dropping me here. Mad at my grandmother for not coming to get me.

After a week of silence, as I sat with Bodhi by the lake, something in me changed. I'm not sure what it was. Maybe boredom. I got up, jumped into the water, and swam over to the dock. I swam around it to see what the Indian was looking at, but his eyes were closed. I knew he could hear me, yet he didn't move a muscle. I climbed the ladder on the side of the dock and sat down a few feet in front of him. His eyes never opened. I didn't say a word. Neither did he. I sat as he did with my legs crossed and watched him. Except for the sound of his breath, I could have sworn he was dead. Several more minutes passed.

I couldn't take it anymore. "What are you doing?" I asked.

"Quieting the mind," he said.

"Is it loud in there?

"It used to be."

"How did you get it to stop?"

"By being present."

"What's that mean?

"Close your eyes."

I closed my eyes.

"What do you hear?" he asked.

I listened for a second. "Nothing."

"Can you hear my voice?" he asked.

"Yes," I replied.

"Now, listen closely. What else?"

"I just heard a bird chirp."

"Yes. And what else?"

"I can hear frogs."

"What else?"

"Something in the water splashed. Maybe a fish."

"Yes, very good. Open your eyes," he said as his eyes remained closed. "Did you know about the frogs, the fish, the birds until now?"

"No," I said.

"You've been out here every morning. They knew you were here. But you didn't know they were here?"

"I don't know," I said. *How did he know I had been watching him? His back was to me the whole time.*

"Why don't you know?" he asked.

I didn't have an answer and offered a shrug of the shoulders as a reply.

"Because you were not here," he said.

Hadn't he said I was here? "Yes. I was," I protested as I pointed to the spot on the rock as if he could see it. "I sat right next to Bodhi. Right over there."

"Your body was here. But you were elsewhere."

"Where?" I asked.

"Here," he said as he placed his long finger on my forehead. "In your mind." His eyes remained closed. "Thinking about other things," he said.

"I don't remember," I said.

"Perhaps, thinking about this strange man who sits on the

dock. Why your mom dropped you here. When are you going home? That you miss your grandmother."

How did he know my thoughts? This Indian could read minds.

"So, even though you were not speaking, your mind was. And speaking interferes with listening and listening is…"

"…the key to knowing," I said.

"Yes, Pahana," he said and let out a laugh. "Yes. It is the key to knowing."

"Why do you keep calling me that?" I asked.

"It's your spirit name."

"What does it mean?" I asked.

"Lost white brother."

"I don't like it. I want another."

"You don't get to choose your spirit name. It chooses you."

"It's like a nickname?" I asked.

"Yes."

He hadn't opened his eyes, yet it felt like he could still see me through his closed eyelids. I looked around, and the lake was calm and smooth, like a soft sheet of glass surrounding us. The old Indian was sitting in front of me, though it was as if he were something else. He could have melted into the dock, water, sky, or trees. They all seemed to be one thing. *How does he do that?*

Silence once again fell over us, but I still had some things on my mind. "My mom is never coming back," I said.

"Give her time."

"Can you take me to my grandma? I want to see her."

He said nothing.

"She went to see friends. She should be back by now."

His eyes slowly opened.

CHAPTER FOUR

The pot's whistle lost its voice as the Indian man took it from the heat. He was chopping, mixing, stirring, and then he turned with two mugs of homemade brew in his hands.

"What is it?" I asked.

"Special tea. It's for your asthma."

I pulled my inhaler from my front pants pocket and showed it to him. "I've got this," I said.

"With fresh air, exercise, and this," he held up one of the cups, "you won't need that," he said pointing to my inhaler. He handed me the cup. "*Hasta al fondo*," he continued and clicked my cup with his.

"What does that mean?" I asked.

"It's Spanish. It means 'to the bottom,'" he said and took a swig from his mug.

"You speak Spanish?" I asked.

"I speak many languages. To the bottom," he said again as he took another sip.

"*Al fondo*," I said and took my first sip. It was sweet with a hint of garden plant and dirt. As we continued sipping our tea, he proceeded to teach me how to say hello and goodbye in Spanish, Italian, French, Mandarin, and Shoshonian—the language of his native people.

"How do you know all that?" I asked.

"Our tribe spoke Shoshonian and English. My grandfather taught me Spanish.

Italian, Mandarin, and French I learned on my travels. Did your grandmother ever speak to you in French?"

"*Un peu* (a little)," I said.

"Did you know she was born in France?" he asked.

"No."

"Do you know where France is?"

"No."

"We have a lot of learning to do, Pahana," he said.

"Where is your TV?" I asked.

"Over there," he said as he pointed to a wall containing what seemed like 10,000 books. "Put your shoes on. We're going for a walk."

Bodhi and I followed him out the front door, around the lake, and along the river. He stopped a few times to show me fish swimming in shallow pools. We crossed the river and followed a trail up a small mountain. The sun was getting low in the sky and Bodhi and I were getting tired, or at least I was getting tired. As we slowed, the Indian started running and I lost sight of him.

I stopped and took a look around. Other than Bodhi, I was alone. *Where is the Indian? He left me out here to die. I know it.* My heart started to race. I thought about going back, but Bodhi ran ahead. Now, I was truly alone. Before I could think, I ran as fast as I could in Bodhi's direction. As I rounded another corner, I saw the Indian sitting on a large rock with Bodhi next to him.

I walked up and stood behind them with my hands on my hips, a move I had learned from my mother when she was mad at me.

"You don't want to sit?" he said, never turning around to look at me.

"Why did you leave me out there all alone?"

"You weren't alone."

"Yes, I was," I said.

"Were there no trees? No leaves? No bushes? No cactus? No

rocks? No birds? No groundhogs? No rabbits? No insects?" he asked.

As I stared at the ground, I could hear the sounds of different birds chirping, and the rustling of bushes from an unseen animal nearby. I looked over to a set of rocks close to my feet as a lizard sat on top posing for the sun.

"Maybe," I said, still staring at the ground.

"We're never alone. Ever. We always have the sun, the moon, the air. Always something with us. If you can learn to live in what most people call loneliness and still be at peace, now that is a true gift." He turned to look at me. "So, you were not alone. Just afraid. And fear is life's biggest obstacle. Facing it, watching it, learning about it, understanding it, is life's gold."

He turned back to look at the sun as it was beginning its escape from our side of the planet. I joined him and Bodhi on the warm smooth rock but sat a few feet away.

"What is the sun doing?" he asked.

I picked my head up and looked to the horizon as the large orange oval began its disappearing act.

"It's moving," I said.

"It only looks like it's moving when in truth, we're moving, and it is still. We call that an illusion. When something is different than it appears."

We sat for a while and said nothing as the light disappeared and was replaced by a bright moon and a billion stars. I'd never seen so many in my life. As I looked up in awe, the Indian pointed to the sky and said, "Konkachila made all of this. And this," he said as he pointed to the land. "And us," he continued.

"Konkach…" I couldn't say the name.

"Konkachila," he repeated.

"Who is that?"

"He is the creator. The grandfather."

"The grandfather of who?" I asked.

"Of everything."

I peeked over at him.

"Are you sure?"

"Yes, Pahana. How else can we be connected to every other thing in the universe?"

I looked up. "Am I connected to the stars?"

"You're made of stars. And the stars are made of you. You're the same."

"No, I'm not."

"You're both made from the same stuff," he said.

"Really?"

"Nitrogen, calcium, iron, carbon, are all in your body. They are also in every star."

As I was pondering that piece of information, a shooting star streaked across the sky and disappeared. "Whoa," I said. "What happened to it? Where did it go?"

"It's an old star that has burned out. Some say it has died. But only its physical form has disappeared. Its spirit is very much alive. We just can't see it with our eyes."

"It's different than it appears," I said.

"Yes."

"It's an illusion," I said.

"Yes, Pahana. It's an illusion."

We sat silent for a few more minutes in the warmth and humidity listening to the sounds of crickets and the other night-time noises of the Texas Hill Country. I looked over and caught the side of his chiseled face as he was lost in the stars. He looked like he was in a trance, like he somehow was silently communicating with the sky, and it with him.

"Konka," I said.

"Konkachila." He corrected me without taking his eyes off the sky.

"It means grandfather?" I asked.

"Yes."

"And you're my grandfather?"

"Yes."

"Then, you're Konka. It's your new nickname."

He turned from the stars and looked at me. "I don't like it," he said.

I didn't turn away. "You don't get to choose your nickname. It chooses you."

He let out a long belly laugh and then another. And another. After his laughing fit had subsided, he asked, "Do you know where your grandmother is?"

I pulled in my legs that had been dangling on the rock and wrapped my arms around them as I sat in a little ball. I noticed my left shoelace was in a knot so I started to pick and pull at it.

"We don't need to talk about this if you don't want," he said.

"My mom said she went to see friends, but I don't think that's true," I finally said.

"Why is that?"

As I continued to work on my shoelace I said, "Before we came here, people started bringing a lot of food and flowers over to our house. Every time someone came to the door, my mom told me to go to my room. When they left, I would look out my window and watch them walk away. I didn't know everyone, but I knew a lot of them. And those were my grandma's friends. So, why would they come over and bring stuff if she was visiting them?"

"So, where do you think she is?"

"I don't know," I said as I freed the lace from its knot. "But the day after she didn't come home from the doctor, I had a dream she was walking toward me through a field of bluebonnets."

I looked at the two shoelaces in my hand and began to tie them just like my grandma had taught me. I could hear her voice in my head. *You take one caterpillar and lay it over the other caterpillar and curl it over and back through the cave and then stretch out both caterpillars.* I took one lace and laid it over the other, turned it back under and through and pulled on the ends.

"She was wearing her favorite yellow dress as she walked through thousands of purple flowers on each side of her. I wanted to run to her but I couldn't."

Then the caterpillar on the left makes a loop and turns into a butterfly wing. I made a loop with the lace on the left.

"No matter how much I tried, my legs wouldn't move. When

16

she reached me, she bent down, gave me a hug and said, 'I'll always be with you.' I couldn't speak."

The other caterpillar goes over and around the butterfly wing and back through the cave. I made a loop around the other lace and began to pull it through. "She got up and walked away until I couldn't see her anymore."

As you push the caterpillar through, it turns into another butterfly wing. I pushed the lace through and made another loop. *Tug on both wings and the butterfly is complete.* I pulled on both loops to tighten. I gazed at the perfect butterfly sitting on the top of my shoe wanting to fly away though it couldn't. "She's not coming back, is she?"

"Pahana. There are two worlds. There is this world we live in, and there is a spirit world. All of us spend some time in this world, and when that journey is over, we go to the spirit world."

"Like the shooting star?"

"Yes, like the shooting star."

"Grandma went to the spirit world, didn't she?"

"Yes."

I looked up from the butterfly on my shoe and into the darkness ahead. "Did she die?"

"Her body did."

"Where did it go?"

"It's with the earth."

"Why is it with the earth?"

"She didn't need it anymore."

I looked back at my shoelaces. "Just like a caterpillar."

"Yes, Pahana. Just like a caterpillar."

"So, I can never see her again?"

"Of course you can. Whenever you want."

I looked at him. "I want to see her now."

"Then look."

I looked at the ground, then straight ahead, then up to the sky to the right, then the left. She wasn't there.

"Your eyes won't help you."

"How am I supposed to see her?" I asked.

He put his finger on my chest. "With your heart."

"My heart can't see."

"Of course it can."

I took a deep breath and pushed my chest out and waited for a clue. It never came. "I think mine is blind," I said.

"It can also hear. It can smell. Touch. Taste. Laugh. Cry. Sing. It can do many things."

"How?" I asked.

"By keeping it open."

"How do you keep it open?"

"Never close it," he said.

We sat for a few more minutes as I envisioned my pumping heart with a set of eyes, ears, and nose. Like a Mr. Potato Head singing, laughing, and crying. The sound of a coyote howling in the distance brought me back to the present.

"Tell me about her," he said.

I let go of my legs and they slid down and again dangled against the coolness of the rock. I looked over to Bodhi, who had moved closer and whose eyes seemed to be watching me. My eyes finally settled to their safe place, the ground. "She smiled a lot. Every time I looked at her, she smiled at me. It made me feel good. My mom didn't smile much, but Grandma did. She was always happy and nice. Even other people said that. She laughed a lot too. Sort of like you. Not quite as loud though. We would lie on the floor, and I would put my head on her stomach and she'd laugh, and it would make me laugh. She read me stories every night. We made cookies together."

"What kind?"

"Mostly chocolate chip. Sometimes peanut butter. We ate them right out of the oven with a glass of cold milk. We played cards. And checkers. We would draw and paint sometimes. She'd let me paint on myself and it was okay. She never got mad. We made forts out of pillows and threw blankets over the kitchen table, and she would let me sleep underneath. On Halloween, we made tie-dye T-shirts and dressed like hippies. Anytime I felt bad she'd always bring me a Big Red soda."

My legs folded back up into me on their own as I again wrapped up into a tiny ball. I reached down and began to play with my butterfly shoelace. "I love her. I miss her. She smells like flowers." Tears began to pour down my cheeks.

On one side, Bodhi moved over and nuzzled next to my thigh. On the other, Konka put his large hand on the back of my neck and shoulders and held me. For the next hour, I was wrapped up safe between Konka, Bodhi, and a billion stars.

I had a new family.

CHAPTER FIVE

Eleven Years Later

Beads of sweat ran down the side of my Shiner Bock as I sat
alone in the empty Scooter's Bar and Grill. The ninety-two-
degree heat outside coupled with the lack of air conditioning
inside made drinking a beer in several quick gulps a necessity. I
was on my second.

It was a tick before noon on Tuesday. My final high school
physics exam was moments away from starting. I wouldn't make
it. Nor had I made my final English literature exam a few hours
earlier.

The grill part of Scooter's didn't exist. Neither did Scooter.
Eddie had taken over the place more than a decade ago from
someone named Stretch, who had dreamed of turning this old
copper mill into a restaurant. He never got around to building the
kitchen. No one can agree on why he named it Scooter's. He had,
however, made this beautiful old wooden bar. Eddie added the
jukebox, the pool table, shuffleboard, a few old tables with chairs,
a small stage inside, a larger one outside, and old Ernest. I imagined at some point Ernest had strutted his one-ton black body and

huge horns through the Texas hillside. Sadly, now the once-proud bull was nothing more than a large ornament above the main door. Of course, I'm not certain that Ernest was actually proud, but I'm sure he hadn't had this in mind as his final resting place. At least he wasn't alone. He had friends. Charlie, a ten-point buck —his mug hung on the back wall. Swifty, an eight-foot rattlesnake, protected the jukebox. Ike, a bobcat, relaxed near the men's room. And Lucy, the hawk, in permanent attack mode, hung above the Texas state flag to the left of the bar.

This was my second home. Eddie had hired me to work for him when I was twelve. My grandfather's place was about a mile up the road. In the summer, other than reading books, playing games, and discussing the world with my grandfather, there was nothing much to do. So, I would ride my bike down and hang around like one of the many stray dogs. I guess Eddie realized I wasn't going to leave, so he figured he might as well put me to work. Maybe he was repaying my grandfather for not charging him to rewire the joint correctly. Supposedly, before Eddie took over, it wasn't an uncommon occurrence to receive a few jolts depending on where you leaned.

I'd spent most of my summer months and days after school doing whatever Eddie needed, which was mostly sweeping, cleaning, and stocking. On weekends and nights when bands played, I became the bar-back. When I turned fifteen, I bartended and became the taxi for anyone who couldn't make it home. Eddie didn't care how much you drank or how shitty you got, just as long as you didn't start fights or drive. If there were any questions about your sobriety, Eddie would make you walk the line. You couldn't miss it. A thick white line painted on the wood floor ran for twenty feet directly down the room. If you failed, you had to sit and wait for a ride home from the taxi: me. If you drove home anyway, you couldn't drink at Scooter's for three months. No exceptions.

The best part of the evening came around closing time when Eddie would line up the usual suspects, cue up Johnny Cash's "Walk the Line" on the jukebox, and let the festivities begin. It became the town sport. How messed up can I get and still walk the line? However, you got one shot at it. If you stumbled, he took your keys.

Leaving the bar unattended in the middle of the afternoon wasn't unusual. If Eddie had to go somewhere, he'd put a sign on the bar that read, "Happy Hour Beer $2 Whiskey $3 Help yourself. Leave money in shoebox. Be back shortly."

Eddie never worried about people stealing from him. People here didn't do that sort of thing. They had their issues, but honesty and integrity weren't them. It was the type of place where you never locked your door, and you could leave your keys in the ignition of your truck.

Sisterdale, Texas was a ghost of a town amongst others about fifty miles northwest of San Antonio. It consisted of the bar, a general store that was no longer in service, a handful of dogs, a few roosters, and sixty-three residents. At least, that's what the census claimed back in the early seventies. The actual number, by all accounts, was closer to twenty, though the number could swell to a few hundred on weekends when Eddie booked live music.

It was more of a pit stop than an actual town. A place for tourists heading to the more famous Lukenbach to the north; antique shoppers making their way to Boerne, just south; or oil-field workers passing through to take a leak and grab a drink.

Nicolaus Zink and his German followers, known as frei-denkers or free thinkers, founded the area in the mid-1800s. These were German intellectuals who advocated reason and democracy over religious and political authoritarianism. The plan was to make the town and surrounding area into a free-thinking society. Days were to be spent farming, and the evenings were for discussing and nourishing intellectual matters.

Old Zink's dream didn't survive. Other than my grandfather, there wasn't a lot of free thinking going on in Sisterdale. One only had to read the bumper stickers on the array of trucks out front on any given weekend night to prove the point. "Eat, Sleep, Fish. There's nothin' else." "Keep honking. I'm reloading." "If I wanted to hear from an asshole I'd fart." And "Hate Fags, Love Bush" were some of the more popular.

Zink should rest comfortably, though, knowing on almost any given evening at Scooter's, thoughts and opinions were shared openly on about any subject possible; the economy, the wars, our Kenyan Muslim socialist president. Does peeing on a jellyfish sting ease the pain? Do plants die of old age? Why do old men go bald yet get hairy nostrils? Would a metal plate in someone's head make it stick to magnets? Can a turtle breathe out of his ass? Plenty of philosophizing was still going on.

I took another gulp of my Shiner Bock when the front door opened and the mayor of Sisterdale sauntered through. It was high noon. Every day, 365 days a year, the mayor would walk through the door at exactly 12 p.m. You could set your watch by it. The mayor didn't say a word or acknowledge my existence, but instead strolled behind the bar, put two dollars in the shoebox, grabbed a Lone Star beer and opened it. He made his way back to my side of the bar sitting two stools to the left and sat silent for about a minute, staring at his beer. He took one large gulp, let out a sigh, belched, and said, "Afternoon, Tag."

"Afternoon, Lefty," I said.

"Where's Eddie?" he asked.

"Haven't seen him."

"Reckon he went to town?"

"Could be," I said.

Lefty wasn't actually the mayor. Sisterdale didn't have elected officials. Eddie had given him the title because Lefty knew everyone in the county. He was a fixture here in the hill country. Lefty had been forced to retire from the oil field two decades previous when an accident on the drilling-rig floor took his left arm and a small chunk of his brain. His cowboy hat hid the head injury, but the missing limb was an open conversation piece for any new patron. And Lefty was more than happy to talk about it. For the mayor's contribution to the town, Eddie gave him his own bar stool and a framed eight-by-ten glossy that hung up behind the bar next to the patron saint of Texas, Willie Nelson.

"Graduation this weekend?" Lefty asked.

"Saturday night," I replied.

"One of the craziest nights of my life," he said, then paused to think about it. "Mary Sue Hawkins," he shouted as he slipped into his other world.

The mayor loved to talk, although on occasion he would pause in the middle of a sentence and wouldn't finish his thought until a later date. The pause could last a minute, an hour, or a few days. But he would always pick up right where he had left off.

"Well, Ernest," I said, looking up into the bull's glass eyes. "I'm going to miss you. Hopefully, my fate has a better outcome."

"Southern Comfort. Bacon grease. Handcuffs and coyotes," continued Lefty.

"I thought you didn't graduate high school?" I asked.

"Hell no! But I partied like I did."

"Coyotes?" I asked.

"They chased my naked body through the brush until I jumped into Sisterdale Creek!"

"Why were coyotes chasing you?" I asked.

"They smelled the bacon grease."

"Why didn't you drop it?"

"I wasn't carrying it. I was wearing it!"

Before I could ask the two obvious questions, Ellie Shane walked through the front door, stopped, and gave me the stare. Now, the stare in itself would've been enough of a hint, but the radiant, reddish energy emanating from her depths and dancing around her noggin like lava made it official. Ellie wasn't here with a message of merriment.

"Afternoon, Ellie," said Lefty.

"Mayor," she replied, not taking her eyes off of me.

"Don't you have school today?" I said.

"Very cute," she replied.

"Yes, you are," I said.

"Why didn't you tell me?"

"I didn't want a debate," I said.

"Why not? You're so good at it."

"I might have lost this one," I said.

"So you admit what you're doing is wrong."

"No. What I'm doing is right," I said.

"Blowing off your two final exams, purposely getting F's, dropping your grade point. You're manipulating the results, the system. Explain to me how that's right."

"It's not an election, Ellie. It's high school. A high school that uses standardized testing to rank intellect. However, it doesn't test for social, emotional, linguistic, logical, kinesthetic, spatial, inter-, or intra-personal intellect. And what about morality or the ability to think critically? They only measure how much crap you can remember. So, I can remember a lot of crap. That in itself doesn't make me the smartest person in our class."

"The only word that made any sense out of all of that was crap. Because that's the only thing coming out of your face right now," she said.

Though he never looked up from his beer, a smile crept onto Lefty's face.

"I told you I'd lose this debate," I said.

"So you just gave Marcy Smitworth the keys to valedictorian."

"She wanted it. She needed it. It means everything to her," I said.

"But she doesn't deserve it. Not like this."

"Yes, she does. She worked hard for it. A lot harder than I did."

And truth be told, she did. Marcy did nothing but study. She obsessed over being first to the point of her hair falling out. She wanted to please her parents. She would make them proud. Besides, Marcy was genuine. She was nice. One of the few people who didn't treat me like an outcast, even though I was the one person standing between her and her dream. Plus, things in school came to me easy, too easy, sometimes almost magically. Answers would pop in my head from who-knows-where. It didn't seem like a fair fight. So, I did my part. Besides, she was doing me a favor. I didn't want to give the valedictorian speech. My high school experience wasn't one I'd wish on any person. A public forum, a microphone, an audience—I didn't trust myself. It would be better for all involved to hear Marcy's "be all you can be" speech.

"I know you've been going through a lot. I know how difficult these past few months have been. But why are you keeping things from me?" Ellie asked.

"You're right, El. I should have told you."

"Is this going to hurt your scholarship?" she asked.

"It'll all work out."

"What are not you telling me?" Ellie asked.

She knew I was hiding something from her. I'd been for a while. Telling her last minute, while not being fair, I decided, was still best. She would know soon enough.

"I don't understand," I said.

"Seriously? You? You don't understand?"

"No. I don't understand."

"You don't understand?" she said louder.

"No, Ellie. I don't understand."

"You ain't tellin' me somethin'," she said. Anytime she slipped into Texas-speak meant only one thing. She was officially pissed. "What is it?" she continued.

"Looks like I'll be the salutatorian," I said.

"Salute this," she said as her upturned middle finger on her right hand sprung to life.

She turned around and walked under Ernest and out of the bar. Lefty sat silent, took a long draw from his Lone Star, and said, "I reckon you understood that."

"Reckon I did," I said.

CHAPTER SIX

I met Ellie Shane in biology class my junior year. We became lab partners not by choice but through attrition. We were the two left standing after everyone else joined up and our biology teacher, Mr. Penthearst, pointed at us and said, "You two, together."

Ellie played the flute in the band and wore braces, thick glasses, a pimple or two, and tomboy clothing. Other than a few bandmates, she didn't have many friends, which was still more than I enjoyed.

My problems with classmates started early. My grandfather was not only my grandfather, but became my father, mother, and best friend. So, I grew my hair long like his. In small-town Texas, I stood out. This was cowboy boots, hats, and gun country. Short hair was the norm. I was a hippie. A girl. I lived with the crazy Indian man. We were poor. At least that's what the other kids told me on a regular basis. Having a different shade of skin didn't help matters. Making good grades made it worse. I was teased and picked on. I ignored most of it and kept to myself.

In high school, things got worse. The summer before my freshman year, a distant cousin named Ray visited us for a few days. It was one of the few summers Ray spent outside the Department of Texas Correctional Institution. Ray had a lot of different philosophies on life. Of course, they seemed to change with each new incarceration. On hearing of my voyage into the high school ranks in a few weeks' time, Ray offered this chunk of wisdom. "Hit 'em as hard as you can right between the eyes."

"Hit who?" I asked.

"The first cocksucker that messes with you," he said.

"Why is someone going to mess with me?"

"Because you're a freshman."

"I'm not worried about…"

"Between the eyes," he shouted. "Don't think. Just bam. Before they know what hit 'em," he said as he slammed his right fist into his open left hand to show me the proper force at which to execute the punch. Ray was looking into my eyes from a few inches away when he said with delight, "If you do, no one will mess with you again. I promise you that."

"And if I don't?" I said.

"You want to be someone's bitch?"

I wasn't a hundred percent sure what he was talking about, yet I was fairly confident being someone's bitch wasn't the high school experience most fourteen-year-olds were looking for.

Ray was a thief and a con man but understood survival. And as it turned out, he could also see the future. Less than two weeks into my high school career, Donny Coledge, a senior football player, snatched James Joyce's *Ulysses* from my hand. Donny, a starter on the defensive line, was a big boy. He had at least six inches and more than a hundred pounds over me. Not someone you pick a fight with unless you were stupid or crazy.

As he stood next to my locker holding stately, plump Buck Mulligan in his large right mitt, I was confident he wasn't too interested in the read. And if he was, I was even more confident he wouldn't understand it. I was on my third attempt and still wasn't sure what the hell Joyce was talking about most of the time.

"It's a great book. Have you read it?" I asked, already knowing the answer.

"Books are for pussies," he said. As if his witty reply wasn't enough of a hint that he was eyeing up his bitch, his next gem was. "And I like pussy."

"Who doesn't?" I said, trying my best to find any common ground on which to worm my way out of the situation.

"Gay-wads," he said.

I then made a huge technical blunder. I didn't mean to. I didn't want to. It just happened. I started laughing. It was like one of those inappropriate laughing fits when things get too serious to handle, like in the principal's office or at a funeral. It didn't help my cause.

"What's so damn funny?" he asked.

"Gay-wad," I said trying not to laugh. "It's a funny, funny word. Gay-wad. It's like douchebag or butt wipe, twat burger, cock bite. You know, it's just in a long line of immature and stupid, yet funny, funny words," I said as my genuine gut laugh turned toward nervous. "You're funny," I continued.

For the first time, I noticed we had an audience. I'm not sure why, but kids in high school can sense when there's about to be trouble. Like blood in the water. The sharks were now starting to hover. Fear was in the air. It was mine. Maybe that's what they sensed.

Playing to his audience, Donny said, "You know what's funny? You washing my truck after school. Now, that's funny."

I didn't see the humor in it.

"And when you're done, maybe you'll get your book back," he continued.

"You can't have the book," I shot back and heard a small controlled collective "Oh" from our audience to let me know that wasn't the correct response. "It's my grandfather's," I said as though that was going to change my predicament.

"Maybe he should wash my truck," he said, which got a few chuckles.

"Can I have the book back?" I said, holding out my hand.

"If you get down on your knees and say please."

It was official. The bitch was in a corner with no way out. I tried another tactic. "Give me the book and go back to class," I said slowly and right into his small brain, hoping it might do some good.

It didn't. "Get on your knees, gay wad!" he said as he shoved me in the chest.

"No," I said.

He shoved me hard in the chest again. And again. Tears on their own decided to make an appearance and cloud my vision. Tears that didn't help my cause.

"I'm sorry, you need to go home to Mommy? Oh, that's right, you don't have a mommy. She ran away."

A sudden surge of energy awakened and began to course through my being.

"Get on your knees, boy," he said as he shoved me again.

"No," I said louder as the wetness in my eyes doubled, and the awakened energy became more intense.

He glanced down at the book and said, "Well then, I guess I'll just keep poor little Grandpa's boo--"

That's when my right fist landed flush across the bridge of his nose. I didn't plan on hitting him. It never crossed my mind. It just happened, just as suddenly as Ray had smacked his open hand during his demonstration, though the sound was much different. Much worse. Like something exploded.

I admit. I hit him when he wasn't looking. I guess that wasn't fair. But he was four years older and bigger. I figured that wasn't fair either.

I walked over and picked up *Ulysses*, which lay next to Donny on the ground. The blood spewing from his face seemed as excessive as Joyce's run-on sentences. Everything slowed. I heard nothing. As I walked away from the scene of the crime, I noticed three other football players. They glanced the other way as I passed. I felt a complete sense of calm. I was at ease, in control. Minutes later, behind the school, I sat down under a tree, started to tremble, then sobbed like a six-year-old whose goldfish had just died.

I hated Ray. I hated myself more. But he had been right. No one in high school ever messed with me again. Maybe it was because the principal issued a warning that any football player harassing an underclassman would be kicked off the team. Or maybe because any freshman crazy enough to clock a senior football star is someone you might want to stay away from. But I think it was the rumors. I heard everything from me pulling a gun, to putting a knife up to his throat and threatening to cut it out. Several years later, the rumors were legend. I could hear the whispers of incoming freshmen about how I ripped both ears off a guy with my bare hands. My favorite, though, was that I bit his tongue off and put it in my pocket as I walked away. Supposedly, I ate it later for lunch.

Regardless of the reason, people stayed away from the crazy, long-haired Indian freak. I was on an island, and no one wanted to visit. Not until Ellie Shane was forced to work with me. The first few weeks we spoke very few words to each other. I tried to break the ice a few times, but she was all business in the laboratory. She wouldn't even look at me and kept her head down most of the time. I understood though. I was the lunatic who bit off a guy's tongue. Then one afternoon during an experiment a disagreement arose. We were given different compounds and elements and had to choose the right amount and correct combination to achieve the desired reaction inside a glass tube that hovered over a Bunsen burner.

As she was about to put element A with element B, I said, "I don't think you want to do that."

"Why not?" she said.

"I don't think it's the reaction we're looking for," I said.

"This will cause it to smoke."

"It will do more than smoke."

"Not if this is the right amount."

"Is it the right amount?" I asked.

"Yes, it is."

"You sure?"

"I've checked this. It's the right amount!"

"I wouldn't put that in there," I said.

"Why, because you think you're smarter than me?"

"No. Because it's the wrong element."

She pulled up her protective plastic goggles, took off her glasses and looked me straight in the eye. "I'm not afraid of you. You can't bully me."

It was the first time since Donny anyone in high school had looked me in the eyes. Hers were beautiful. They were large and this crazy shade of green. Those eyes sucked me in, and I was lost. I looked down at her lips. They seemed a little too big for her face yet so soft and inviting. I had this sudden urge to kiss them when it occurred to me. Ellie Shane was a swan. In a few years, after the camouflage of youth fell away, she would make men stop and turn. I couldn't speak.

"What? You have nothing to say?" she said.

"You're beautiful," I mumbled.

"What?"

"You're a beautiful girl," I said into those emerald beauties.

Our eyes stayed locked together as the gravity of my comment took hold. It hit deep. A boy had never told her that before. The reality of the situation struck, and she panicked. She poured element A into our heated glass tube that held element B and another compound. I grabbed her goggles and slid them back into position as our glass tube blew up. The classroom went silent. All eyes pointed to us as Mr. Penthearst ran through the smoky room in our direction and screamed, "What did you do?"

"You put the wrong two elements together," I said.

"It wasn't the reaction I was looking for," Ellie said.

She looked back at me. I looked at her. In an instant, we were connected. Being caught off balance we both had revealed something inside that had never been exposed before. It was raw, it was pure, and the fact we saw it in each other at the same time made it safe.

We became friends after that. Months later, we were more than friends.

CHAPTER SEVEN

I t was the day before graduation as I opened my eyes and looked out over the water to the hills. The visual cue didn't break the connection. I was part of everything I could see, hear, smell, and feel. It, part of me. I'd spent almost every morning with him on that dock being present or attempting to be. In that oneness, that stillness, I could still feel him. His calmness. His laughter. His joy. His peace.

As everyday consciousness began to awake, I looked over at the rock that used to be Bodhi's chair. It was empty. It had been for over a year. He'd left first. Konka followed eight months later. In twenty-four hours, it would be my turn to leave. I guess all of our trips were planned; theirs by time, mine by fate.

I stood up on the dock, took one last look around, dove into the water, and swam to shore. My journey was about to begin. Although I still didn't know where I was going, I knew it was time to leave.

As I began putting the last items of clothing I owned into a duffel bag, I heard a car coming from over the hill. It was El. I'd tried to talk to her at school the past few days, but she was having none of it. She knew a conversation was coming; one she didn't want to have.

I went out to the porch and sat down on the steps as her car pulled up. I saw her expression through the windshield. My stomach churned seeing it. I loved this person. What was I doing? She didn't deserve this moment. She got out of the car, walked over, and sat down a few feet away.

"They get mad at you for missing the tests?" she asked.

"Disappointed is the word they used. They offered to let me still take them," I said.

"And when you said no?"

"They assured me I'd regret my decision later in life."

"No, you won't," she said.

"Probably not."

"You're leaving, aren't you?"

"Yes."

"When are you coming back?"

"I don't know."

"So, us going to college together isn't happening?" she asked.

"No."

Tears began to roll down her cheeks. "Is it me or college you don't want?" she said as the flow of tears increased.

"Hey," I said and turned her face with my hand to face mine. "I love you. I always will. Nothing is ever going to change that. You're the most important thing I have left in this world."

"Then why are you running from me?"

"I'm not running from you. I'm running toward something else."

"What?"

"I'm not sure. I wish I knew. Something is missing, and I need to find it," I said.

"You're just scared," she said.

"Of course I'm scared."

"Then why are you running?"

"I'm not scared of anything here."

"Sure you are. Everyone you've ever loved has left you, so you're worried eventually I'll leave you too. To gain a sense of control over it, you're leaving first."

"Death is part of life. It makes you mad. It makes you cry. It

34

makes you ache. But I accept it. I miss them. But I'm not haunted by it," I said.

"Bullshit!" she yelled.

As usual she was right. I accepted it because I had no other choice.

"And your mother?"

We sat in silence as I stared at the dirt between my feet. The same dirt I stared at the last time I saw my mom.

"I don't want you to go," she said.

"I don't want to leave you either."

"Why are you?"

I didn't answer.

"Why, Tag?"

I looked up. "I miss him."

"I know," she said.

"I feel like he was leading me in a certain direction. Now he's gone, and I don't know where to turn, who to ask, what to do next. Every night that I stay in this house, every time I go into the barn, sit on the dock, take a run, walk up on the hill, it feels like he's still here with me. And he is, I know he is. I can feel him speaking to me. I don't know what he's saying, but every ounce of my being is telling me to go, to leave, to find, to discover what he was leading me towards."

She looked up at me with those large green eyes. "Then go," she said.

We both sat silent for a few more seconds. I looked back over to El, but her eyes were searching the distance.

"What about us?" she asked.

There it was. The question I couldn't or didn't want to answer. Had I turned into my mother—dropping off and moving on? I suppose that was my plan. But I had underestimated El, which made it worse.

"You don't need to answer. I already know about us. I get it. To do this, you can't have strings attached," she said.

"El, it's not like…"

She put her hand on my knee. "It's okay. Go. Find what you're looking for." She paused as more tears ran down her cheeks. "I'm going to be fine."

"I'm sorry," I said.

"Don't be. You're being honest."

"Thank you."

"I have one favor, though."

"Of course," I said.

"Will you come to graduation? I'd like that. Us graduating together."

The truth was, I hadn't been planning on it. The plan was to leave later that night. "I don't have a cap or gown. But I'll be there," I said.

"Good."

She slid into my chest. I wrapped my arms tight around her. We stayed that way for another hour.

CHAPTER EIGHT

The morning of the graduation ceremony, the air conditioning units above the high school auditorium decided they had had enough and quit working. Those in charge simply moved the ceremony to the football stadium a few hundred yards away, which made perfect sense. At 5 p.m. the temperature gauge read 96 degrees, but with the humidity, it only felt like 105.

I met Ellie in the parking lot a half-hour before the festivities. She was wearing a stylish blue poncho gown that smelled of dry-cleaning chemicals, and a funny hat with a gold tassel. I was in my usual uniform—sandals, jeans, and a T-shirt that read "Love is my religion." We both were sweating.

"Thanks for coming," she said.

"Thanks for inviting me."

"I was being selfish. I needed a cute boy to take a picture with."

"You're using me?"

"I'm afraid so. How's your smile?"

I gave her a big fake toothy grin.

"It needs some work, but it'll do."

"Love your outfit. Did you pick it out yourself?" I asked.

"Indeed, I did. In fact, I loved it so much I got you one."

She reached into her car and tossed me the blue ceremonial cape and headdress.

"Oh, you shouldn't have," I said.

"Couldn't have the second smartest person in school wearing jeans and a T-shirt on stage."

"And Principal Hitchins thanks you."

"Plus, it would've messed up my photo op," she said.

"El," I said.

"Yeah."

I looked at her and tried to say something but the words wouldn't come.

"I know. Me too," she said. "You leaving tonight?"

"I need to stop off to see Eddie, but after that, yeah, that's the plan."

"Can I stop by before you leave? I want to give you something for your trip."

"Of course."

She came over and gave me a big hug. It lasted for a while. I heard a slight sniffle, and her body tensed as she fought back tears. She took a big breath, gave me a big slap on my butt, and said, "Let's do this." She grabbed my hand, and we walked toward the stadium.

When we got inside, Ellie went to her seat in front of the stage, and I, being the salutatorian, got the honor of sitting on stage next to Marcy, Principal Hitchins, Vice-Principal Hurst, a few members of the faculty, and His Holiness, the Reverend James B. Stukey. He was one of twelve, by my last count, Protestant ministers within a ten-mile radius who could have given the invocation. I wondered if he'd like my T-shirt.

Principal Hitchins kicked off the ceremony with a few bad jokes, a welcome speech, and, with the help of the high school band, a rousing rendition of the school's fight song. Aside from everyone being drenched in sweat, things seemed to be going smoothly until moments before Marcy was to give her valedictorian speech. Then tragedy struck. Marcy was overcome by stage fright and threw up on herself. She also caught the left pant leg of Principal Hitchins. He was not amused.

I didn't see the real tragedy until Mrs. Hurst informed me that I'd have to read Marcy's speech. She was in no condition to go on. *Are you kidding me? How the hell did that just happen? This was Marcy's moment, not mine. I made sure of it.* Before I could think my way out of the situation, Mrs. Hurst handed me Marcy's speech and proceeded to the microphone to introduce me.

Before I knew it, I was walking with speech in hand toward the podium. Despite my best efforts to avoid it, I stood in the one spot where I didn't want to be. I guess you can't outsmart fate.

I looked out on all of my classmates. How ironic and odd this moment seemed. People I never spoke to, people who had never listened to a word or thought from me, were now being forced by this yearly ritual to pay attention, or at least pretend. The same ones who had pointed, stared, laughed, who had whispered or yelled, "half-breed," "redskin," "Geronimo," "orphan," "loser," "freak" or, worse, just plain ignored me as I walked past them in the hallway.

It was a good thing it wasn't going to be my speech. I didn't want to talk to them and even if I did, I couldn't. I didn't know them. I didn't go to parties, text, tweet, or Facebook. Hell, I didn't even own a phone. El was the only person my age I talked to. Yet there was no need to panic either. It would be easy. It would be quick. I'd read Marcy's words and be done with it. Unfortunately, as I looked down at her speech for the first time, two major obstacles stood in my way.

First, the title: "Possibilities—The Roadmap to the Future." Now, Marcy could tell you every capital in the world, discuss the US Constitution, and show you the difference between a derivative and an integral, but I was sure she didn't know anything about the future, much less own any roadmap. Unless, of course, her roadmap was possibilities. If that was the case, I guess it was possible that she was going to say that anything is possible. Mathematically speaking, this was true, but it's more likely impossible than possible, especially with this group. How could I read it with a straight face? I'd never get through it. I couldn't bear to look at the first sentence. Which, as it turned out, I couldn't see anyway because Marcy's lunch covered most of the first page. Before I could think, I flipped the speech over to avoid making direct eye contact with the rest of what looked like an egg salad sandwich and a grape soda.

I glanced over at Marcy, who not only looked like she had seen a ghost but indeed looked like a ghost. Her pale, white face was pointing to the ground and expressionless. Mrs. Hurst was steadying her with both hands.

I peered back up to the audience for my next move. No help from them. They were still stirring around in their seats. I looked over to Principal Hitchins. The large, round sweat stains from the pits of his powder-blue suit weren't helping my cause, but his stained left pant leg was priceless, though it didn't match his tie. He smiled broadly as his eyes bulged and the pulsating vein in his left temple seemed to be larger than usual as the seconds ticked by.

I looked back over the crowd but couldn't stay in the moment. My mind went elsewhere, and I let it. I thought of Konka. He always talked about living more, experiencing more, and growing more. As a person, as a species, as a civilization, he believed it was our goal and duty. To create a better society, a better civilization, citizens must continuously and actively pursue knowledge, truth, and understanding of not only the world around us but also the one inside. He would often say, "Follow knowledge like a sinking star, beyond the utmost bound of human thought." A quote from a poem by a favorite poet.

I closed my eyes and for some reason remembered standing with Konka in the middle of a field discussing another great poet, Walt Whitman, and the life of cows when I said, "Ladies and gentlemen, classmates, parents, teachers, friends, Romans, countrymen, any members of the press, and Brad Pitt." I pointed into the audience where he was sitting.

Of course Brad Pitt wasn't there, but it caused quite the commotion and bought me a few more precious seconds.

"If I have one piece of advice to give to you and my fellow students, it would be this…"

I paused for a few more seconds, not knowing what was coming next from my pie hole, when out of nowhere I looked into the audience and said with utmost confidence, "Don't be a cow."

The rustling from the audience I had heard earlier was now gone. I guess I had their attention. "Not unless, of course, you want to end up as a ribeye on the neighbor's grill," I continued.

The vein on Mr. Hitchin's head looked like a snake that had swallowed a rat.

"Of course, a cow has an easy life. It eats, sleeps, and fertilizes. That's it. No cares in the world. No stress. No mental torment. No worries about acne. No worries about boys. No worries about being cool, or being in the right group, or having friends. No worries about sex, money, food. What a simple and wonderful life that must be. And you can have that life if you want it. The formula is simple. All it takes is your forehead, a chisel, a hammer, and some gumption."

I wasn't sure but was willing to wager Mr. Hitchin's melon was seconds away from exploding.

"Now, on the other hand, you can choose greatness. That's what we're told from the time we can speak, "You can be anything you want to be," and we believe our parents, our teachers, and our coaches. And the truth is, we could be great. We can be great. But to become great, I mean truly great at any one thing, the experts say it takes at least 10,000 hours of practice. That means if you spent eight hours a day, every day, on one thing it would take you almost three and a half years to become great at it. Say you spend four hours a day, every day of the year, it would take you nearly seven years to become great at something. And really, who has that kind of time? Less than half of one percent of the population has the dedication, the discipline, the drive, to pull that off. Now, let's be honest. Does that sound like any of you?"

I looked out into the crowd waiting for a reply. It never came, so I kept going.

"To be truthful, most of us will end up wallowing around in mediocrity. And I say there's nothing wrong with that as long as we don't become complacent. Instead, try and do new things. Eat new things. Talk to different people. Read different books. Read any book. If you like country music, listen to hip hop. If you like hip hop listen to classical. If you hunt and fish, try chess, if you're Christian read the Koran, if you're Muslim read the Bible. Step out of your comfort zone and walk in other people's shoes. Be curious about things you don't know. Stretch yourself mentally and physically. It's a big world out there. Get to know it."

The blank look on their faces suggested that might not happen anytime soon.

"We're here today because over three billion years ago there was a one-celled organism—let's call him Stuart. Now Stuart, either for survival's sake or out of sheer boredom, decided to try something new. So, Stuart started to evolve. Had Stuart been content with his situation, all of us would still be a pile of goo in the ocean."

For some reason that made Reverend Stukey squirm in his chair.

"Stuart wasn't great. He was average, but he was curious. He was peeking around the corner at something new, something different, and it changed him. It changed him for the better. It changed us for the better.

"So, at the end of the day, you don't have to be the best. You don't have to be great. You don't have to be the next Einstein. You don't have to be the next Shakespeare. You don't have to be Da Vinci, or Newton, or Plato, or Columbus, or Gandhi, or Mother Teresa. Or even Elvis for that matter. You don't even have to be you. Just don't be a cow."

For some reason, there was no standing ovation, just an eerie silence hanging uncomfortably in the air. I guess I had reached them. I walked back to my seat.

Mr. Hitchins walk-sprinted to the podium and moved to the next phase of the evening without congratulating me on my fine speech. I guess he was overcome with inspiration.

The festivities moved on, though for me it was a blur. I suppose I had moved on as well.

CHAPTER NINE

I strolled into Scooter's to find the usual cast of characters at the bar. It was slow for a Friday. The band Eddie booked had canceled, and without live entertainment, there was no reason to make a trip to Sisterdale on a Friday evening. Conway Twitty crooned from the jukebox as the boys sipped their whiskey and beer. It was going to be one of those nights. Old school. Nothing but Merle Haggard, Charley Pride, Tammy Wynette, and a little Hank Williams. I'd spent many a night watching as the regulars would drift away into memory land when their favorite songs came on.

Eddie taught me never to get too close during those moments or be subjected to the dreaded man love-stare. I did my best to avoid it at all times, but I was no match for this common ritual. It usually was a surprise attack from behind. An arm thrown over the shoulder and neck and firmly being pulled in close with nothing but the smell of cigarettes and cheap whiskey sharing the few inches between our faces. Then, a soft slurred whisper aimed into the pupils. "Now Tag, this is a good song. You know, when country was country. When life was simpler. When things were good. You know what I mean."

I never did.

The tight grip on the back of the neck held me in place as the aggressor got further lost in the song and his past. And then would come the moment. The man love-stare. That slight second where everything gets really weird as you're looking deeply into another man's eyes and you see both love and rage and don't know if you're about to be kissed or punched. Luckily, neither ever happened.

This "manly" behavior usually surfaced on slow nights, which were most nights. The recipe was simple. A little booze, an old song, and they would transport into another reality. A reality they seemed to enjoy more than the present one, one they liked to visit as often as possible. Some nights, if the right song came on at the right time, you could witness a half-dozen men sitting in absolute silence at the bar, all within a few feet of each other yet miles apart, lost in regret for how things could have been.

"What are you doing here? Shouldn't you be out celebrating?" Eddie said from behind the bar.

"I'm meeting El later," I said.

"Tag," yelled Johnny Blu from the pool table. "I heard Brad Pitt was at the graduation."

"No, Blu. He wasn't there."

"Yes, he was."

"I'm pretty sure he wasn't."

"My niece Susan said one of her friends Erika saw him and a friend of Erika's talked to him."

"She's mistaken, Blu," I said.

"Nope, he was there."

I was no match for the rumor mill of my small Texas town even though I was the rumor's author.

"Was he wearing one of those beret-type hats?" I asked.

"Yes. I think he was."

"Really good-looking?"

"Yeah, that's what Susan said."

"I guess he was there."

"I told you."

Before I could turn back to Eddie, a chill went down my spine. I froze with panic. I couldn't breathe. Donny Coledge had walked into the bar and was headed right toward me. Surely, he was here for his revenge. It made perfect sense. I was now out of high school. I'd put on some weight and was six foot two. I was fair game. He had come to collect his pound of flesh, all those years waiting and waiting to rearrange my face. The anger he'd been holding onto for all those years was now a few yards away. I had no out. My mind and mouth couldn't move fast enough to avoid the inevitable, and my fists were of no use. If I wasn't certain after that fateful day four years earlier that I would never again harm another human being, the moment I read the story of Gandhi and India, well, that clinched it. If Gandhi and his people could win a war without violence, surely I could live a life in the same pacifist mode. *Why did I read that damn book?*

"Tag," said Donny as I looked down at those oversized mitts.

"Can I help you?" I said waiting for the customary invite outside.

"I saw you speak tonight."

"You were at graduation?" I asked.

"There are a few kids in your class who are in my weekly church group. I went to celebrate their achievement," he said.

"That was nice of you," I said, anticipating the first punch.

"I came here to apologize," he said.

"For what?"

"I was mean to you in high school. I was not a good person back then," he said.

I paused with confusion, not knowing how to react when "You called me 'gay wad'" came flying out of my mouth.

"It wasn't very Christian of me. I said a lot of things unworthy of our Lord to my fellow brothers. I'm still trying to make amends." He stuck out his right mitt to shake my hand. "Please, forgive me," he said.

I shook his meat-hook of a hand. It was surprisingly soft.

"I'm sorry about hitting you," I said.

"It wasn't you. It was God."

"God hit you in the face?"

"He was trying to make me see," he said.

"See what?"

"Him."

"Did you?" I asked.

"Not then. Too busy thinking about me. It took several more years, and few more slaps upside my thick head before the blinders came off."

"You can see him now?" I asked.

"I'm looking at him," he said directly into me, sending another chill down my spine. "Don't worry. He's in everyone. You'll see him one day. If Jesus can save me…" he laughed.

Maybe Jesus had saved him. Who was I to argue? But one thing was for certain: That night, He saved me.

Donny and I talked for a while more. He handed me his card in case I ever wanted to visit his place of worship with him, patted me on the shoulder, and walked peacefully back out the bar.

"Eddie, I need a shot and a beer," I said.

"I don't believe you're of legal drinking age," he said as he poured two Cuervo shots and tossed up a cold Shiner Bock.

"Hell if I'm not," I said and threw down Cousin Ray's old driver's license.

He took a look at it and asked, "Aren't you doing five to ten in Huntsville?"

"I got time off for good behavior."

Eddie raised up one of the tequila glasses and said, "Congratulations."

"*Al fondo*," I said.

We clinked glasses and shot 'em down.

"A chisel, your forehead, and some gumption. Nice words of wisdom…What? You thought I wasn't going to be there?" he said after seeing the expression on my face.

Hell, I didn't even know I was going to be there. I never thought about asking Eddie. "No, I didn't," I replied.

"I guess you're not so smart after all."

"Right now, I feel plain stupid," I said.

"It's good for ya on occasion. Helps with perspective."

Other than Konka, I'd spent more time with Eddie than any other person. I'd worked with him for the past five years. He was there for me when Konka passed. He had helped with the ceremony on top of the hill near the house. He offered for me to stay at his home so I wouldn't be alone. When I refused, he came by to check on me when I wasn't working or in school. I'd been in such a fog since Konka left, I guess I never noticed all he had done.

"I'm sorry, Eddie."

"For what?"

"Not inviting you to graduation."

"Obviously, I didn't need an invite."

"I know, but…"

"Tag, I'm not losing any sleep over it."

"Thanks for coming," I said.

"So, what are you doing here?"

"I need a favor."

"Shoot," he said.

"I was wondering if you would keep an eye on the house."

"Where you going?"

"I don't know."

"How long?"

"Don't know that either."

"Sounds like a well-thought-out plan."

"It's the best I've got."

"What about college?"

"Putting that on hold."

"I could tell you what I think, but a smart guy like you wouldn't listen anyway."

"Probably not."

"Let me guess. You want to go out and see the world."

"Something like that."

"Well, it's not always a pretty place out there."

"But it's a different place."

"Listen, if you get your butt in a bind, and you're gonna get it in a bind, call me."

"I might," I said with a smile.

There was a long, awkward pause, neither of us knowing how to say goodbye. Charley Pride's "Kiss an Angel Good Morning" was blaring out of the jukebox. That's when Eddie grabbed me around the neck, pulled me in close, and whispered, "Now this is a good song."

I laughed and replied, "When country was country."

He pushed me away and yelled, "Now, get the hell out of my joint and don't be asking for your job back next week."

I walked toward the door, winked at old Ernest, and left the bar.

CHAPTER TEN

I arrived home to Ellie's car out front, and I walked into the house. Music was on, and candles lit the room. Between the strange orange glow, my shadow flickering on the wall, and the melodic classical music playing, I was either about to witness a satanic ritual or something good was about to happen. When Ellie walked out of my room wearing nothing but my T-shirt, I knew the devil was nowhere in the vicinity. And if he were, he'd have a new member of the club shortly.

A surge of adrenaline stormed through my system, or was it out-of-control teenage hormones on the loose? I wasn't sure. I didn't care. This was happening. This was happening now. I walked over and gave her a long, soft kiss. I grabbed her hand and placed it under my shirt, and she started to rub my chest as we stared into each other's eyes. Within seconds her hand made its way to the top button of my jeans while mine slid down under her panties and over her butt. Her lips barely touched mine as the first button of my jeans came undone. She kissed my bottom lip, and another button was free. A long slow kiss and another button lost. She was taking her time, and it was driving me crazy. And she knew it. It's a game we'd played many times before: undressing each other with one hand while making good use of the other. Our game had always ended before our virginity was compromised, but I tried. Oh, how I tried, and tried, and tried. However, my hormones, enthusiasm, and technique were no match for her beliefs.

Ellie hadn't wanted to have sex, not only because she was saving herself, but also because as it turned out, she was terrified of Hell. Her Baptist preacher and weekly Bible-study group had done their job. Yet she was no prude. It seemed she and her deity were okay with about everything else.

Her mother, on the other hand, didn't share the same view. I know this for a fact because one late evening on their living room floor as I was writing the alphabet with my tongue in and around Ellie's happy place, I peeked up between Ellie's bent knees when my eyes connected with Mrs. Shane's as she rounded the corner. I guess she wasn't asleep after all.

Though the look lasted a split second, it seemed to linger for eternity. At that moment, I understood Einstein's theory of relativity. Mrs. Shane's look pierced deep down into my soul. How could I be doing such a horrible thing to her precious little girl? Her innocent Ellie still kept stuffed animals on her bed to keep the bogeyman away. Ellie was a good girl. An honor student. A Christian, for Christ's sake! I'd just gotten busted for stealing a piece of candy. I was caught on camera. The store manager saw the whole thing. I was guilty. There was no escape.

I couldn't move. I was frozen with fear when Mrs. Shane let out a loud, "Oh," took the Lord's name in vain, did a one-eighty, and walked out of the room.

Within the span of a minute I had heard the daughter moan, "Oh God," and the mother scream, "Oh my fucking God." Now, I'm still wrestling with the idea of the Almighty and his existence. Though by all accounts, he was on hand that evening.

I wasn't allowed back in the house. I saw Mrs. Shane a few times more. We never looked each other in the eye.

As the music bounced off the walls of my house, Ellie had removed my shirt and pants from my body. She pulled away from a kiss and said, "I want you. I want you now."

She walked away and disappeared into the bedroom. I took

one step to follow when some crazy lunatic in my head screamed, "You can't do this."

It stopped me in my tracks.

Yes, I can. Sure, I can. Watch me, I thought.

But I couldn't move. Ellie was doing this for me. All for me. In the morning, or the next day, or week, when I was gone, and she had time to reflect, she would regret this. She was betraying her faith. And while it was her faith and not mine, I couldn't be the one. I should be the one. But I couldn't be the one. I'd be taking something she wasn't ready to give. I couldn't do that to her. I wouldn't. Her beliefs would probably change before she got married, but it hadn't happened yet. I couldn't take advantage. Oh, but how I so wanted to take advantage! Then, a voice inside me started to scream. *Are you kidding me? What are you doing? This isn't fair. You want it. She wants it. No one is forcing anyone to do anything they don't want to do. Come on. This is your life. Live it. Experience it. Peek around the corner and see what's inside.*

As I stood in my jockey shorts at full attention, convincing myself to walk through the door, the other voice in my brain kicked back in. *You're seventeen. About the same age as your grandmother when she had your mom and the exact age as your mom when she had you; the unexpected gift that altered their lives and forced them to become adults at a young age.*

Was I about to follow in their footsteps? Was history repeating itself? I didn't have any protection. I doubted El did either. Was this some sort of weird karmic test?

Maybe it was fair after all. More than fair. I give up this one moment, and the cycle is broken.

I can't say I made the decision. But something or someone inside me did.

"What's wrong?" Ellie asked as her head popped out from the bedroom.

I didn't say a word. I didn't have to. One look at my now baggy jockey shorts, and the answer was clear. Moments later, she walked out of the bedroom fully clothed and got all the way to the front door before she turned and looked at me. I got one last look at those big green eyes behind a wall of tears.

As the water from my eyes started to swell, she gave me one last half-smile and slipped out the door. A minute later, I walked out on the front porch in time to see the rear lights of her car vanish over the hill. The same hill my mother had made her escape. The same hill my grandma never made it to.

I stood alone in the darkness as bullfrogs filled the night silence with their deep voices, calling out for company.

CHAPTER ELEVEN

For my fifteenth birthday, Konka had found an old beat-up Dodge van from the early seventies sitting in a junkyard. It was complete with shag flooring, ripped velour ceilings, bubble windows, two captain chairs, an overused bed, a kick-ass stereo system (if you considered an eight-track kick-ass), and a box of accompanying eight-track tapes ranging from Al Green to David Bowie. The original paint job was faded and peeling, but you could still make out the swirling purple, yellow, and gold acid-induced design.

Konka and I spent two months rebuilding the engine. I spent at least that much time cleaning up the interior. She wasn't pretty, but she was reliable, which was good because not only was she my ride but also my new home.

In Konka's will, he left me the land and house. In his papers, I also found letters from a sister who lived in Arizona, where he had grown up. I had been planning to write after he moved on but decided on going there and telling her in person after graduation. There was so much he'd taught me, yet so much I didn't know about this man. Maybe she could shed some light on the missing pieces.

On the evening he left to the spirit world, he gave me a package. He said it was my graduation gift and not to open it until afterward. Though my curiosity was high, I still wasn't ready to see what was inside. I hoped I'd soon get to a place where that was possible. Until then, it was me, the road, my thoughts, and a box of old eight-tracks.

The Mystery Machine, the name El had given the van, was loaded with my clothes (all of which could fit in a single drawer), a tool box, an old ice chest, and some books.

I jumped in, headed up the hill, stopped at the top, rolled down the driver's side window, and took one last look. The sounds of the small creek kept me company as my eyes drifted from the barn to the house, to the lake.

Speak to me, Konka. Speak to me.

A strong warm Texas wind blew through the van as the clouds pulled back their curtain to reveal a full moon. I looked back to the lake, and my heart almost stopped.

I saw a silhouette of a man sitting motionless on the dock, facing the other direction.

It couldn't be. Is my mind playing tricks on me, or is this just a weird shadow from the sky?

"Konka," I whispered.

He turned and looked back up at me in the van on the hill. It was him. Still as the night. I could see the outline of his chiseled face smiling. I took a deep breath.

"Thank you," I said.

Another gust of wind blew through the van and across my body and face. It lasted for a few seconds, then the clouds overtook the full moon, and he was gone.

A minute later, my taillight's vanished over the hill, and so was I.

At three in the morning, I was somewhere in the middle of Texas heading northwest toward Arizona. I was tired and should have waited until the morning to leave, but I needed to put some distance between myself and the past six months. Konka used to say the best time to begin anything new is now. As in right now. Any hesitation of movement in the new direction is just a veil of fear. The greater the fear, the faster you need to jump into it. If not, the fear grows, and fear doesn't need much growth before it can stop a man cold in his tracks as hesitation slips into procrastination and morphs into apathy in the blink of an eye.

So forward I went into the night, knowing movement was my ally, my friend. I rolled down the windows to let the warm Texas wind keep us company, grabbed an eight-track from the box, inserted it into the dashboard, and turned up the volume as Grand Funk Railroad joined our party rolling down Highway 87. I'm not sure what makes a highway versus a road, but nothing on this small, dark two-laner suggested its superiority.

As the miles started to pile up, the eight-track player indiscriminately decided it didn't want to play any songs from track two or four and repeated "We're an American Band" three times in a row like a love-struck drunk at the jukebox with a pocket full of quarters. I decided to pull out the cartridge and give it a rest. That move left me with the road ahead and my thoughts, which I wanted to avoid for a few days. Invariably those thoughts would turn to Ellie. While I didn't want to forget her, I also didn't want to carry her around in my head. I'd let go of her physically by leaving, but if I couldn't let go of her mentally, what was the difference?

I'd hoped to keep my mind blank or occupied with other things for as long as possible. However, since a calm, blank mind can be the neighbor of sleep, driving with one in the wee hours of the morning is a recipe for disaster. Fortunately for me, I didn't have to make a choice—other things were just around the corner.

As I rounded a bend in the road, I saw a pickup truck off to the right had slammed into a ditch. I pulled over, jumped out, and ran over to help. The headlights were still on, as well as the light in the cabin, but nobody was home. Steam and water spewed out of the totaled front end. I peered into the cabin for any clues, but everything seemed normal, whatever normal is after one plows into a ditch. Whoever the truck belonged to must have started to walk to the next town, twenty miles away. As I was about to turn and head toward the van, a voice in a slow country accent said, "See something in there you like?"

Standing a few yards in front of the truck's headlights was the shadow of a man who looked seven feet tall, wearing a cowboy hat. Before I could reply he said, "Awful late being out in the middle of nowhere all alone."

"I'm not alone," I replied.

He strode over and stood a few yards in front of me. He was only about six foot four. The cowboy hat and headlights exaggerated his height, or maybe that was my imagination. I looked down, and in his right hand, he held a large buck knife covered with blood. So was part of his shirt. That was not my imagination.

Goodbye, journey; hello, spirit world.

What are the odds of this—stumbling upon a murderer? Make that mass murderer once he starts to fillet me. You could win the lottery several times over before walking up on this. Get struck by lightning in a rubber room before this. Get killed by a flying duck on a roller coaster. If I had more time I could do the math. But I'm going to go out on a limb and say big cowboy didn't care about probabilities. My options at that point numbered two. Fight or flee. I'd already given up the fight game years earlier, and even if I hadn't, I didn't want to dance with this cowboy. He seemed to have more experience doing the two-step. I knew I could run. I'd started following Konka in the hills when I was about eight. The little kid who couldn't run to the mailbox without getting asthma could now run fifteen miles without losing his breath. One glance at big cowboy's Tony Lamas and I knew I had my out.

With the calculations finished, but before I could make the first step, big cowboy grinned. "Got-damn axis buck. Nearly got me killed," he said as he folded up the knife and put it into his back pocket.

"You okay?" I asked as my heartbeat began its way back to normal.

"Oh shit. I'm fine. But that poor deer got tore up pretty bad. After he hit the front of my truck he stumbled across the field over there and fell. Broke both front legs. He couldn't move. Had to put him out of his misery." He stuck out his bloody right hand. "I appreciate ya stoppin'. Kicker Tom's the name."

I guess I didn't win the lottery. I shook his blood-soaked hand. "Tag," I said. "You want a ride?"

"Does a whore wanna get paid?"

I took that as a yes.

He went to his truck, cleaned off his hands and knife, changed shirts, grabbed a bag, and off we went.

"You want me to take you somewhere?" I asked.

"Right now, whatever direction you're going is fine. You mind if I grab a smoke? Killing one of God's creatures up close and personal like that got my nerves a little rattled now the adrenaline's wearing off," he said.

"Sure. No problem."

He pulled a joint from his front shirt pocket and settled it between his lips, lit it, and took an enormous hit. He held the smoke in and proceeded to roll down the window, put his long right leg out, and rested his boot on top of the side mirror. He paused for another ten seconds, leaned his head back on the headrest, and let out an endless stream of smoke. He held up the joint toward me with raised eyebrows.

"Maybe later," I replied. "So, you a religious man, Kicker Tom?"

"Hell no. I use the word God in a more liberal sense these days. Used to be, though. When I was 'bout your age."

"What changed?"

"Seven tours of duty in Iraq and Afghanistan."

"I guess that would do it."

"It's funny. It wasn't the killing or the death, or even the stupidity of it all. It was a simple moment of complete clarity. We'd been in a three-day firefight in this small town in the middle of fuckin' nowhere. It was late one night and me and another guy were on watch, and he was reading his Bible. And it just struck me kind of funny. Here he is reading and praying to his God to keep him safe and to be victorious, which basically meant killing the other guy across the road. And I'm sure the other guy across the road is reading his version of the Bible and praying to his God to keep him safe and to kill us. So, are there two Gods? And if so, who's in charge? And if not, then whose side is he on? I'm guessing neither since both men are acting like a bunch of jackasses and trying to kill each other. If neither of these guys is right, then they both got to be wrong. So, either there is no such thing as God, or he is something completely different we got all wrong—that mankind has all wrong. Talk about a huge fuckin' worldly blunder. But hell, that's man for ya. I tell you what. Show me a perfect moment, and I'll show you a man in charge waiting in line to fuck it up."

As we cruised through the blackness of the Texas countryside, I wanted to add in my two cents, but Kicker Tom didn't seem to need my help. So I let the roller coaster continue.

"And every one of those shit asses has two things in common. They're afraid and paranoid. Afraid of anything slightly different and paranoid of losing what they have. Hitler and the Jews—fear and paranoia. Vietnam—fear and paranoia. Stringing up Jesus—fear and paranoia. Iraq—fear and paranoia. American Indians, Muslims, blacks, Mexicans, gays, hell that's different than me, well fuck then, let's just shoot 'em, take care of that real quick. All a bunch of dumb fucks, men at the top. And education? What the hell they studyin'? How to be stupid? Job well done, boys!"

"Be fearful of a fearful man," I said.

"That's right. Absolutely right. I like that. Be fearful of a fearful man. Who said that?"

"My grandfather used to say it."

"Hell, I like that a lot. I'm goin' steal that if ya don't mind. I tell you what you should be fearful of. Misguided patriotism. That shit'll kill ya. One minute ya sign up to protect your country from those Al Qaeda bastards and the next you're sittin' next to a tank during a sandstorm somewhere in the middle of Iraq. I-fucking-raq! How the fuck did that happen? Those fearful, paranoid power freaks is how that happened. And they used good ol' fashioned American patriotism to pull it off. And me and thousands of other idiots bought it hook, line, and sinker. Those tricky fucks."

Kicker Tom took another hit off the joint and handed it to me. I

59

took a long look at it in my hand and decided maybe this was a roller coaster I might not want to miss. I took a hit and proceeded to cough for the next minute and a half.

"Whoa, whoa, be careful, that's not your garden-type ragweed varietal. That's Southern Samoan Pineapple Crush. Finest sativa in America, son. It'll make your nut sack sing," he said with a smile.

I wasn't sure what all that meant but was surprised to find out my testicles had a voice. The first day of my journey and I already learned something new.

"Old marine buddy makin' a pretty damn good livin' over in California growing medical marijuana. Thinks I saved his life, so he sends whatever I want."

We rode in silence as America's finest sativa began to do its thing on me. That silence was broken a few minutes later when a nighttime bug was in the wrong place at the wrong time and splattered onto the middle of the windshield. I turned on the wipers and watched the blades and water wash it away.

"Did you?" I asked.

"What?"

"Save his life?"

Kicker Tom paused and seemed to be momentarily lost in time. "They gave me a bunch of useless medals for it. It's funny. It worked out to be about for every twenty pieces of metal in my leg, back, and ass I got a medal for my chest. I wonder who in the hell figured out that ratio. They wanted me to go to Washington to receive them but no damn chance."

"Why not?"

"I didn't want one kid seeing that propaganda shit on TV or a photo of it in the paper and the next day go enlist. They got me. Fine. My fuck-up. But they sure as hell weren't gonna whore me out. Plus, I didn't deserve the attention. I'm alive and in one piece. So what if I might've saved a few lives. I was doing what I was supposed to. Ya know, my job. But there's 4,000 of my brothers, and at least another hundred thousand innocent people, all dead over there cuz those paranoid fucks at the top didn't do theirs.

Hypocritical a-holes. But hell, how can you blame them? It's our fault. We're the real idiots. We hired a C student to run the world. What were we expecting?"

He took another hit off the joint. I passed this time around after noticing the speedometer had dipped to thirty and was heading south. I tried to regain some focus and got the Mystery Machine back up to the correct speed limit of fifty-five.

"Holy shit. Is that an eight-track?"

"Factory installed," I replied.

"Does it work?"

"Sometimes. Kind of has a mind of its own. There's a box of tapes right behind your seat."

He rifled through the box and tossed in the greatest hits of Seals and Croft. "Summer Breeze" came through the speakers, and the warm Texas breeze rushed through the van as the Southern Samoan Pineapple Crush continued doing its thing.

"My aunt used to play this type of music when I was a kid. I loved that time of life. Not a care in the world. Shit. If you could bottle that feeling you'd be a rich man," he said.

"Maybe you can," I said.

"I'm afraid not, Tag. That innocence, that peace, that joy, slowly slip away with each passing birthday. And it don't come back. It's just no match for life. Hell, I'm only twenty-nine, and it's already beat the fuck out of me. Kicker Tom, biggest badass in the whole damn town, and it whipped my ass without as much as a please or thank you. It don't care who you are. Life ain't preju-diced, it's an equal-opportunity employer. It'll kick the shit out of anyone. And the older you get, the meaner that son-of-a-bitch gets. So, I decided to quit."

"Quit what?" I asked.

"Life. I'm officially retired from it. Given up my union card. Going on permanent vacation."

"You planning on killing yourself, Tom?"

"Hell no. It's more like a divorce."

"How does one divorce life?"

"Still working out the particulars but basically, just don't participate. It seems if you don't pay it much attention it don't pay much attention back."

"How's it working for you so far?" I said as I took another peek at the speedometer to make sure the Mystery Machine was keeping its proper pace.

"Pretty damn good until that deer ran into my truck," he said.

"Maybe that was life throwing you a raft."

Kicker Tom took a hard look at me. "No. Just its lawyer wantin' more alimony."

He tipped his cowboy hat over his eyes. "Where you headed?"

"Northern Arizona," I replied.

"I'll pay for gas if you don't mind a passenger."

"Sounds good."

He fell asleep, his leg still hanging out the window on the side mirror.

Konka once said, "When you're ready to learn, a teacher will appear."

That teacher can come in many forms, with life being the greatest. In every moment there is a lesson, but only when you're in it. Really in it. But at that moment, I wasn't in it. Not near it. I was a blind man. I knew this for a fact because the song "Diamond Girl" had made its third or fourth consecutive repetition. Neither I nor the sleeping cowboy to my right nor the Pineapple Crush had noticed. Now, I had smoked pot before. Konka introduced it to me to help me understand reality and perspective. We also would take a small toke before a long run in the hills. Zen runs, he would call them, when ten miles would go by in a flash, leaving you wondering who ran them. But this Samoan sativa was different. It could make you see things. I could see the future, the past, and the present all at the same time. Not only that, the future could see the past. The past, the present. The present, the future. It was all one. I could not only see it but understand it. How simple it seemed. How beautiful. How perfect. *How long have I been driving? Where am I? Is this all a dream? It must be.*

I say that because I turned to look at my new teacher to the right and he wasn't there.

I turned and glanced at the back of the van and yelled, "Tom!" No answer. I was driving sixty miles an hour non-stop and Kicker Tom had disappeared. Yet, on closer inspection, his black cowboy hat was sitting in the seat next to me. I took a look at the open window, and it hit me. Kicker Tom had just divorced life. And I'd helped him. *Is this happening!?*

I turned on the inside light and took another look at the back of the van. I could see his bag and the empty bed. That's when I heard a loud thump on the windshield. I turned and came face to face, eyeball to eyeball with the upside-down face of Kicker Tom. Only glass and a foot of space separated us. He let out a couple of loud, wild screams as if he was on a carnival ride. I took a look at both windows and saw his fingers holding on for dear life. How in the hell had he climbed out on the roof without my noticing? The joint in the ashtray chuckled. I slowly dropped off the accelerator and made no sudden moves toward the brake. Another minute passed before I could bring her to a complete smooth stop. Kicker Tom rolled off the roof, over the hood, landed feet first in front of the van, did a little victory dance, and started howling at the moon.

He ran over and jumped back into the van. "Sorry, got a little bit too high. Had to readjust. All better now. Oh shit! That felt good! Real good! Need that jolt every once in a while. Good to go! Good to go! Want me to drive?"

"Never," I said.

He let out a loud Texas laugh. "Hell, I wouldn't let me either. Shit no. Not unless you're some type of madman."

I put the van in gear, and we rolled back onto the blacktop as Kicker Tom changed the eight-track.

As I got the Mystery Machine back up to speed, a smile crept onto my face. I didn't know how, but for now, I knew I was on the right highway.

CHAPTER TWELVE

M y left eyelid opened as I noticed rays of orange-reddish light streaming about. The right side of my face was smashed against a soft surface, my body limp, mind dazed, senses confused. I couldn't quite make out the high-pitched voice singing —sounded like a bad fifth member of the Bee Gees clan. *Where am I? What time is it?*

Another moment had passed when an image of a large cowboy driving the Mystery Machine came into focus. I popped up, realizing I'd been sleeping in back. That could only mean one thing. Kicker Tom was at the control panel. A quick glance forward to the back of a cowboy hat bobbing to the music confirmed my theory.

I peeked out the side window to see the sun bouncing off elongated walls of reddish-orange rock. It was a color I was not familiar with. It seemed manmade. Fake. However, its radiance was dreamlike and intoxicating. I moved forward and took a seat next to the captain. His cowboy hat was still dancing to the music. He turned up the volume and sang with the chorus.

"You don't strike me as the Bee Gees type," I said.

"Closet fan. Shit, man, those boys can sing. Makes you wanna dance."

I was starting to learn you couldn't put a label on Kicker Tom. He was no stereotype. At least, that was my first impression.

"What happened to you not driving?" I asked.

"Thought it was important for us to...." He turned up the volume again and sang, "...stay alive!!!"

I reached over and turned it down.

"Shit, Tag. Sometimes things change and you're forced into an adult decision," he said.

"When did that happen?"

"When you started swerving to miss objects in the road that weren't there."

"You get some weird shadows at night," I said.

"It was nine in the morning."

I glanced out the window at the wall of reddish-orange. "How long have I been out?

"About six hours." He turned down the volume further. "Ya know, between you and me, you might want to get a hold of your pot smoking." He let out one of his big Texas laughs. "Ah, shit son. You were dawg-tired beat. Hell, you couldn't have stood up to a wet noodle. Had to practically carry ya back there myself."

"Where are we?"

"Entering Sedona."

"Already?"

"I might not've driven within the confines of the allocated speed parameters set forth by state or local officials."

"Of course not," I said. I glanced out the window again and got lost in those crazy-colored walls of sandstone. There was something peculiar about them, but I didn't know what. They seemed alive. "Pull over," I said.

"Not too fond of my driving?"

"Just pull over."

He pulled the Mystery Machine to the side. I jumped out and ran down a small hill to a dry creek bed. Surrounded by those magnificent walls and rocks, I looked up and was lost in their presence and power when Kicker Tom strolled up.

"What ya lookin' at?"

"Can you feel that?" I asked.

"Feel what?"

"The energy."

Kicker Tom looked around. "Hell, can't even feel my ass right now."

I ran back up the hill, jumped into the van, threw off my sandals, and replaced them with running shoes. Heading back down the hill I passed Kicker Tom, who was relieving himself on a cactus.

"Where're you going?" he yelled.

"For a run," I said.

This place was calling me, and I had to go check it out. I was at least a mile in on a trail that looked to be heading deeper into a canyon. With each step, the energy of this place seemed to get a little stronger. I had felt this energy before, usually during deep meditation when my mind would temporarily go on vacation. I had also felt it anytime Konka was in deep concentration when working on something. But this was a touch different. This was easily accessible. It required no work on anyone's part. It seemed to just be out there, like water in a pond or oxygen in the air, effortlessly penetrating past any guard at the door. It was thick. I could breathe it, taste it, chew it—it was so prominent I could almost see it. For whatever reason, I was plugged in. Deeper and faster into the canyon I went for many more miles. A magical Zen run at its finest. No mind. No body. Someone else was in charge.

After many miles the trail got tighter, the walls got higher, the sky grew darker, and then the trail vanished altogether, which left no place to run. I stopped, looked up, and noticed I was now deep inside the canyon. I closed my eyes and could hear my heavy breathing and pumping heart. I kept them closed for a few minutes as my system began to come back down to normal.

When I opened them, they were greeted by extreme quiet and calmness. My friend, energy, was still present. He floated in and around every speck of dirt, rock, tree, and cactus; his force powerful yet easy, peaceful, and harmonious. He invaded everything in his presence, including me. He felt like a trusted old friend. One I hadn't talked to in a long time. One who knows the answers.

But why was energy's presence so strong and available? Was this canyon a special place? Did the high walls form a natural container, trapping and holding this energy like a pressure chamber? Maybe I was just experiencing a deeper connection with Konka. He was born in this area. He must have run in these canyons. Was it his spirit I felt? Or was this just me? Had the long ride, sleep deprivation, and Samoan sativa opened up some brief window allowing me to experience it?

I had no idea. As long as it didn't disappear, I didn't care.

I made my way back toward the van, letting this force carry me all the way there.

On arrival, I found Kicker Tom sitting on the ground, leaning up against a large rock and smoking a cigar. Minutes passed and no words were spoken. He puffed away as the adrenaline from my run was starting to wear off.

"Got damn, son. You run like a deer. Thank the lord I didn't have a rifle or you might be dead," he said.

"Haven't you killed enough deer today?"

"Oh, hell, that's right. Don't want to go over my limit." He took another puff of his cigar. "You still feel it?" he asked.

I looked around. "Yeah. You?"

"No. What's it feel like?" he asked.

"Like someone else is in the room with you but nobody's there."

"People in white coats have a name for that."

"Bad example. It's like an invisible power source," I said.

He put his hand over his sternum. "Can you feel it right here?" he asked.

"Yes. That's it. So, you do feel it?"

"Nope. But the Afghans talked about it when they guided us through their mountains. They called it Qudra."

"You never felt it?" I asked.

"Nope. Was focused on other things." He put out his cigar in the dirt. "Tell you what. Why don't we go into town. You can bring Qudra, and I can invite vodka. It'll be like a double date," he said.

I put my hand out, helped the big cowboy to his feet, and we made our way to the van.

CHAPTER THIRTEEN

After dropping Kicker Tom off at the Village Tavern, I drove a few miles out of town and pulled the van into a small parking lot of the Sedona Inn. The address was the same as the one on the letter from Konka's sister, Iris. The Inn sat sandwiched in between 300-foot-high walls of reddish-orange sandstone that hugged the two-lane road on the left and an easy-going river that ran parallel to the cliffs and sat 100 yards down the hill on the right. Ten small cabins were sprinkled among the tall pine trees, all with small decks overlooking the river. The little office was empty, and except for a few cars there seemed to be no sign of human life. I slid my hand through the hole in the glass of the office window and pushed the help button. No one appeared.

As I waited, I walked over to the edge of the parking lot, looked down, and listened to the sound of the water rushing over the rocks. It occurred to me. *This woman doesn't know I exist. How am I going to explain who I am? How am I going to tell her that her brother has passed?* Before I had a chance to figure out my approach I heard a voice say, "Tag."

Standing in front of me was a familiar face. Yet one I'd never seen before. It was the eyes. They were the same as Konka's. Exactly. She wasn't as tall and didn't have quite the chiseled face, but there was no mistaking the resemblance.

She saw the puzzled look on my face. "You look like your picture," she said.

She walked over and gave me a long, strong hug. It was warm and motherly. It reminded me of my grandmother. I was a six-year-old boy again—safe, happy, and not a care in the world. I didn't want to let go.

"I'm glad you made it. Let's go inside. We have a lot to talk about," she said.

As she made us tea, I stepped out onto the deck that looked out over the river. The reddish-orange light flowed through the pines. The energy I'd experienced earlier was still present, yet less intense.

"Nature's heartbeat," she said as she handed me a cup of tea.

"It's strong here," I said.

She put her fingertips on my chest. "Stronger for some than others."

"Is that important?" I asked.

"My father said, 'You can't hunt with a dull arrow.'"

I had no idea what she meant so I changed the subject. "Do you work here?"

"Work, live, own. Your grandfather bought the land for me forty years ago. He built the office and the first four cabins. I've added six more since."

"He had money?" I asked.

"Yes," she said.

"But we were poor," came off my tongue without thought.

"Poor?" she said with a quizzical look on her face. "Did you have a home?"

"Yes."

"Clothes to wear?"

"Yes."

"Food?"

"Yes."

"Love?"

"Yes."

"Was there anything you needed you didn't have?"

70

"No."

"How were you poor?"

My flippant choice of words had left me with no move. Checkmate.

"Teaching our children to live simply is one of the best gifts we can give them," she said.

I wanted to explain myself but thought it wise to keep my flytrap shut and listen. She seemed to sense my embarrassment and grabbed my hand and led me inside to a large, spongy couch in her living room that was next to a stone fireplace. Though the warmth coming through the open balcony doors suggested a fire wouldn't be necessary.

"Did you move here from the reservation?" I asked as she sat down next to me.

"Yes."

"Is it close by?"

"Not too far. A few relatives still live there. I go to visit and participate in different ceremonies, but it's a hard way of life. No electricity. No running water. It suits some."

"Why did he leave the reservation?"

"Joseph, your grandfather, was seventeen when our grandfather left to the spirit world. Like you, he was lost. He wanted to know more about the world around him. The world outside of the reservation. How it worked. What it was about. How he wanted to live in it. But his options were limited. So, Joseph asked our father's permission to join the US Army and become a pilot. Our father refused his request."

"Why?"

"In his eyes, Joseph wanted to join the same government and military that took land from us, that lied to our tribe and others over and over. That arrested and sent our tribal elders to jail."

"Why did they do that?"

"The government wanted to assimilate the next generation of Native American children to their customs and ways. They built schools for this purpose. When any parent refused to send their kids to one of these schools they were arrested and jailed. Our

71

father's two uncles spent over a year in Alcatraz. So, as you can imagine, the resentment in my father toward the government ran deep. However, Joseph's desire was too strong. He felt a greater force pushing him. So he joined anyway. Our father was heartbroken. He felt Joseph had turned his back on him, the Hopi, and our way of life. He was ashamed and told Joseph never to return. A year later, after Pearl Harbor, other Hopi and Navajo men enlisted and served. But our father was a proud man. He couldn't forgive Joseph. They never spoke again."

"He was seventeen when he joined the army?" I asked.

"He told them he was eighteen. They never questioned it."

As the light from the outside began to fade, she got up and lit a plethora of different-sized candles that decorated the room before going into the kitchen to check on something that was in the oven. I'm not sure what it was, but it smelled like home. I looked around the living room to all the paintings that decorated the walls. I stopped on the largest one hanging directly across from where I was sitting. It looked like two roads on top of each other that split apart as they moved into the distance. "What's that?" I asked as she came back into the room with a kettle of hot water.

"You've never seen it before?"

"No."

"Koyaanisqatsi is the Hopi word for a world that is out of balance. Our grandfather first drew a scene representing this idea many years ago. This is my interpretation of it."

She poured more hot water into both of our cups.

"What does it mean?" I asked.

"Our grandfather believed all life would cease on this planet unless everyone learns to live in peace and harmony with each other and nature. This ultimate destruction will come in the form of floods, earthquakes, fires, eruptions, and other severe weather disruptions as a result of our continued abuse of Mother Nature. That's of course if we don't kill each other first."

"Do you believe it?"

"I wish not. But even your science agrees this is so."

"What does the top line mean?" I asked.

She put the kettle down on the table in front of the couch and walked over to the painting. "That is the path we're on now. It represents the path of technology that has shown little respect for earth and lacks any type of spiritual balance. It's a path deeply out of balance with nature."

"The white man's path?" I asked.

"Yes."

"Why are those people's heads not connected to their bodies?" I pointed to the figures walking on the white man's path.

"It represents the separation of our minds from our hearts and souls."

"And the lower line is the way of the Native American people?" I asked.

"Yes, it's the red road, the sacred way. But you can see there is only one person on this road, showing few people are still on this path."

"Why?"

"Indigenous clans are disappearing. Small towns are disappearing, ranchers and farmers are disappearing, rural communities are disappearing. And as those lifestyles are destroyed, humanity is being forced into the urban sprawl for work. For the first time in the history of our species, more people live in cities and urban areas away from nature than in the countryside."

"Society's arrow is getting duller," I said.

"Yes."

I looked back to the painting. "And the line connecting the two paths?"

"It's a way back. A path of possibility. A way to bridge these two opposites, to move from ultimate destruction to peace and harmony."

"Konka often talked about our society moving in a dangerous direction."

"When we get here," she pointed to the wavy line on the end of the white man's road, "it'll be too late to act."

"Is it too late?" I asked.

"We're getting close."

I took a sip of the hot tea and looked at her long braids of white hair, her tan skin, and her perpetual smile. She was as stoic and calm as he was. I couldn't take my eyes off her. It was as though I was looking at him. "I apologize, I don't mean to stare, it's just that you remind me of him."

"You miss him, don't you?" she asked.

I looked into the still flame of one of the large candles. "Very much," I said. *How did she know he was gone? How did she know I was coming here?* She seemed to have the same quality he did. They knew things, saw things, felt things on a different level. Somehow connected to something the masses are not privy to. I tried to ask but couldn't get the words out. "I don't understand…"

She walked back over and sat down next to me. Our knees were touching. She grabbed my hands and looked into my eyes. "On the night he passed into the spirit world, he visited me in a dream. He said you would come through on your journey. I've been expecting you."

"Did he say anything else?" I asked.

"No. He just smiled and laughed."

"Did he crack himself up?"

She started laughing. Which made me laugh. "Yes. Yes, he did," she said.

Her laugh was much different than his but just as contagious. We both sat there laughing, each laugh tickling the other's funny. Back and forth this went on until the tears of surrender appeared. It felt as though he was in the room with us. All of us, laughing uncontrollably together. It was my first real belly laugh since he left.

"That felt good," I said as I melted into the couch.

"Tonic for the soul," she said.

I missed that the most about him, that laugh. He did it with such ease. Such spontaneity. Such grace. It was as easy and sincere as breathing. His laughter had laughter. It had joy. Delight. You could feel humanity in that laugh. It was automatic, and it came from somewhere deep inside.

"You know, I never saw him angry, frustrated, annoyed. Ever. He'd laugh at the first sign of life's inconvenience: a stubbed toe, a broken wrench, a flat tire. The worse the situation, the harder the laugh. I wish I had that," I said.

"You do. It just needs more polish."

"But he did it without effort," I said.

"You got to see the finished product. It takes much practice to tame the wolf."

"I don't think I'm the wolf-taming type," I said.

She took a sip of her tea and a long look at me. "Our grandfather was a medicine man. I was too young to remember much about him, but Joseph was very close to him. He saw the same thing in Joseph that Joseph saw in you."

"What's that?" I asked.

"Pahana."

"That was the spirit name he gave me."

"Do you know what it means?" she asked.

"Until a few years ago, I thought it meant lost white brother. I thought it was Konka's sense of humor. Me, showing up out of nowhere on his doorstep. When I got to high school, I did some research. I believe it's a Hopi prophecy. Something about two brothers being separated. Many years later, the lost white brother, or Pahana, returns from the east with knowledge that brings purification and peace and again can join his brother. During this purification, all evil would be destroyed, and true peace and brotherhood would flourish."

"There are many versions, but that is the gist of it."

"But if Konka was the Pahana, how can I be the Pahana?" I asked.

"He was Pahana, not the Pahana."

"Pahana is not a person?" I asked.

"No."

"The story is a metaphor?"

"Yes. Most of our stories are told in such a manner. That's why the white man dismisses them as farcical and myth, because on the surface they are."

"Konka said the same about most religions. Their words, their stories, their Bibles are usually taken as a literal translation. That's the mistake. That's what gets them in trouble."

"Among other things," she said.

I got off the couch and went over to a table in the middle of the living room that held most of the candles. I looked past them to the outside. It was completely dark.

"So, Pahana is searching for knowledge?"

"Yes."

"And Konka discovered that knowledge?"

"He did."

I brought my attention back inside and gazed at all the candles that were illuminating the room. "And I'm looking for this as well?"

"That is the reason for your journey, is it not?" she asked.

"Well," I paused to think about it, "I think so. But to be truthful, I'm not sure what I'm looking for."

"Because you are lost, Pahana. White brother is lost. But that's okay, being lost is a good thing. Most people are lost. They just don't realize it. You do. How wonderful."

"Wonderful?" I asked.

"Only when one discovers they're lost do they begin the search."

"Did your grandfather ever get lost? Was he also Pahana?" I asked.

"No. He didn't need to be. He never left the red road. He went deeper on it. But, of course, it was a different time. A simpler time. Then the white men came to our world, and everything started to change."

I walked over to the large painting and pointed to the top path. "The white road?"

"Yes."

I traced my hands over the two paths as they moved further and further apart. "So, is Pahana someone who is searching for his

76

way back to the other path? To the red road?" I pointed to the vertical line connecting the white road to the red road.

"Yes."

"And Konka found the way?"

"Yes."

"And that is the road he was leading me down?"

"I'm quite sure."

"Why?"

"Maybe so you could show other people the way."

"Why me?"

"It's young people who change the world." She gave me a big smile, went into the kitchen, and prepared us a wonderful dinner of sautéed trout, steamed quinoa, roasted squash, tomatoes, and cornbread, which we washed down with a homemade beer called Iris's Brew. She held court for several more hours as I picked her brain about Konka and life.

CHAPTER FOURTEEN

It was nearly midnight before I made it back to the Village Tavern. I wondered if Kicker Tom was still there. If he was, I hoped after the date with his Russian friend he would still be the Kicker Tom I'd known for the past eighteen hours. I'd seen it before. The metamorphosis, as Eddie called it. A perfectly normal, fun-loving guy transformed into a raging lunatic after an evening spent with the devil elixir, vodka. Oh sure, tequila, whiskey, gin, and rum were no saints either, but for some reason vodka seemed to bring out the worst in people. Add in the fact that while Kicker Tom seemed fun-loving, from what I'd witnessed, normal wasn't in his DNA. Hopefully, his get-together with little Miss Stoli was purely social, though I doubted that.

Within a few steps of entering the tavern, it was clear my assumption was correct. Kicker Tom had made her his girlfriend, but at least they weren't fighting yet. They were obviously still much in love. They had to be. I mean, how else could one explain a large, drunk cowboy on a karaoke stage singing both parts of "Endless Love" to an empty chair. The fact he couldn't pronounce most of the words didn't seem to matter. What was left of the bar crowd cheered him on anyway. They appeared to be having as much fun with it as he was. I caught his eye after the song ended.

He stumbled off the stage to a partial standing ovation and ran over. "You came back," he said, astonished.

"That was the plan," I said.

He came in and before I knew it had me in a man-love-stare grip around the neck. He pulled me in close and whispered with drunken sadness, "Sometimes plans change and people don't tell you."

I had no idea what he meant. And at the moment didn't care. I knew the sooner we got out of there the better. I wasn't sure he had drunk all of Russia, but by the amount of fumes hitting me in the face, I was sure most of the motherland was dry. "Let's go, I got a place for us to stay," I said.

I attempted to help Kicker Tom walk toward the door. But why do that when you still have a bar full of booze?

"You need a drink, Tag. Come on. I'm buyin'."

"No. I'm good."

"Come on, brother. One for the ditch," he said.

"Isn't that where I picked you up?"

"Oh, yeah. Hell then, we'll have two drinks. One for that ditch and one for the next ditch." He made a motion toward the bar and promptly fell into it. "Oh hell, did you see that? The room moved."

I tried to get him turned in the right direction when the room shifted again, and he fell back into the bar and bumped a guy sitting there. Unfortunately, the wrong guy.

"What the hell is your problem?" the guy yelled.

"Sorry. No problem, just a little stumble," I replied.

"Not talking to you, boy. Talking to hoss," he said.

I'd learned the worst kind of person in a bar isn't the drunk person but the angry person. You can have 200 people in a joint and the angry one will find someone to fight. His first choice is always the other angry guy. For the simple reason: it's easy. Automatic. No invitation necessary. No wasting time. Finding each other is basic physics. Pure gravity. Some kind of weird rotational pull. A magnetic force. Anger attracting anger. Booze making the anger and attraction only stronger. And the easiest way to get the anger out is to fight. Pulverize or be pulverized or both. Winning isn't the goal. Getting out the anger is. I'd witnessed this at Scooter's on many occasions. I sometimes drove one of the bleeding and bruised participants home. They all told me the same thing. They fought because of how it made them feel afterward. With the anger gone, they felt nothing at all. It was the only time they experienced peace. Tranquility. One guy told me it made him feel closer to God. But the feeling was temporary. Anger is like the worst form of cancer. It comes back. Usually stronger.

"No problem, we're on our way out," I said.

"What's wrong, big boy can't speak?" he replied.

Now, when an angry guy can't find another angry guy, he opts for plan B. Big guy, mainly because big guys don't usually back down. After doing a quick survey of the room, I was pretty sure angry guy had found his mark.

Kicker Tom slurred in my ear, "Why's he so mad?"

For some stupid reason, I whispered back, "Anger is the weak man's high." It was one of Konka's sayings. And while it may be true, this wasn't the time or place for a philosophical discussion. My point was proven in short order.

"Anger is the weak man's high," Tom said out loud like a preacher to his flock.

"What the hell does that mean, cowboy?"

Kicker Tom thought about it for a second in his drunken haze, and then looked at me for an explanation.

"Uh...well," I said. "Anger is like, like..." I spotted a bowl of potato chips sitting on the bar and grabbed them. "Like these potato chips. Once you eat one, then you have to have another and another. They taste so damn good. They make you feel great, momentarily. Yet everyone knows that potato chips are bad for you. Bad for your cholesterol. Bad for your heart. Eventually, if you eat enough of them, they'll kill you. But once you start, you're hooked, like a meth addict. And only a strong, confident man can put down the potato chip bowl." I held the chip bowl out to angry guy. "Are you a strong man?"

Without hesitation, he slapped the bowl out of my hands. I had my answer. Kicker Tom stepped in front of me before the bowl hit the ground. "I guess that means you don't want to be friends," he said.

"Go fuck yourself, cowb--"

Before the word "boy" could come out of angry guy's chip hole, Kicker Tom slammed the man's head against the bar and pinned it there with his left forearm. Tom's right arm had angry guy's right arm twisted behind his back. The place was silent for the next minute, the only sound coming from Tom's whispers into angry guy's ear. When he let go, angry guy didn't move.

As I helped Tom walk out, he said to me, "He was just confused. He wants to be friends now."

We performed a combination do-si-do and a drunken version of the Texas two-step all the way into the van.

Any time you have a large human vessel full to the brim with fermented grains of ethanol, you might want to stay away from winding roads. Moments after pulling the van over, Kicker Tom released Moscow and St. Petersburg from his body. Then, violently, came Samara and Kazan. For the next twenty minutes, other parts of Russia I couldn't spell or pronounce flooded the Sedona hillside with reckless abandon. Finally, there was nothing left to say, and like most bad relationships, this one had come to a sad end. Though if my short history had taught me anything, those two would date again. However, I was guessing it might be a while.

I managed to get Kicker Tom back into the van. On the drive to the Sedona Inn, he was quiet. Still awake but empty. Every bit of thought and emotion left back on the side of the hill. That changed the minute I got him into the room. As he fell onto the bed, he started garbling to himself. "I'm sorry," he said.

I didn't respond. I was too busy getting his lizard-skin Tony Lamas off his size- fourteen feet.

"I'm sorry, Jacob. I'm so sorry. I'm not a bad person. I was wrong. I'm so sorry," he mumbled over and over.

I stood in the doorway looking down at this giant man. Somehow, seven years of war hadn't killed him, though it was now apparent something had.

I turned out the lights.

CHAPTER FIFTEEN

The stilling of the mind was central to everything Konka taught me. He called it the cultivation of attention. The secret to this was learning how to concentrate and focus.

Our morning meditation was the beginning of my training, though I never thought of it as training. To me, it was always a game. How long could I focus on one thing until my mind wandered elsewhere? This became a competition with myself. Each week, each month, each year, I got better and better at calming the child in my head and teaching him how to sit still. Our mornings on the dock were only a start. Konka said, "Every moment is a chance to participate. An opportunity to learn." He routinely stopped me and asked, "Where is your mind? Is it here now?" He did it so often I began to ask myself the same question. Eventually, I didn't have to ask anymore. It would happen on its own without prompting from me. *Where is my mind? Is it here now?*

I have no doubt that's why I did so well in school. It's not that I was smarter than anyone else. I just had the ability to stay in the moment and pay attention.

Yet, I knew a grander reason existed for this discipline. I had a suspicion it held the key to the path he was leading me down though it often puzzled me as well. Stillness seemed to be in direct opposition to evolution's driving motor: action and movement. But if Konka was right, somehow those two counters tangoed effortlessly.

I didn't know if that was the reason I still got up in the mornings to meditate. Maybe it was out of sheer habit. Maybe it reminded me of him, of our time together. Maybe it made me feel like he was still here. Regardless, it's something I did. Today was no different.

Kicker Tom was in the same position I'd left him in seven hours before. The occasional bearish snore alerted the world the Reaper hadn't stolen him in the night. I walked about a mile down a trail next to the river looking for a place to sit. The energy I'd experienced the previous day was out of bed early and beginning to yawn. Not completely awake, its force, while palpable and present, hadn't yet penetrated my being like the day before. It casually and quietly hung in the air like the morning dew clinging to the vegetation.

I found a large rock, took a seat, closed my lids, and listened to the running water and the world around it. Twenty minutes had passed by when I heard footsteps coming my way. They stopped about fifteen feet in front of me. Whoever they belonged to didn't say a word. They just plopped themselves on the ground. Any curiosity to open my lids and see my company had been programmed out of me long ago. "Don't give in to the urge," Konka would say.

It wasn't easy. It took many years not to react like a nervous puppy to every sound or movement. He had taught me to treat all those sounds with equal weight. To him, there was no difference between a waterfall or a car crash. It wasn't the sound that was important. It was our reaction to it, and his reaction was always the same. Balanced, even, and at total peace, as if nothing had changed. "Find the silence amidst the noise," he would say.

I hadn't quite mastered the technique at his level, but I could handle the presence of another human being. Any desire to take a peek vanished. The presence melded into the stew of running water, wild bird chirps, and the occasional plane in the distance. When my eyes eventually opened, I was a bit startled to see someone sitting across from me. Between his silence and my meditative state, I'd forgotten someone was there. Other than my eyes opening, I hadn't moved a muscle. He didn't notice any change, because he was in his own meditative state. He seemed as focused as I had been, yet all of his attention was on whoever he was texting. I figured he hadn't disturbed me by saying anything, so I thought it only right to return the favor. Besides, he seemed to be in deep conversation judging by the lightning-fast movement of his thumbs. I thought it best not to interrupt his flow.

He looked maybe a few years older than me, wore jeans, T-shirt, designer Nike shoes with the laces untied, and a backward baseball cap. His flying thumbs continued their rapid pace for several more minutes when out of nowhere he looked up as his thumbs kept motoring along. "You're awake, bro," he said.

"You can text without looking?" I replied.

"Ah no, bro. Not texting. Slinging some birds. Level fourteen. You play?"

"Not much of a gamer," I said. The truth was I'd never played one in my life.

"Me neither, bro. Only when I need to kill some time."

The fact he was on level fourteen led me to believe he had killed his share of it.

"You want to see the cave?" he asked.

"Cave?"

"Where your great-great-grandfather lived. Our great-great-grandfather lived."

"Who are you?" I asked.

"I'm your cuz, bro. Louis. My bros call me Sweet Lou. Iris is my grandmother."

"Technically we might be second cousins, but who's keeping score?" I said.

"Yeah, bro. Second cousins. Sweet! You're my two-cuz."

"I guess I am," I said.

"Ready to roll, bro?"

"Sure."

"Sweet!"

Can't imagine how he got his nickname.

CHAPTER SIXTEEN

After thirty minutes with Sweet Lou, I still didn't know any more about him other than he liked loud music and enjoyed driving fast while keeping the majority of his attention glued to his phone. I wasn't sure if he was texting, checking Facebook, tweeting, or killing more time. But I was sure that if he continued to use the loose gravel off the right of the road as a casual reminder to straighten the wheel or the line in the middle of the road as a mere suggestion, then things other than time could soon be on his kill list.

"You want me to drive?" I yelled through the cranked music and wind that flowed through his roofless Jeep.

"What?" he yelled back.

"Drive?" I yelled again as I pantomimed me holding on to the wheel.

He leaned closer and screamed, "No problema, bro. I can do this in my sleep."

"Sweet," I said.

Luckily, we left the main road. I say luckily because our rate of speed reduced dramatically and thus my odds of survival grew proportionally. The lack of speed must have made him a touch nervous because he tossed his phone on the dash and committed both hands to the wheel as we crept along a single dirt path that led us deep into a canyon.

I turned down the music. "Are we on the reservation?" I asked.

"Yes and no," he said. "This is now considered Navajo land, but years ago it belonged to us until the government redrew the map."

"Why'd they do that?" I asked.

"Because they're idiots."

"My grandfather used to say the land belongs to no one," I said.

"It don't matter, bro. Times change. You either change with it or you don't. A lot of people like to live in the past. Not me, bro. It's all about the future."

I grabbed the dashboard with my left hand and the doorframe with my right to keep me steady as we began to move up and over large-scale boulders that littered the dirt path.

"You have a plan?" I asked.

"Success, bro. Sweet, sweet success."

"You going to school?"

"Three non-consecutive semesters at the local JC. But it wasn't my thing, bro. I figure Jobs, Gates, Zuckerberg dropped out and they did all right. Plus it got in the way of my music career," he said.

"What do you play?"

"Mostly spin and rap."

"Spin?"

"DJ, bro. Everybody knows the fresh sounds of Sweet Lou. Local king of EDM."

"EDM?"

"Electronic dance music, or as I like to call it, MEDS. Music. Electronic. Dance. Sweet!!!"

"You make money doing that?"

"Yeah, bro. Plus, I got my side businesses."

I was afraid to ask.

"I'm throwing a rave tonight, bro, and you're coming. It'll be off the hook. Sweet Lou style."

I wasn't sure what his style was, but it didn't matter. It was the first time in my life anyone had invited me to a party. To be honest, it felt good. Really good. I didn't care if he was family or not. Someone close to my age had asked me to do something. Something inside me felt intoxicated. It was a feeling I didn't want to let go of. While I knew that was a mistake, I held on to it.

We went over one last large boulder, and Sweet Lou stopped the Jeep. He grabbed a flashlight out of the glove compartment and we jumped out. Handing the flashlight to me he pointed to a path twenty yards away. "Follow that for about a mile or so until it dead ends. Then start climbing. You can't miss it, bro."

"You're not coming?"

"No cell service up there, bro. Got to take care of a few details for tonight's show." He turned around and again became one with his phone.

I hoped Sweet Lou was as good a DJ as he claimed, because any future as a tour guide would be ill advised. After I walked a mile the path disappeared, and I proceeded to walk at least another three. Maybe I should have realized "or so" in this case was short for *I don't know*. But he was right about one thing. I did get to a dead end. However, the "you can't miss it" part might have been a bit optimistic. It was another twenty minutes of climbing up rocks and over ridges until a triangle-shaped hole in the side of the canyon finally appeared.

While Sweet Lou might have oversold the ease of finding the place, he also undersold the best part. In fact, he didn't sell it at all. The view. It was spectacular. Majestic. Standing at the entrance of the cave, you could look out over the whole valley and see every nook and cranny, yet from the valley floor I had walked, you wouldn't know this cave existed unless you stumbled upon it. And as my last hour and a half had taught me, this wasn't a place you stumbled upon, even with the help of a Sweet Lou. But maybe that was the point. You could see everything from the cave while being invisible yourself. If you wanted to see, but not be seen, this was the place.

I wondered if my great-great-grandfather had chosen it for that reason; to remain in touch with the world while in complete solitude.

The cave turned out to be just that. A cave. Nothing else. No markings. No drawings. Nothing. It was so barren inside it looked as if no human had ever been there, much less lived there.

The sun came through the entrance and lit up the insides like a natural giant chandelier reflecting off the bright reddish rock. I wasn't sure why Sweet Lou had given me a flashlight. Maybe he'd never entered the cave himself and assumed it would be dark. It wasn't big either. Maybe the size of a small living room. The walls, however, went up at least twenty feet on all sides and narrowed as they grew toward the ceiling. I say at least because it started getting dark about fifteen to twenty feet up, and that's where the walls disappeared into the darkness.

As I looked up at those walls, I wondered if maybe that was what the flashlight was for. I turned it on and looked for some clue high above where I was standing. Sure enough, I saw a spot that looked like a ledge hiding in the darkness. I put the flashlight in my back pocket and went to the back wall looking for a path up. The way the rocks jutted in and out of the walls you could use them as a natural ladder, so I did. Halfway up you could see where someone, presumably my great-great-grandfather, had cut notches here and there to make the climbing a bit easier. I had traversed my way to below the edge of the ledge when I made a rookie mistake. I looked down. From my new point of view, it seemed much higher than my estimated twenty feet, with nothing but hard rock to soften the fall if I slipped. Before I could let my mind dwell on that fact a moment longer, I pulled myself up onto the ledge.

From a few feet back, one could stand and have a perfect view down without being seen. I wondered if my great-great-grandfather and those who came before him had used this cave as not only a place for solitude but also safety. I turned away from the light below and total darkness greeted me. When I turned on the flashlight, a narrow passageway several feet back appeared. I walked through its winding, dark path, and the darkness faded away as I entered into another cavern. Inside, I turned the flashlight off as the sunlight streaming in from a hole above provided plenty of illumination.

This room was different from the one below. It had been lived in. A dug-out hole near one wall of the room was home to an old fire pit. The charred red rocks from years of smoke passing through the small opening way above gave evidence of that.

Something felt alive here. You could sense it. A worldly presence. Like an old library, history and knowledge hung in the air. Literally. Hundreds of drawings and diagrams covered the walls. Was this the essence of my great-great-grandfather's life? His discoveries? His path? Secrets of the red road? Well, if it was, unless Sherlock Holmes or Robert Langdon appeared, I wasn't going to figure them out. I could make out this image was a buffalo, and that image the sky, and on and on. But what relationship did they have with each other? And what did it all mean?

I thought about going to get Sweet Lou for his insight but then thought better of it. I was sure his analysis would be summed up in one word. Sweet!!! Regardless, I made mental pictures of everything in hopes that either Iris or time would reveal their truths.

As I surveyed the room, an image caught my eye, and I walked over to the north wall and took a closer look. It was a circle. Inside the circle was a square filled with different geometrical shapes. As I traced my fingers over the pattern, I searched for the necklace under my shirt and pulled it out. Its design was similar to the image I was looking at. The necklace was the only piece of jewelry I'd ever owned. Konka had given it to me the night he left for the spirit world. He called it a mandala and told me Buddhist monks used them in their meditative practice. He also gave me a passport at the same time and said to let these be my guides. I think it was his way of saying never stop traveling. The passport represented outward travel while the mandala represented the inward journey. Konka had painted and drawn many versions of the mandala and placed them in and around our home.

As I looked further around the cave, I noticed another of my great-great-grandfather's mandalas. It was across on the south wall at the same height as the first one. I spotted two more, one on the east wall and the other on the west wall, at the same height facing each other. As I stared at the mandala on the west wall, another image caught my eye. Above the mandala was a large drawing of the two roads picture that Iris had painted and hung in her living room. My great-great-grandfather's version was much simpler and basic, but there was no mistaking the resemblance. My eyes followed the top line, which represented the white road, to almost its end when they came upon another line, or road, that headed back down and connected to the red road below it. I fixated on the line between the white and red roads.

The path of possibility. The bridge between the two opposites. The way back.

I looked back down at the mandala below, then over to the mandala on the east wall. I walked over and stood in the center of the four mandala images, which put me just about in the middle of the cave. I sat down, lay back, looked up, and to my surprise, more drawings appeared. High above, a twenty-by-twenty-foot rock with a flat surface made for a perfect canvas. On it was an image of a white wolf and a dark wolf looking directly into each other's eyes. The white wolf was expressionless. The dark wolf was showing his sharp teeth and seemed to be in attack mode. Below those images was a bright, radiant sun and an Indian chief sitting just below that. The rays of sunlight permeated from all different directions right through a circle above the Indian's head and into the center of his chest.

As I tried to make sense of the scene above, I wondered how my great-great-grandfather had drawn those images. They were straight up over twenty feet off the ground and in the middle of the cave. How did he get up there? What did he stand on? Did he build some kind of crude scaffolding? Did he hang from the rocks above like Spiderman? Levitation?

As I thought of him hanging up there painting the ceiling, my thoughts turned to Michelangelo. Not that this was in any way, shape, or form a Sistine Chapel. This ceiling was by no means an artistic masterpiece. It was, however, an expression of ideas, an expression of thought, a philosophy on life. There was something in there he wanted the rest of the world to know, to learn, not to forget, but I had no idea what that was.

I wondered if there was some weird connection between the two ceilings or to Michelangelo himself, or if my imagination had gone off grid. If there was a connection, I wasn't going to figure it out at that moment. I knew little about the Sistine Chapel or Michelangelo. In my small-town south-Texas classroom, we didn't spend a lot of time on sixteenth-century Italian artists, even the great Michelangelo. Now, if Davy Crockett had painted the Sistine Chapel that would be a different story. We spent a whole semester on the Alamo.

When I walked out of the cave, I was surprised to see my two-cuz Sweet Lou waiting for me. His face was buried in his phone and by the look of his thumb motion, he was killing more time and birds.

"Not much to see, huh?" he said as he looked up.

He obviously had never made it up to the penthouse portion of the cave.

"Not sure why Grandma wanted you to see it so bad. But hey, that's what she wanted," he said.

"So, do you believe the stories about him?" I asked.

"You mean our great-great-grandpapa, him being superhuman and all? Magic powers, see in the future, read people's minds, be at two places at one time. Listen, I love my grandmother, but she's old school. That stuff is nothing but a bunch of old stories told by old people sitting by a campfire. Don't get me wrong, I respect my native peeps, but at the end of the day Sweet Lou believes in one thing. Reality. And right now, the reality is, Sweet Lou has a show to put on and gots to go."

CHAPTER SEVENTEEN

S weet Lou dropped me off at the cabins, where I was expecting to find a large cowboy still paying for his previous night's indiscretions. I was wrong. Kicker Tom was gone. A perfectly made bed was my evidence of that. I guess once a Marine, always a Marine. A note on the table read, "Gone Fishing" with an arrow pointed upstream.

After about a mile hike, I found Iris in waist-deep water casting her fly rod hoping to find lunch. Kicker Tom, catching a few rays, sat half-submerged next to the bank, his arm around a bucket of Iris's brew.

"I see you found a new girlfriend," I said.

"She's much nicer than the one last night," he replied.

"How's your head?"

"Nothing this cold water and a few of these won't fix," he said as he took a long swig. He yelled to Iris, "Need another beer, my good lady?"

She looked back, smiled, and shook her head.

"You getting Iris drunk?" I asked.

"Hell, no, she has more sense than that. Unlike myself," he said and took another swig. "Did I say anything crazy last night?"

"You didn't do a lot of talking after we left the bar."

"Yeah, don't remember that part."

"Don't worry, you didn't miss anything worth repeating," I said.

I slid off my sandals and started to walk toward Iris. All was good until I dipped my foot into the river. A shock went through my system. The water was freezing. Iris had proper fishing gear on, but how in the hell was Kicker Tom handling it? He looked like he was sitting in a hot tub. With each step, I went deeper until the water was almost up to my waist.

Iris could sense my discomfort. "You'll get used to it," she said.

"When?"

"When you train your mind to disassociate pain with something that's bad or..." she paused as if lost in thought.

"Or?" I said.

"Or when you get a pair of these," she said, pulling on her waders. She let out a loud laugh, then another.

That was such a Konka joke.

I stood next to Iris and we laughed for a bit as she continued to cast. Then the pain of the freezing water sobered that laugh right up. "Last night you said to tame the wolf," I said.

"Yes."

"Which one?"

"There is only one wolf."

"But in the cave, there are two wolves. A white wolf and a dark wolf."

"It's the same wolf." By the look on my face she could tell I had no idea what she meant. She reached into her fishing vest and handed me a coin.

As I looked at the top side of it, she asked, "What do they call that side of the coin?"

"Heads."

"And the other side?"

I flipped it over. "Tails."

"Yet, it is the same coin."

"An illusion," I said. "Why didn't you tell me about the cave last night?"

"I wanted to see."

"See what?"

"If Pahana was awake."

"It was a test?"

"Only an awakened Pahana goes places, finds things, sees things others don't. Only an awakened Pahana will find a way back."

"But I was taken there."

"Many have been taken there. Many have been there. Only a few have found the room."

"Konka?"

"Yes, right before he left for the service."

"But, what does everything mean?"

She didn't say anything.

"Those walls were like reading a foreign language. I didn't understand any of it."

"You will."

"When?"

"When it's time to know."

"And I'm guessing now is not that time."

She smiled. "Patience and persistence," she said.

I knew the phrase well. Konka used to say, "If you want to excel in life all you need is patience and persistence." Patience and persistence. Over and over he would say it, any time I was learning something new. Like their cousins stillness and movement, they seemed to contradict each other. But at least I understood their relationship better. I had learned how to wait while still never giving up.

"On Konka's travels, did he ever go to Rome?" I asked.

"That's where he learned Italian."

"Did he see the Sistine Chapel?"

"I don't know. He never mentioned it."

She made another cast with her rod. I followed the fly as it hit the water on the other side of the stream. I wanted to tell her my plans but couldn't get the words out. Without taking her eyes off the other side of the river she began to reel and asked, "What so concerns you?"

"I'm thinking about leaving tomorrow."

"I know."

"How do you know?"

"Sharp arrow," she said.

"But I like it here, it feels like home. I don't want to leave, but something is telling me to move forward, and I don't know why."

She looked over to me, "Because…" she made a quick motion with her rod as a trout hit her line. The loud thrashing of water eventually subsided as she carefully reeled him close to her body. She scooped up her lunch in a net, and then pulled him out by his lip with her fingers. Lifting up her catch, she looked at me. "Because your trout is in another stream."

A sudden pain shot through my legs. It felt like someone was jabbing needles into them. I suppose there was more than one thing telling me to leave.

"I don't think my mind has quite yet mastered the disassociating technique," I said.

"Yes, that takes many years of practice. The wader method is much quicker. Maybe it's time for dry land," she said.

"I don't know if I can."

"Why not?"

"Because my legs won't move."

Iris helped me drag myself out of the river and back over to Kicker Tom basking in his ice bath and brew.

"Ahh hell, son, doesn't it feel great?" he said as the water cascaded over him.

"For someone divorcing life, you sure seem to be having lots of fun."

"I guess it's working, my friend," he said.

CHAPTER EIGHTEEN

K icker Tom decided to play DJ and had selected the best of the Steve Miller Band as we headed toward Sweet Lou's party, or as he called it, "The Dance in the Desert, Part Three." He told me part two was not to be believed and part three was going to be part two on steroids yet much, much sweeter. I had no doubt, nor did I care. I was just glad to be invited.

As "Fly Like an Eagle" was pumping through the speakers, the Mystery Machine waddled like a duck trying to find the next turn on the pitch-black road. Shockingly, Sweet Lou's directions were not quite up to scale as we headed deeper into the Hopi reservation. When all seemed lost, two cars flew by us on the left, the insides of both glowing with bright reds, purples, greens, yellows, oranges, and blues. We were no longer lost. We had two pace cars ahead of us, so we followed along.

I looked over at Kicker Tom. He was in his mandatory riding position, cowboy hat hung low and right leg hanging out the window resting on the side-view mirror.

"Where would you like me to take you?" I asked.

He looked over and gave me a puzzled look.

"I'm taking off tomorrow."

"Why?"

"Because my trout is in another stream," I said.

His puzzled look got more puzzled.

"What do you want to do?" I asked.

As he listened to the music he said, "I want to go to the coast, the ocean, the water. There's a little town just south of San Diego. But hell, I don't expect you to take me. I appreciate ya taking me this far. Drop me off on the side of the road when you need to go in the other direction. I'll take the reins from there," he said.

"You going to hitchhike?" I asked.

"Hitch, jump a train, bus, hell I don't know. I'll figure it out."

Now, I hadn't planned on going to the west coast, but then again, I didn't have a plan. I was still directionless. At that point, the wind was my direction and it seemed to be blowing toward San Diego.

"I'll take you," I said.

"You sure?"

I didn't know why, but I liked Kicker Tom. He was authentic. He was who he was and made no apologies. At the core, he seemed to be a good person—had a good heart. I was sure there was more I could learn from him and maybe him from me. Or maybe I wasn't ready to be alone yet.

So, I said in my best Kicker Tom impersonation, "Ah hell, son, why not?" I turned the music back up and we followed the glow.

We arrived at what turned out to be an old airstrip and hangar built by the United States government during the Second World War. Once it was no longer needed, the government kindly gave it to the Hopi people as a gesture of goodwill, which was awfully nice considering it was their land to begin with. The airstrip was overrun by time and the elements, and the hangar hadn't been used in fifty years. In fact, it wasn't used until a certain enterprising young Hopi had convinced the elders to let him use it as a place to bring young people from different tribes of life together and celebrate and praise that life in the form of dance.

Now, I don't know if that is what convinced them or if it was their cut of the ten-dollar donation for anyone to pass through the doors of the old hangar. Whatever the reason, Sweet Lou had the perfect place to throw a rave: a place in the middle of nowhere

where you could be as loud or illegal as you wanted to be. I soon discovered Sweet Lou had taken liberty with both of those advantages.

The party was in full gear as we entered the belly of love. The building, stoic and cold from the outside, was warm and alive on the inside. Music blared as hundreds danced to the shifting beats while surrounded on all sides by giant light screens morphing in and out of every color in the spectrum. Light rays shot from all angles as the colors danced along with the bass beat. Everything and anything tangible glowed or sparkled: hats, belts, necklaces, earrings, shoes, shirts, skin, beach balls, and sticks. It all looked like a glowing, dancing rainbow had thrown up on itself and its surroundings.

I stood fixated on this young mass of humanity dancing without limitation or inhibition. Everyone seemed unafraid and free—that openness and unabashed freedom calling me to join, to jump in, yet the mere thought scared the living shit out of me.

I could never do that. I'd never danced. These freedom kids would laugh me out of the building. It would be high school all over again, but on one grand stage in a single moment. My intimidation turned to pure fear with each step. What was I doing here? I didn't belong. These were the cool kids. It was just a matter of time before I was discovered or, worse yet, ignored. What a horrible idea this was. What had I been thinking? I was in way over my head. *Don't panic,* I thought. *Kicker Tom is here. Stay close, and it'll all be okay.*

It was at that moment two young twenty-somethings dressed from head to toe in nothing much more than glitter and glow jumped in front of my protector.

"My name is Happy," said the first.

"And I'm Bliss," said the other. "Let's dance, cowboy."

They grabbed him by both arms and before he said a word led him into the middle of the happy madness. In a flash, my safety blanket vanished.

I walked around the sea of jumping, pumping, sliding, stomping, twisting, gyrating flesh and made my way up front to a set of stairs that led up to the DJ booth that hung high over the crowd. Looking up, I saw Sweet Lou doing his thing. I thought about walking up to him, but next to Sweet Lou stood a large, older Indian man. His body language and facial expression said, "Don't even think about it." However, he must have caught my lost puppy-dog gaze, because he tapped Sweet Lou on the shoulder and my two-cuz looked down.

Half a minute later, Sweet Lou was running down the stairs. "Two-cuz, you made it," he yelled.

"I don't mean to bother you while…"

"Don't worry, bro, I've got it on a pre-recorded track. I've got a few minutes."

"Who's your buddy up there?"

"That's Big Mountain. He's the advisor."

"The advisor?"

"About every half hour or so, the joy gets the better of someone and they insist on playing D.J. Big Mountain advises them not to." Sweet Lou put his hands up like a ringmaster at the circus showing off his spectacle. "Whataya think? Sweet, huh?"

I looked around. "Extremely," I said.

I suppose I said the right thing because he put his arm around my shoulder and led me on a tour of the rest of his empire. We couldn't get more than a few steps without someone coming up and saying hi, giving him a hug, candy, or something that glowed.

And with each new person, it seemed I had a new friend. Sweet Lou introduced me to all of them. They hugged me as well and insisted we hang out later. It all seemed real, genuine with no strings attached. What was happening? Why was everyone being so nice? Then it occurred to me. I was with the most popular kid in school and he had his arm around me—coolness by association, instant credibility, instant friends. To be truthful, while it felt good, at the moment, it felt like I was wearing someone else's coat; it didn't fit. Yet I didn't want to take it off either.

Sweet Lou led me to an area of small tents and tables. Here you could buy anything and everything you might need to have a good time yet forgot to bring. And Sweet Lou owned it all. By the look of the crowd, it appeared he was doing a brisk business, particularly in the water tent. When we walked in, I noticed two lines. The shorter line was for water that cost three dollars and the longer line for water that cost twelve dollars.

"Does the twelve-dollar water taste better?" I asked.

"Much better," he said. He pointed to someone behind the table who threw him one of the bottles. He opened it up and handed it to me.

I took a drink. "It tastes like water," I said.

"Because it is water," he said.

"Why pay twelve dollars for it?"

"Flip it over," he said.

I flipped the water bottle over, and taped on the bottom was a little blue pill in a clear pouch.

"What is it?"

"A tab, a bean, a happy pill." He saw by the look on my face that it didn't compute. "Ecstasy. Molly. MDMA. But not just any ecstasy. Good, pure, pharmaceutical-grade ecstasy, not like that shit they sell ya on the street. That's why that line is so long. They know my shit is the best. Clean, safe, fun, and happy. It's all part of putting on a great show. I'll sell about 2,000 tonight."

"You make these?" I asked.

"I got a guy."

I guess the United States government knew what they were doing. It might have taken a few generations for someone to assimilate to their customs and ways, but they'd finally succeeded. Sweet Lou was a true-blue capitalist.

As I looked around, a hand grabbed mine and took my little blue happy pill.

"This is Sama," said Sweet Lou.

"Hi," I said.

She gave me a big hug as if we were long-lost friends. This was a touchy-feely crowd.

"Sama is going to be your guide tonight," said Sweet Lou.

"My guide for what?"

"For the best night of your life. Gotta go, bro, Sweet Lou is back on in a few. PLUR, my two-cuz." He put up the peace sign in front of me and held it there.

"PLUR?" I asked.

"It's what this night is all about. Peace. Love. Unity. Respect." He showed me the PLUR handshake, which started out with us touching the tips of our two fingers that made up the peace sign and ended with our hands together as one. He slid a piece of bracelet candy from his wrist onto mine. It read "Sweet."

"Enjoy," he said and walked away.

"Your name's Tag?" Sama asked.

"Yes."

"That won't do tonight. You need another."

"My spirit name is Pahana," came blurting out to see if that might be more accommodating.

"Pahana, I like that. What does your spirit name mean?"

"Lost white brother."

She laughed and then put her right hand under my chin and moved in close. "Well, Pahana, tonight I'm going to help you find your way." She opened her other hand, which held two blue pills. Before I had a chance to ask a question or object, she put one on her tongue, then mine. I suppose I was already committed. We proceeded to wash them down with the twelve-dollar water.

Sama pulled me toward the dance floor and before I had the chance to dig my heels in, we were in the middle of the fray. I stood flat-footed watching everyone around me moving in their own particular way to the beats of Sweet Lou. No one seemed to mind that I was standing with my feet covered in cement blocks. Including Sama. She danced around me like I was a pole holding up the roof, occasionally touching my face, arm, back, and neck. Before I knew it, several other girls had caught on and I was surrounded by a flurry of skin, hair, beads, and glow, moving around my wooden body. I wanted to move but was frozen with fear. But fear was no match for Sama and her female dance troupe. She moved up from behind, wrapped me up tight with her arms and body, and forced me to go with the beat of the music as the others took turns doing the same in front of me. "Close your eyes and listen," she whispered in my ear.

I knew the command well. So I followed it with complete confidence and slowly found the beat of the music and eventually the rhythms of her movements. I don't know how long she stayed with me, but the beat, the movements of her warm body, and the smell of the others' perfumes put me into a relaxed state, a trance.

I didn't want to open my eyes and bring the rest of the world in, afraid it might break the spell. So, I kept on moving with the beat in my own world until I felt a hand on my face as another whisper entered my ear. "Pahana."

I opened my eyes to a smiling Sama and realized I was dancing on my own. Not great, but I was dancing. Dancing without hesitation, without fear. It wasn't long after that realization that it happened. My first surge. I wasn't sure what was going on, but I started to feel different. My head, stomach, arms, and hands were all awkward and disagreeable. I guess the little blue pill was starting to do its thing, and I wasn't sure I was going to be a fan. My vision seemed off a bit. Getting sick entered my thoughts. I didn't know why Sweet Lou called it a happy pill, because I felt things were moments away from spinning out of control. Sama could sense my unease. She gave me her water bottle and I took a big swig as she yelled, "Dance. Dance. Dance."

I listened to the music and kept on going. As if on cue, Sweet Lou cranked up the beat. It got stronger and faster, and so did I. I looked over and saw two guys dancing in a whole different way. It was more of a bounce and shuffle, a bounce and a shuffle. I did my best to copy what they were doing without much success. One saw my incompetence, jumped over, put his arm around me to help, and we bounced together. The other guy joined me on the other side, the three of us bouncing and moving to the beat. I wasn't sure what I was doing but didn't care. Neither did they. We eventually broke off but not until a perfectly timed, three-way chest bounce off each other, as though we'd scored the winning touchdown. *Where did that come from?*

I looked over to Sama, who was in the groove. The girl could dance. She flowed like a jellyfish in honey yet still matched the tempo and beat. I could have watched her all night. That soft brown skin glistened off the reflection of the lights, her long black hair held up by a combination of glow sticks and beads, her contrasting, super-white teeth that smiled without trying, and those deep, mysterious brown eyes that if you looked at too long, you might never return. She was exotic. She was mesmerizing. She was different than anyone I'd ever seen.

It was at that moment that a sensation came over me like I'd never experienced. Warmth, energy, joy, love, happiness ran through every cell in my body with such intensity a howl of ecstasy exploded without consent from the depths of my soul, rained out loud over the dancing mass, and left me with a permanent grin from ear to ear. The lights and colors seemed more intense. My energy level was an eleven, yet I felt calm and in control. A feeling of love and empathy for anything and everything around dominated my being. I wanted to help people. I wanted to talk and hug everyone in the room. Sama would be my first, but before I could move she wrapped her arms around my shoulders and held me. I held her back. It was the greatest hug in the history of time. As we pulled away, I said, "Thank you, I love you."

She kissed me on the lips and said, "I love you too."

The kiss wasn't sexual. It was one of pure joy, compassion, and understanding.

We continued dancing hard for the next hour, with each other, alone, and with strangers. The whole time, the smile never left my face.

I looked around at all these people: black, white, Indian, Mexican, Asian, and every blend in between, yet nothing but a big melting pot of love—no cliques, no hang-ups, no hate, no judgments. Brothers and sisters, sisters and brothers celebrating harmony, unity, tolerance, respect, freedom, and love through dance.

But how had it happened? Most of these people were a few years removed from high school. Had everyone changed? Had they grown up and dropped all the petty bullshit? Or were these the outliers, the outcasts like me, who found each other, found a place to go, a place to meet, a place to express themselves, be themselves, without worry of retribution. Was this the start of a movement by young people that would lead to a better and more peaceful humankind? Was this the path back to the red road? Or was this the result of that little blue happy pill? If it was all the pill's doing, we needed to slip it to the people who needed it the most. Maybe try a test run in the Middle East? What's the worst that could happen, a hug-fest?

We danced our way up front and I sprung up the steps toward Sweet Lou. I had to say thanks. And, of course, give him a hug. My mad dash was stopped cold in its tracks when I came face to face with Big Mountain a few feet away from my destination. He wasn't smiling. I guess the advisor forgot to take his happy pill.

"Loloma, wuko tuukwi," I said, which meant, *Hello, Big Mountain* in his native tongue. Though I began to question my verbal accuracy, for Big Mountain stood and looked as if a deer had spoken to him.

Before he could say a word and send me on my way, Sweet Lou gave him the thumbs up and I was safe to pass. I saw Sweet Lou was in a deep groove, so I stood several yards away and let him work while I looked down from my high vantage point over the dance floor. Everyone was in their own world, doing their own thing yet somehow still dancing with each other, dancing as one, and like a puppeteer, Sweet Lou was in control of them all. With each new beat, each subtle change, they changed. The joyride he was leading them on made me want to jump over and give him a bear hug of gratitude. Damn, I loved him. But I think I started to make the advisor nervous, so I turned my attention back to the dance floor.

I looked for Kicker Tom but couldn't locate the big cowboy. Intermittently, the lights would turn all one color and the dance floor below seemed to stop. Motion didn't exist, only stillness. Yet inside that stillness, I knew there was constant flow and activity. Movement and stillness. I felt like an astronaut from space looking down on the stillness of earth yet knowing the bustling of energy was taking place on its surface; an energy I wanted to get back to as soon as possible. I wanted to roll in that energy with my new friends. I wanted to dance again.

Sweet Lou was still in his work trance, so I ran over to Big Mountain, gave him the hug instead, and said, "Kwakwhay," which meant *thank you.*

He didn't hug back, but I swear a hint of a smile escaped for a brief moment. "Kwakwhay," he said.

I ran down the stairs hoping to jump back into the earth of dancers but was met by Sama. She had other ideas. She grabbed my hand and led me down a glowing hallway and a set of stairs away from the music. We ended up in a dimly lit room filled with couches, pillows, beanbags, and other cushy things to sit on. Soft, mellow music blended in with library voices that occupied the space. We walked through other hallways and passed several more rooms of the same variety. "This is the chill wing," she whispered to me.

That explained the different-sized groups that sat and talked while they held and massaged each other. I wanted to stop and join all of the conversations, all the touching, all the holding. I wanted to talk to everyone, wanted to make sure they were all right, wanted to know where they were from, why they were here, what they liked, what they didn't, what they wanted from this world.

That would happen soon enough, but first, it was Sama and me, and for that, I was the luckiest person on the planet. We found a spot in a corner on the softest, most kind pillows I'd ever imagined existed. It was pure mush.

"How do you feel?" she asked.

"I didn't know you could feel this way. It's the most intense happiness I've ever experienced."

"Good."

I felt the surge of goodness in my arms, neck, and hands. Then a small chill went through my body.

Sama knew the symptoms well. "This will warm you up." She

leaned over and held me. I held her back. We stayed wrapped in each other as routine surges of ecstasy coursed through our bodies.

"Thank you," I said.

"For what?"

"For hanging out with me tonight."

"Don't thank me. I want to hang out with you. I told Lou I'd dance with you, get you on your way, and make sure you were okay. And are you okay?"

"More than okay."

"But this here right now was my idea."

"It was a great idea," I said.

"I agree, but to be honest, I'm taking advantage."

"No, you're not," I said.

"When I'm feeling like this, like you are, I love to hold, I love to hug, I love to touch, I love to kiss, I love to love, but with most guys, I can't be that way."

"Because they want more," I said.

"Yes."

"I can understand why they would. You're gorgeous."

She smiled and ran her fingers through my hair. "I was thinking the same thing," she said. We got lost into each other for a moment. "But you're different," she said.

"How?"

"The way you hugged me on the dance floor and when you said you loved me, it was pure, authentic, it was innocent. I loved that. It made me feel safe. It made me feel like I can do this." She leaned over and gave me a long kiss on the lips.

It sent another surge of exhilaration throughout my body. "That was nice," I said.

"Yes, it was."

I kissed her back.

"Even better," she said.

"Okay, I'll let you take advantage," I said. I wish I could explain why my hormones weren't in charge, but they weren't. Not that they weren't still alive. They were, I'm sure, somewhere in the background lurking and hoping Sama would change course. But tonight they were no match for the bliss that ran through my being, a bliss even youthful hormones couldn't sabotage.

We held each other in our puddle of gooeyness and talked.

"Is your full name Samantha?" I asked.

"No, Sama is the name my grandmother gave me. She grew up in Iran. In that culture, Sama is a type of meditation created by song and dance. When I was small, she would play music and I'd dance and dance and dance. So, it stuck."

"And you're still dancing."

"It's the only time I can be free. It's the only time when I feel perfect. When I am perfect."

"You don't feel perfect right now?"

She smiled. "This would be the other, but it's a little different when I dance."

"You feel this good?"

"The joy, the happiness is not as intense, but yes I feel this good and in certain ways better. When I dance, the best part of me is left. It's that part of me I want to show the world. It's that part of me I want to live with day to day. It's that part of me that I want to share."

"So why do the happy pill?"

"That happy pill allows me to do this." She looked at me and touched my face. "It allows me to have deep, in-depth connection with another, to have a conversation, to hold, to touch, to kiss, to share me, to share that same best part of me with another. I haven't figured out a way to dance and still do all that. When the music stops, that part of me for some reason goes away."

"Why?"

"I don't know, but I think it has something to do with listening. Sama means to listen. When I dance, that part of me can hear and it wakes up and wants to be alive, it wants to be heard. Like you tonight—it took a while, but you listened and that part of you sprang to life and started to dance on its own without my help, without your help. You weren't dancing, it was dancing."

"Then the music and movement stop and it goes deaf and leaves," I said.

"Yes."

"Maybe it's shy," I said.

"Maybe."

"But it's not shy right now?"

She leaned over and kissed me again. I had my answer.

Is this what Konka had tapped into, that vein of gold that made everything so wonderful, that made the everyday magical, a connection that opened you up and let your true being sing? If it was, he'd not only found a way to access it, he'd learned to control its flow and was able to release the right amount. Like a water faucet he could turn it on and off, he could let it trickle or he could let it surge when needed. Unlike now, where it was a constant deluge of euphoria, though I wasn't complaining.

"I don't want this feeling to end," I said.

"Me neither," she said.

So, we didn't. Sama pulled out two more happy pills. She put one on my tongue, and one on hers. We washed them down with more of the expensive water.

We spent the rest of the evening and morning alternating between the dance floor and the chill wing. I talked to more people, danced with more people, and made more friends that evening than in my previous seventeen years of existence. I felt like a new person and I had to give full credit to that little blue happy pill.

It wasn't so much that it gave me confidence, but it filled me with so much love that it suffocated fear and self-doubt. I wanted to be that person, always, like Sama when she danced, like Konka at all times. I wanted to be free. I didn't want to go back to the old me. I didn't want the night to end. I didn't want to see the pumpkin.

But time was on a different schedule, and the music stopped and the lights faded.

I said thanks and goodbye to Sweet Lou, Big Mountain, and all of my new friends. I found Kicker Tom, and I'm pretty sure I announced my love to the big cowboy.

The last hug of the evening was saved for Sama. It lasted the right amount of time and as we pulled apart, we ended our night with a PLUR handshake. With our hands holding tight she slid a candy bracelet onto my wrist. It read "DANCE."

CHAPTER NINETEEN

The morning came and went without much notice, but that's bound to happen when you don't say goodnight until the birds wake up. As my left eyelid tried its best to separate himself from my pupil, the sun sent a death beam of light into my cornea, which apparently pissed her off, for I know of no other reason why she turned on the jackhammer in my skull.

The love, the joy, the beauty, the goodness from the previous evening had vanished and was nowhere to be found. A thief had taken it all and then some as I slept and left no clues to if or when I would get it back.

Note to self. Scratch idea of little blue pills to the Middle East. They'll hate each other even more the next morning.

My mind was a bowl of overdone spaghetti, my nerve endings confused about their function. I had violated Konka's golden rule and was paying the price.

"Excess is the enemy," he would say. He believed you should experience everything in life. Try everything at least once. See what works for you and what doesn't, what you like and what you don't. He'd have a drink every night yet never more than two. I never saw him drunk. I never saw him take more than a small puff off a joint. He used things, did things to enhance life, not to subtract from life.

The problems start as soon as you overdo it. Abuse it. That's when things turn out bad. However, the only way to know excess is to try it. And last night, we'd gotten acquainted.

As I stood up, every muscle in my body yelled at me. That tends to happen when you jump up and down, back and forth, and side to side for hours at a time. I walked over to Kicker Tom's room and was greeted with a perfectly made bed, which was my cue to get my act together. I eventually did and headed outside.

Kicker Tom had loaded the van and was talking to Iris. "Afternoon, love bucket," he said to me.

I managed to let out a fake smile.

"Looks like you had a good time last night," said Iris.

"Good time? Good time? Hell, I'd say falling in love constitutes a great time," said Kicker Tom

"Falling in love with?" I asked.

"With everything and everybody. You loved the music. You loved the lights. You loved the people. You loved the air, the dirt, a pole, a rock. Hell, son, you hugged a cactus."

There was a long pause.

"Oh, that's right. I did hug a cactus," I said as my memory was coming back. "It was a nice cactus."

"An absolute beaut," he said. "Probably a good idea if I drive the first leg."

There were no arguments from me. He thanked Iris, gave her a big hug, and jumped into the van.

As I stood in front of Iris, I didn't know what to say, and even if I had, a sudden lump in my throat would've prevented it. Tears started to well up, and I was lost. Being here it was as though he had never left, and now I was leaving. Being torn away again.

She gave me the same loving hug as when I arrived. I guess her faucet flowed at the correct rate. She grabbed my hand and walked me to the passenger's side of the van, and I got in.

"When will I know I'm on the right path?" I asked.

"What makes you think you aren't already on it."

She pulled something from her pocket and handed it to me. "This will help," she said.

It was a little picture frame that held in place an old, yellowing piece of paper with handwritten words that read:

Turn Me
Into We
Be Free

"It's a poem your grandfather wrote many years ago," she said.

"I don't suppose you're going to tell me what it means?"

She gave one more smile and walked away.

I hung it on the rearview mirror as Kicker Tom put the Mystery Machine in motion.

CHAPTER TWENTY

A s the Sedona Inn disappeared from the rearview mirror, an image of El popped into my skull. With it, a thread of guilt wormed its way into my being. And without the deluge of euphoria from the evening before to kill it in its tracks, it began to grow. Had I betrayed her? Us? I suppose I hadn't totally let her go. Before the guilt had a chance to swallow me whole, I put my focus on the road ahead and the yellow stripes that ran down its middle.

Twenty minutes passed and not a word was spoken. Kicker Tom sensed I wasn't in a talkative mood and didn't push it. He did, however, offer half of his breakfast burrito, which I turned down. My stomach wasn't ready for food. I barely got down the water I was sucking on. Apparently, the ingredients that made up the happy pills the previous evening had done a number on the stomach and appetite. I eventually was able to squeeze down a few bites of a banana and started to feel like a personality of some sort might emerge. Many more miles had passed when I noticed a sign reading 89A North.

"Isn't San Diego southwest of here?" I asked.

"It is indeed," said Kicker Tom.

"Why are we headed north?"

"Taking the scenic route."

"How scenic?"

"Canada," he said with a straight face.

As I pondered the route, he said, "Ah hell no, just kiddin'. You ever seen the Grand Canyon?"

"Until a few days ago, I'd never been out of Texas."

"Well damn, son, it'd be shame to get this close and not take a peek. Eighth wonder of the world and all."

"Isn't the Houston Astrodome the eighth wonder of the world?"

"Maybe it's the seventh wonder then, or the sixth wonder. Hell, I don't know, I wasn't paying attention when they were givin' out the awards."

"Sounds good, you're in charge today," I said sounding half alive.

He pulled a joint out of his shirt pocket and handed it to me. "Take a small offering from this. Purple Marin Magic Kush. It'll clear up what's ailin' ya."

The last thing I wanted to do was put something else foreign in my body. I handed it back, and he proceeded to take his usual dosage. I guess Kicker Tom hadn't gotten the memo on excess is the enemy. In fact, it seemed excess was his friend, a friend he liked dearly.

"So, what's it mean?" Kicker Tom asked as he looked at Konka's poem hanging on the rearview mirror.

"I'm not sure." And I wasn't. I hadn't given it much thought at that point because of the last half hour fighting the nausea and the moving van. However, I took a stab at it anyway. "My grandfather talked a lot about being connected—to each other, to the world around you, to the universe. To be free, he'd say, 'one must not be separate from the whole.' I guess he captured that thought in a simple poem. If that's what it means, I guess that sounds strange to you," I said.

"Why?"

"Because you're trying to disconnect with life. Divorce it."

"There's more than one way to freedom, Tag."

"I suppose you're right," I said.

"So, is that why you're out here? Looking for freedom?" He asked.

"I guess you could say that."

In his stoned haze, he thought about that for a minute. "Well shit, Tag, it looks like we're looking for the same thing."

"Sure seems that way."

"It's pretty damn simple then. All we got to do is find this We," he said.

"Any idea where it's hiding?" I asked.

"I'm pretty damn sure mine's just south of San Diego. But hell, I've been wrong before. And shit, yours could be anywhere. I mean anywhere. And we don't even know what he looks like. Ah hell, son, seek the We! Seek the We! In order to be free, we must seek the We!" he yelled with delight over and over.

Obviously, the Purple Marin Kush was doing its magic on him. We passed a sign that read, "Grand Canyon, 85 miles."

"What ya say we hike down and camp near the river?" he said.

"Not a good idea."

"Not a good idea? Not a good idea? It's a great idea! Maybe my best ever."

"Don't think we are quite prepared."

"Well shit, son, we'll get prepared."

Now, getting out of the van and taking a hike, I was all for. A good sweat would do me good, but taking an eight-hour hike down the Grand Canyon to the Colorado river in 100-degree temperatures with a stoned cowboy after the night we'd had would have to be put in the plain stupid category. Though by the look in Kicker Tom's eye, stupid was where we were headed. Hopefully, though, the Purple Kush would wear off soon, and the big cowboy would have a change of heart.

"Possible, that little bastard the We is waitin' for us down there. Comin' to get ya, We! Comin' to get ya!" he yelled.

Then again, maybe not.

CHAPTER TWENTY-ONE

W e stopped in Flagstaff at a sporting goods store, and Kicker Tom went in and grabbed some gear. We loaded up on food, water, some adult beverages, and off we went. Over an hour later we passed the main entrance to the Grand Canyon Village. Either he was still too stoned and didn't see it, or, hopefully, he'd changed his mind.

"Wasn't that our turn?" I asked.

"That's the tourist turn. We're taking the road less traveled, my friend."

"Any particular reason?"

"You think the We is just walking around amongst all those tourists? Hell no. Freedom is a loner, my friend. You think the We is just sitting in some crowded coffee shop having a latte and scone with everyone else? Shit no. Not possible. If he's out there, and we find him, fuck sure we're going to find him by himself."

Okay, I was wrong: he was still stoned. "So, where is this road less traveled?" I asked.

"The guy I bought the gear from showed me a map."

"Where is it?"

"The map?"

"Yes, the map."

"Don't need it."

"Why?"

He pointed to his head. "Got it right here."

Kicker Tom must have been bipolar, or manic, or some other disease that's neighbors with crazy that I didn't know about or have the experience to deal with. I mean, who in the hell travels into the Grand Canyon without a map? This whole thing started on a whim, an impulse. He saw a road sign, and now we're here. And I was following right along. Maybe I was the one who was crazy.

I turned away and looked out the side window.

"Tag, it's all good. That's what I did for a living. Read maps."

He also killed people for a living, though I thought it best not to bring that up.

Like a hound dog, he smelled my hesitation. He pulled the van over to the side of the road, rolled down his window, and struck a familiar pose. He put his left leg out, rested it on the driver's side mirror, pulled what was left of the Marin Magic joint from his shirt pocket, and took another long hit. Looking straight ahead, he said in one breath, "Tag, a few miles up this road will be a sign that says Kaibab National Forest, when we get there, we'll be greeted by a fork in the road, we're goin' to stay left at said fork and cross some railroad tracks for 'bout a mile or so until we get to an intersection where we'll take a right in the westerly direction on Farm Road 328 and drive sixteen miles to a gate that marks the Havasupai Indian Reservation. After paying the Havasupai tribe for the kind use of their land, we'll proceed for another 1.7 miles to a four-way intersection where we'll turn right in a northeasterly direction and travel another 1.9 miles to the Forest Service boundary fence, at which point you'll jump out and open the gate as I drive this beautiful van through. You then will shut said gate to keep the local cows out of said park, and we'll proceed north passing a deserted ranger station and maintain that northerly direction over difficult terrain for almost four more miles at which time we'll have arrived at the starting point of road less traveled. Now, I have the rest of the map to this trail up here for safe keepin'," he said as he pointed to his noggin. "I've got a large knife, a compass, a lot more weed, and a better sense of direction than Rambo."

He handed me the stub of the burning Purple Kush. "You still in?" he asked.

I grabbed the dying roach and took the last hit Kicker Tom style. He had my answer. He returned the Mystery Machine back to the road as I let the smoke release from my lungs.

"Who's Rambo?" I asked.

He shook his head. "Ah hell, son."

Every turn, every marker, every distance, was as he described. That would be the last time I doubted Kicker Tom.

When we arrived at our destination, it indeed was the road less traveled. Only a handful of trucks were parked and scattered throughout the area. We got our gear ready. My backpack was loaded with food and water. I don't know what was in Kicker Tom's, but it was about three times the size of mine.

"I can take some of that," I said.

"Ah shit, son, this is light."

I changed my sandals for some old trail shoes and threw on a baseball cap. Kicker Tom kept his cowboy hat on, but I was relieved to see he was leaving the Tony Lamas behind. He laced up a pair of beat-up army boots that looked like they could tell a story or two.

As we approached the trailhead, Kicker Tom had a different way about him. He walked with a purpose. His attitude reeked of confidence. He was focused—on a mission. This was not the same impulsive man as back in the van. Marine Tom had taken over and was now in charge.

"The guy said it should take five to six hours to reach the bottom. However, we need to do it in about four, unless, of course, you want to hike in the dark," he said.

Now, I ran almost every day in the Texas heat, was in great shape, and despite not feeling my best wasn't that concerned. However, big cowboy looked as though any physical training might have ended when his duty was up. Not that he was fat, but

I'm confident there weren't many tacos left over at the dinner table.

"Lead the way," I replied.

He grabbed two waters out of my pack and handed one to me. "Take a little every half hour," he said and he headed down the trail.

Whatever concerns I had about Kicker Tom's fitness vanished within the first half hour. We weren't running, yet moved at a good clip as we descended the narrow trail with 300-foot drops on either side depending on the turn. We didn't speak a word for the first hour.

We arrived at a flat area covered with some vegetation. He stopped, took a sip of water, and walked over to the edge. I followed. The view was breathtaking, inspiring, an absolute natural high. What was left of the Purple Kush in my system only added to the experience. We stood for a few minutes soaking in the beauty. All was calm. All was right. Out of nowhere, Kicker Tom yelled at the top of his lungs, "I am Kicker Tom."

A few seconds later his echo returned and he screamed, "I am seeking the We."

As soon as that echo returned, he looked at me. "Your turn."

I paused.

"Got to let the world know your purpose," he said.

I yelled at the top of my lungs, "I am Pahana."

After the echo had returned I yelled, "I am seeking the We."

As soon as my echo returned and silence reappeared, Tom said, "No turning back now."

With that, we continued on our hike down. At times the heat was bruising, yet we managed to keep our pace. Despite all the switchbacks, crossing trails, and a lack of signage, Kicker Tom didn't miss a beat and navigated the trail as though he'd done it before. We made the big sandy beach next to the Colorado River with plenty of daylight to spare.

CHAPTER TWENTY-TWO

The past three-plus hours had flushed out whatever remnants of the happy pills and Purple Kush that remained in my system. I felt like a new man, clear headed, the adrenaline pumping through my system overriding any fatigue brought on by the hike down.

We dropped our packs on the sandy beach. The same one we shared with at least fifty other people. About 200 yards west, several rafting outfits made this their overnight campground as well.

Kicker Tom grabbed the six-pack of Coors Light from my pack, walked over, and placed them into the river. "Nature's icebox," he said. He began to assemble our tent.

"You need help?" I asked

"Only one rooster in the hen house."

As I walked away and let him do his thing, I looked up. I had been so focused on the hike down that other than our first stop I hadn't taken in the enormity of my surroundings. And enormous it was. You could fit the canyon I ran through in Sedona in here 50,000 times over, maybe many more. It was hard to fathom, much less do the calculations.

I had gotten a small taste of it from the top, but from the river looking up, it was plain overwhelming. There was no hiding, no running. You were surrounded. She was in charge and in complete control. She had you wrapped up inside her and you knew it.

The first time you feel connected to something that large it is intimidating. Yet, once you learn it's on your side, also quite comforting. There's a weird power in feeling so small yet knowing you're part of something, in touch with something so big.

Before I'd had time to sit, meditate, and soak up all the energy within those grand walls, Kicker Tom had put up the tent. I suppose it wasn't his first.

He ran over to the water's edge, kicked off his boots and socks, and put his feet in the water. I took my shoes off as well but kept my feet on dry land. I wasn't going to make that mistake again. He grabbed two beers, threw one to me, popped the top on his, and took a hard-earned swig. "Now, who in the hell is Pahana?" he asked.

I'd known that question was coming. I don't know why it had come flying out of my mouth earlier. But I guess I knew Kicker Tom was right. You have to let the world know your purpose. Until you do, until you surrender, until you let her know, you're nothing more than a boat without a rudder, motor, or sail, letting other people, other forces, shape your fate.

So over the trickling waters of the Colorado River, and under the fading light of the day, I gave Kicker Tom the short version of my life's tale.

Kicker Tom cracked another beer. "You ever think about her?" he asked.

"Who?"

"Your mother."

"Not much anymore."

"Ever try to get in touch?"

"El looked to see if she was doing any of the social media stuff once. She wasn't. But other than that, no."

"When's the last time you heard from her?"

"After she left, she'd write me letters, send birthday cards, and a Christmas present every year. But as time went on, the letters became fewer and fewer, shorter and shorter, and then stopped altogether. Then the Christmas presents stopped. On my thirteenth birthday, I got a card with the number twelve on the front. On the inside it said, 'Mom.' And that was that. No more. Never heard from her again."

"No interest now in trying to find her?"

"It was clear my mother wanted another life than the one she was handed, a life that didn't include me. I made peace with that years ago. And, if she is still on this earth, I hope she is happy, I really do. I hope she found that life she wanted. But I have no need to see her again."

"Hell, son, she's still your mother."

"It takes more than giving birth to be a mother."

"You sure you've made peace with it?"

"Totally."

"How in the hell is that?"

I took a sip from my beer and looked at the slow-moving water in front of me. "As soon as my grandmother died, my mother knew she'd have to take care of me every day. Be my mom every day. How do you do that job when the person you're taking care of is a daily reminder of your mistakes, of your life, a life you don't like? A life you don't want. When she dropped me off at my grandfather's, maybe she was being selfish. But wouldn't it have been more selfish to raise me? She'd have ended up hating me, and me her. But sitting here now, I have no hate for her. No malice. I wish she could have been a different person, a stronger person like my grandmother. But she wasn't, and at least she knew it. So, she did what was best for me, and if that also happened to be best for her, I'm fine with that. When she left that day, she relinquished the role of mother. She let me go. Soon after my thirteenth birthday, I did the same."

"Ah shit, son, that's a sad-ass story."

"It's the one they gave me."

The light was all but gone, so we grabbed the remaining beers and headed back to the tent. Tom pulled a small lantern out of his gear to give us some light. I picked an assortment of fruits, berries, and nuts to snack on while Kicker Tom lit up a stogie and cracked another beer.

"What's your sad-ass story?" I asked.

"Don't have one."

"Really?"

"Really."

"Who's Jacob?"

He paused. "So I was talking the other night," he said.

"More like mumbling."

He took a long draw on his cigar and let out the smoke. "He was my son."

"Was?"

"Court thought it best if I wasn't in his life."

"That makes no sense."

"If you nearly kill his stepfather and hurt his mother, it does." He stared down at the ground for a while.

"We don't have to talk about this…"

"When you fuck up, you face the music, simple as that. And I fucked up." He took a Kicker Tom gulp from his beer. "My high school sweetheart and I were supposed to get married and then 9/11 happened. I enlisted and everything got put on hold. And shit let me tell ya, being away from your honey eight to ten months a year for almost eight years isn't the proper recipe for a harmonious relationship. Each year got harder and harder. Then, three years ago, Jacob was born. He was a blessing. What a beautiful, beautiful boy. He made her so happy. Made me happy. The happiest I'd ever been. He brought us closer together, like it was in the beginning. But damn if I didn't get redeployed one last time. It was supposed to last six months. It lasted almost two years. And she sure as shit wasn't handling it very well. The last year of it I could hardly get her on the phone."

He took another swig of beer. "The day arrived and I'm at the airport with all the other guys coming home for good and everybody is running to their families, and hugs and kisses and tears, and when the chaos cleared I still couldn't find mine. No Jacob.

No Marie. So, I called her cell and it was disconnected. Went to our apartment and someone else was living there. Went to where she worked and they said she had quit several months ago and they didn't know where she was."

"What'd you do?"

"My best friend Ted had helped her and Jacob out on many occasions, so I thought he might know something." He took another long draw from his cigar. "Turned out I was right. He did know something. When I got to his house I noticed my truck in the driveway. Still, though, I didn't think nothin' of it. Before I could get to the front door, Ted stepped out and met me on the lawn. I asked where's Marie and he says inside. Still, no bells going off. He says we need to talk and puts his hand on my damn shoulder and that's when...that's when..."

He paused and took a long swig of beer. "I get this sick feelin' in my stomach. He said something about Marie, and how he was just trying to help or something, and things just escalated, and they, they, they...were in love, and some shit about them getting married, and her being pregnant with his child, and, and, and, and...that's all I remember hearing, the word *and* over and over and over again. Funny how that happens...It was kind of a fuckin' blur after that. Until five or six policemen pulled me off him and cuffed me. In the melee, Marie had come out and got hurt, but hell, I don't remember even seeing her. As they were draggin' my ass away..."

He paused and stared at his cigar for a long while.

"I look up and I catch...I catch my son Jacob's eyes. He is lookin' at me through the kitchen window. My son...who doesn't know me other than in pictures and stories, just watched this animal, this monster, this beast, do this horrible act."

He took another gulp of beer.

"That's the fuckin' gift I gave my son. The look of terror in his eyes. I'll never get that image of his face out of my mind. Ever. And I shouldn't. I deserve that. Over and over, I deserve that. That's my penance for what I did to that innocent boy and that's not even close to justice. I should be strung up, and I'd have done that shit myself, but that would've been the chicken-shit way out of it. As long as Jacob has to deal with what I did to him, I don't get the easy way out."

"Did you go to jail?"

"I wanted to. I deserved to. But because of my war record and on account they said I probably had post-traumatic stress disorder, the judge let me off."

"Probably had?"

"Hell, I don't know. It was never properly diagnosed."

"Why not?"

"Backlog at the VA for whoever in the hell makes that determination."

"Even with all your medals?"

"Tag, once you're done they don't give a shit about you. Hell, we'll spend a couple billion every year on new tanks we don't need that will never see a day of action, but fuck, man, we can't seem to find an extra dime for another doctor or therapist." He took another long draw from his cigar. "You know the really fucked-up thing? I spent eight years of my life thinking I was doing something good while all I was really doing was making the situation worse. I was just continuing the cycle."

"What cycle?"

"In war, people get killed. A lot of them are innocent people, good people, and when good people get killed, it turns other good people into bad people. People who just want to raise their kids, go to work, go to school, get drunk, have a laugh, are now taking up guns, learning how to make bombs, wantin' to kill, wantin' revenge. Fuck, man, I just turned good people into horrible people, a happy person into an angry person. That's all I fuckin' did. Poured more gasoline on the fire. Somebody with a set of brass balls needed to jump in and stop that shit. Stop that craziness. Enough of that stupid shit. But it wasn't my government and it sure the fuck wasn't me. I was too young, too stupid, and too angry."

He stared at his beer. "I'm no damn different than the guys who flew the planes into the World Trade Center."

"You weren't trying to kill innocent people."

"Tell that to their relatives, friends, neighbors, kids. You think they give a damn about intent? We fuckin' blew it. I fuckin' blew it. Nothin' more than a damn bully with a gun. That's all we were. That's what I am." He finished the rest of his beer and sat in silence for a while.

"Are you going to ever see Jacob again?"

"I agreed to give up my rights as his father. Thought it was best for everyone involved."

"Even you?"

"My vote don't count no more. I lost that right. Plus, it's better this way."

"How so?"

"Ted isn't a snake. He's a good man. He really is. He'll be a good father to Jacob. Hell, I don't blame him for what happened. I don't blame Marie. Shit, man, she was lonely. I wasn't doing my part. I guess I was more worried about my guys in the field than her. They're not to blame. I'm to blame. I did this."

"So, you left town?"

"I wrote her and Ted a letter apologizing for everything and wished them the best. I wrote Jacob a letter for when he gets older, letting him know I loved him and trying to explain everything. I drove about 200 miles to a friend's house and spent the next eight months gettin' drunk on his couch. Then his wife started to get irritated for some reason, and hell, I figured I'd messed up enough relationships so I left there too. About a month later, you found me in a ditch."

I took the last swig of my beer. "Now that is a sad-ass story," I said.

"It's the one they gave me." He put out his cigar in the sand, crawled into the tent and passed out.

I slid into my sleeping bag and looked up to the stars, all billions of them, but couldn't get the image of a frightened little Jacob out of my head. I knew that feeling well. Afraid, alone, and confused. My stomach suddenly felt like an empty pit. I slowly morphed back into a six-year-old boy. *Why didn't she love me? Why did she run away? Why didn't she come back? What did I do wrong?*

I zipped up my sleeping bag the rest of the way. It held me tight. I suppose I needed a hug. And I suppose I hadn't truly made peace. Not totally.

As the big cowboy's body lay motionless in the tent nearby I whispered,

"Goodnight, Kicker Tom."

The Colorado River serenaded me until my lids decided to call it a night.

CHAPTER TWENTY-THREE

Early-morning sounds from the belly of the canyon stirred me awake. I looked over at the tent where two large feet hung out and weren't moving. I decided to let them wake up on their own. After getting up, I made my way to the river's edge, walked upstream for several hundred yards, and plopped down for my morning sit. If one ever wanted to learn the art of meditation, this was the perfect place to start. Even the chattiest mind is lulled into submission here. It has no choice. Calmness and serenity run the show.

I kept my eyes open for most of the time, a practice Konka had taught me during moments like these when the connection seemed simple. It was a way to bring another sense into the mold, training it to still see and be without it triggering the mind to talk. Konka would say when you mastered the ability to be open to all five senses at once, yet still maintained the present moment, then and only then could you truly see.

I was still a work in progress.

After an hour, my morning session came to an abrupt end as there was a loud scream and the nude body of a large man flashed in front of me and disappeared into the water. Kicker Tom and his feet were awake.

"What's with you and cold water?" I asked.

"Ah hell, son, it keeps you alert." He looked down. "But it sure doesn't do much for your manhood." He looked back up. "Talked to a couple of river guides this morning, and I think that little bastard the We is runnin' downstream somewhere."

"Maybe he's right here."

He took a deep breath, looked long at his surroundings, and said, "Nope, not here, definitely downstream. But he's moving fast so we better get it in gear."

"You plan on swimming after him?" I said.

"Hell no, got us a ride."

"With?"

"Reverend Willy."

"Reverend Willy?"

"Don't worry, he's a brother. Ex-marine. He's got forty years' experience on this river."

"What about the van?"

"We'll pick it up later."

As it turned out, Reverend Willy's party had needed to cut it short. The reverend had dropped off a father who was having heart issues and his family the day before, so the park rangers could get him to the top. Not sure why Reverend Willy invited us. Maybe he was doing another marine a favor? Maybe he wanted the company?

Regardless, we had a ride.

CHAPTER TWENTY-FOUR

Reverend Willy must have been in his sixties by the look of his weathered face, but his body spoke of a man half that age. Lean muscles protruded from his beat-up T-shirt, and his handshake was pure granite. He owned a relaxed gaze that lingered long enough to make you think he knew something about you that you didn't, and a smile that indicated he didn't have a care in the world, a smile that was permanent that never went away. He also had a wonderful sense of humor; at least I thought so. Why else would anyone name their river raft *Titanic*?

As we climbed into our vessel I was sure it wasn't its maiden voyage. The once bright-yellow rubber raft had faded from its time in the sun, and the number of off-color patches suggested she had already had a few altercations with icebergs. The raft wasn't overly large but could have still fit a few more.

After securing our gear, the reverend handed us two paddles and we were off without so much as a hint of instruction. Kicker Tom manned the left side of the boat and me the right. Reverend Willy lay back on the front portion of the raft with feet up and watched us paddle. At least I think he was watching us. Dark sunglasses covered his eyes, and he didn't say a word. Twenty minutes in, the reason for our invitation became clear. We would be the motor during the long stretches of still water. And, as I learned, there were a lot of long stretches.

It was eerily quiet with nothing more than the sounds of our paddles hitting the water when the smiling reverend raised his hand for us to stop paddling. We sat in silence for about a minute when Reverend Willy said in a soft, happy voice that had seen its fair share of cigarettes and scotch, "You hear that?"

We listened, yet I heard nothing. Another few seconds of silence had crept by when the small sounds of rustling blue water began to speak.

"Poetry, boys. Poetry," he said. He put his hand down, which was our cue to put the oars back in action, and he began to whistle as the sounds of the river started getting healthier.

I noticed the water up ahead begin to dance and saw that we were about to become partners. Reverend Willy hadn't moved a muscle and was whistling away in his own world. Thirty yards out and the size of the waves and swells became evident. And they weren't playing. The calm, pretty blue water had morphed into frenetic brown-and-white chaos.

"All right, boys, pay attention," said the smiling reverend. "Tom, seven strokes real hard right now and Tag, hold your paddle down." The raft veered sharply right and almost sideways when Reverend Willy pointed to me and yelled, "Give me five," then to Kicker Tom, "three on your side," and like that we were around a large rock and into the fray. Kicker Tom threw his left knee over the side of the raft to give him more leverage. I did the same on the right.

For the next hundred yards, Reverend Willy called out our stroke count like a coxswain to his crew while never looking ahead. We followed his instructions as we bounced our way in, around, and over the swells, and before I had time to think we rolled back into the calm, still stuff.

"Ah hell yeah," screamed Kicker Tom.

His excitement was contagious. I followed with a howl of my own.

Reverend Willy didn't move. He sat as stoic as before. He'd

133

seen our reactions a thousand times. Maybe that was the reason for that perpetual grin. "Just a little warm-up, fellas," he said.

And a warmup it was. We spent the next several hours alternating between the calm water and rapids, stillness and movement, movement and stillness. There it was again, stillness and movement, taunting me to make some sense of their relationship. Still, nothing was registering in my attic, and the river hadn't offered any suggestions, at least, none I could see.

Through each new set of rapids, Reverend Willy continued to verbally navigate as Kicker Tom and I found not only our rhythm but our confidence. Each run got smoother and smoother. Each run the reverend spoke less and less, as our ability to integrate our strokes became almost seamless. But what impressed me the most was the reverend's knowledge of the river. He knew every cliff, bend, curve, rock, wave, curl, and note she sang. He either knew it from memory or had eyes in the back of his head. He didn't turn or peek forward the whole day. As he said, "After a few decades, you get to know a girl's plumbing."

We hit another long stretch of calm water and Reverend Willy still wasn't talking. I looked over to Kicker Tom and whispered, "Doesn't talk much for a preacher."

"Maybe he's sleeping," said Kicker Tom.

"I'm right here, boys, I can hear you," he said, still smiling.

"You okay?" I asked.

"Don't I look okay?"

"Kind of look like a dead man with pretty teeth," Kicker Tom said.

The reverend's smile got wider. "Playing hurt today, boys."

"What's wrong?" I asked.

"My mental and verbal abilities have been severely compromised, though I do believe they are starting to return. It seems last night while telling stories at the campsite with a few other fellow guides and their groups, I might've ingested more than my fair share of the devil water better known as Bookers."

"What's that?" I asked.

"It's bourbon," said Kicker Tom.

"A-hundred-and-twenty-proof bourbon," said the reverend. "I generally take only a small sample of the gut-burning fuel just to prime the pump and crack the door a bit, but last night I got on a roll. The heavens opened up and supplied me with all the relevant information for my audience with pristine accuracy and wit. My muse was alive and kicking and she seemed to enjoy the whiskey. So, as long as she hung around I kept feeding her. Unfortunately, she hung around all night."

"That's why we're doing all the paddling?" I asked as I picked my paddle out of the water.

"One reason."

"There's another?" Tom asked.

"Getting you boys prepped for tomorrow."

"What happens tomorrow?" I asked.

"You two get to tackle the baddest-ass rapid CC has to offer. All by yourselves."

I guess CC was his nickname for the Colorado River, and though I wanted to inform the reverend he had one too many Cs, I thought it wasn't my place. "Are you going somewhere?" I asked.

"Nope, just along for the ride. Now I could do it for you, but what fun would that be?"

We paddled around a bend and were greeted by direct warm sun, which was a welcome relief for my cold, wet, drenched shoes and shorts.

"Where'd you get the name Reverend?" I asked.

"Used to be one," he said.

"What happened?"

"I might've had intimate relations with someone in my congregation."

"I guess that's against the rules," I said.

"It is if she's married. But that's not the reason I stopped preaching the word. I finally realized I was preaching the wrong word. I realized God didn't live in a church. I learned that this," he stood up and looked around with his hands held high to the velvety orange rock structures against the clear sapphire sky above, "that this is his church. That this is his temple. That this is my temple, your temple, and everyone's temple. The Native Americans had it right. Eastern religions had it right. Buddhism, Taoism, Hinduism, and several other 'isms,' including science's religion 'quantum physics-ism,' had it right. God doesn't live in a penthouse apartment in the sky making judgments. He's here. She's here," he said pointing to the chocolate- and yellow-colored banks and the vegetation of lavender, magenta, and green that was sprinkled everywhere as we floated by. "It's all right here, right in front of you: the air, the water, the trees, every speck of dirt, every atom, every electron, proton, and every quark. Why in the hell would you waste your time inside a church? You want to praise the Lord, get outside and talk to the wind, pray to the water, soak up the sun."

I guess he still was a reverend. I knew one thing for sure, he and Konka prayed at the same altar. We paddled around another bend into an inlet of clear blue water that was as still as the cavernous rocks that protected them. The reverend, still standing, didn't move a muscle as he took in the silence that now surrounded us.

"Yes, gents, organized religion as we know it trashed God's reputation. They selfishly abused it, hijacked it, prostituted it, for their own convenience, for their own purpose. Religion killed God," he said in a softer voice.

"How'd they manage that?" I asked.

"They made God a he. God isn't a he. Or even a she. God isn't good. God isn't bad. God doesn't save. God doesn't judge. And certainly doesn't get angry, hurt, punish, or kill. God doesn't have emotions. And please don't tell me he has his reasons. God doesn't read, write, or speak, at least not in any literal sense. That's what we do. That's what humans do, that's us. We made God like us, in our image."

"Why'd we do that?" I asked.

"Because we're a bunch of egomaniacs. Yep, ya don't need organized religion, boys. It's like asking the local junior-college astronomy department to be in charge of the stars. No one can

136

be in charge. You don't need permission—just breathe, fools."
With that, he took in a large inhale of air and slowly let it go.
"Now, excuse me while I wash away all my sins from last
evening." He fell backward into the river as the sound of his
body hitting the water bounced off the nearby walls. When he
popped up he screamed, "Come on, boys. Let these waters
purify your soul."

Kicker Tom stood up and took off his cowboy hat. I followed,
yet wasn't sure about the cold water. As it turned out, I didn't
have to make up my mind, Kicker Tom had already done that. He
pushed me in and then followed.

The shock was immediate and unnerving. My breath was
gone. My instinct was to climb back in the boat, but I decided to
give the baptism a chance.

Reverend Willy was floating on his back communing with his
church as Kicker Tom decided on a slow, relaxed breast stroke. I
took off into full freestyle sprint, hoping to keep my muscles
warm. It seemed to work. The cold was still present but the pain
wasn't. Maybe the disassociation method was in full effect
without my knowledge. Whatever the reason, I didn't care. My
body was awake, and my mind alert.

I glanced over to Kicker Tom, who seemed transfixed on the
massive canyon walls that surrounded us. He had moved into
another world, a world of tranquility brought on by either the
canyon, its cold waters, or the reverend's sermon, perhaps all
three.

Reverend Willy floated by and said, "Once you swim in her
veins, only then do you start to know her. And once you know
her, it's hard to get her out of your veins."

Hopefully, for Kicker Tom some of her serenity would stick.

Reverend Willy swam back to the raft, flipped himself in,
pulled off this T-shirt, and wrung it out. He then reached into a
cooler, cracked a beer, and downed it. "Oh, thank you for that,
Lord," he said as he lay back and took in the sun. Kicker Tom and
I eventually crawled back over the squeaky rubbery sides and into
the raft but with a lot less poetry than the reverend had. I also

took off my T-shirt, wrung it out, and took in the warmth of the sun.

Reverend Willy opened the cooler again and tossed us each a beer. Kicker Tom didn't open his. Something back there had gotten to him, and he wasn't ready to let go. The reverend knew what to do. Without a word being spoken, he changed places with Kicker Tom and grabbed his paddle. We paddled slowly and sipped our beer as a soaked Kicker Tom continued to look at the canyon walls.

I turned in the opposite direction and took a look back. Up high on my left I could make out the top of the North Rim of the canyon, and up to my right the edge of the South Rim. From my angle, the two canyon walls moved away from each other. The angle reminded me of Iris's painting of the white and red roads moving farther and farther apart. Technology and nature continuing in different directions, on different paths.

Kicker Tom turned around again.

"This used to be one. All of this was once together. It was one."

The reverend and I stayed quiet.

"Over millions of years it slowly split in two."

Again we said nothing.

"And somehow it has managed to remain as though it's still one, still together, still at peace with one another."

I guess Kicker Tom was still in her grasp. I'm sure the reverend had seen it often between those canyon walls. Kicker Tom opened his beer and took a standard-sized gulp.

"Such beauty, such grace," he said.

"That's what you get when nature splits something," said the reverend.

Kicker Tom thought about that for a moment. "How come when man is in charge, his split gives you the atomic bomb?"

I looked back and up to the North Rim. "He's on the wrong road," I said.

"Ain't that the truth," said Kicker Tom.

"Amen, brothers. Let it set you free," the reverend yelled.

After fifty miles on the river, Kicker Tom's awakening, and the reverend's all-day hangover, we made camp on a small sandy beach. The evening affair was calm and tame. The reverend and Kicker Tom spent most of it trading war stories over a burning fire, while I attempted to converse with the stars. It was a game Konka had taught me soon after we first met. It was another form of meditation practice. I would pick any star in the sky and stare into it without blinking or at least attempt to without blinking. When I got comfortable enough with that, I started to imagine the star came in through my eyes and illuminated the inside of my body. Any time my mind wouldn't shut its lip, which often happened late in the evenings, I'd go outside and converse with the stars. It's what got me through school. All the negative thoughts built up after a terrible day would vanish. When my troubles at school first started, Konka would patiently listen and say, "Go to the stars." As I got older, he would put up his hand as I started to complain and say, "Go to the stars." Eventually, I stopped complaining altogether and went to the stars the moment the need arose, which was most nights.

As I laid near CC, my body was exhausted and wanted to sleep, but my mind was in full gear trying to figure out, understand, put into place, debate, talk over, discuss, explain, analyze, and solve the last few days.

Will life on our planet really cease unless everyone learns to live in peace and harmony with each other and nature? Is technology really to blame? What were the walls of my great-great grandfather's cave trying to tell me? What knowledge should I be searching for? Where do I go next? What am I suppose to show other people? Am I truly on the right road? The right path?

My mind wasn't ready for shut-eye. He was on a mission and wasn't stopping until he got his answers. So as the reverend and Kicker Tom discussed rifles, bullets, mortars, ambushes, and the United States war machine and its profiteers, I went to the stars.

CHAPTER TWENTY-FIVE

For some reason the water in the calm parts of the river today was an incredible emerald green. The same as Ellie's eyes. Now, I don't know if credit should be given to a disciplined mind or a plain busy one, but I had only thought about Ellie once. However, sitting on the right edge of the *Titanic* paddling through all that deep gorgeous green water, she was once again with me. Those eyes, those lips, that smile, the smell of her neck, the curve of her back above her butt, all with me as though I had never left. With each stroke of my paddle, I became more lost in her and didn't want her to leave. I wanted to hold her again. I missed her, and with that came a sudden ache in my stomach, the same as I had given her when I left, I suppose.

As much as I'd wanted to stay with her at that moment, I knew it wasn't wise, it wasn't healthy. But she was now on the raft with me and was in no hurry to leave, and why would she? I was the one who invited her, so how could I now ask her to please go away? Maybe I didn't want her to even though it was best. As it turned out, I didn't have to make that decision. The reverend saw my dilemma and exorcised my demon. He grabbed an oar and flicked it at the cold water, which came rushing back and splashed me in the face.

"Wake up to the glory of the moment, my son," he said.

And just like that, El was gone and I was back.

"Be careful of the past and future, they're very seductive. Don't let them put you in their prison," he whispered with that gravelly voice.

Maybe it was a good night's sleep or the lack of a whiskey bath, but Reverend Willy's sermon had started early. He stood up and shouted, "CC is alive and awake, boys. Better bring your A-game, she's not fooling around today."

Kicker Tom and I looked around as we sat in the calm, silent water. It seemed like the day before. I guess the reverend was trying to get us pumped up and mentally ready for the day's ride and the Colorado's baddest-ass rapid.

"Hell, Rev, nothin's movin'," said Kicker Tom.

"Something is always moving. You just can't see it. It's invisible, but it's there. And today, it's moving with purpose," he said.

"How do you know?" Kicker Tom asked.

"She is singing to me, boys," he said.

Kicker Tom looked around again. "Hell, Rev, don't hear nothing either."

"You're listening with the wrong instrument," the reverend replied.

"Movement and stillness?" I asked, hoping he could shed some light on those opposites.

"Yes indeed, movement and stillness, the one who moves while not moving, the unmoved mover, movement in stillness, stillness in movement, and in both is where true power, the ultimate power, the ultimate energy, the ultimate truth plays. To know it is to know the universe," he screamed.

"How does that work?" I asked.

The reverend crouched down at the front of the raft as he held both sides. "Perfect stillness and infinite movement are the same things: the alpha and omega, the beginning and the end. That stillness, that calmness that sits around us is just..."

"An illusion," I said.

He pointed at me. "Yes, that's right, it's an illusion. That stillness is made up of billions of vibrations, of waves, and if you add

141

them all up, it gives you a wave of zero hertz, absolute perfect stillness. Movement and stillness at the same time."

Kicker Tom sat dumbfounded, looking at the reverend.

"Don't know if I follow you, but hell, it's your party," said Kicker Tom.

"It's not my party." The reverend looked all around. "It's the good Lord's party. I'm just dancing to his music." He stood up and did a little jig.

"CC is always moving, always talking, always communicating. That's her job. You feel that?" He looked around as the water started to churn around us.

"Why do you call her CC?" I asked.

The movement of the water picked up as we approached our first rapids of the day. The reverend stood still as Kicker Tom and I started to paddle with more urgency as we were now in it.

"Corpus Colorado. She's the nerve center, boys, the substance. She contains a vast body of knowledge," the reverend screamed.

We were now at full speed, bouncing, moving, and flowing through the rapids as the reverend continued his sermon as though he was standing on solid ground. "She runs smack down the middle with millions of nerve endings pulsating between..." he slapped my side of the raft as it rose, "the right side," he slapped Kicker Tom's side as it rose, "and the left side. And if we are doing our jobs and carefully listen to the information given we should stay in perfect..." The rapids had run their course, and we were back in steady calm water as the reverend stood over us. "... balance. Now, if the left side decides to take over and dominates the rowing or if the right side decides it has had enough and takes a nap, then we get out of balance and things can get messy. And today is not the day for things to get messy."

For the next twenty miles through numerous rapids, we continued to practice, work in unison, and follow CC's every command in our preparation for the big one. I noticed the rapids that day seemed more turbulent, more violent than the day before. Maybe it was my imagination, or maybe the reverend was right, CC wasn't playing around today.

A few hundred yards before the big one, we pulled over to the bank and hiked a couple of stories above it to get a better look and make a game plan. It was midday and the sun was beating down hard. As I stood over CC looking into her, I knew she was in a bad mood. How else could you explain the violence and mayhem that swirled below?

"Either of you like a-holes?" asked the reverend as sweat fell from his brow.

I assumed that was a rhetorical question.

He looked back toward CC and pointed out a large hole that spanned the middle third of the river. It apparently sucked boats and people into it just because it could. "That is the a-hole. And not any garden-variety-type a-hole, but a big, nasty, steal-your-grandmother's-life-savings type a-hole. You do not want to be near the a-hole. You do not want to make friends with the a-hole. And most importantly, you do not want to go into the a-hole."

"Amen," said Kicker Tom.

"Amen," I repeated.

The reverend showed us our line of attack and other obstacles to avoid. After he said a quick prayer asking CC for her guidance and cooperation we geared back up, got into our positions, and off we went. The reverend was up front, but this time, facing the music. He was on his knees holding on tightly to the rope rigging on both sides of the raft. Our navigator looked more like a cowboy prepping to ride a pissed-off bull.

From 200 yards out you could hear the angry roar, a mother-bear-protecting-her-cubs kind of angry roar. We were moments away from a face-to-face meeting. The speed of our boat picked up dramatically, and now we were flying. So was my pulse rate. The reverend barked out orders to keep us on the correct line, but Momma Bear screamed at the top of her lungs and it became more and more difficult to hear him.

Fifty yards out and you could see the monster. A wall of angry water a story high, stretching from the a-hole to the bank, was waiting to say hi. When we got there I hoped she didn't misinter-pret my silence as rudeness. I had lost the ability to speak. The reverend, however, had not. He let out a loud scream to let Momma Bear know we were at her doorstep.

Kicker Tom and I paddled to the tune of the reverend's beat, but it soon became apparent we were not in charge. Rows of waves threw us right, then left, then up, then back, then suddenly changed direction for no good reason. The reverend yelled instructions but they became just background noise. Kicker Tom and I tried to correct the raft with each new onslaught. It felt like we were in a heavyweight bout taking constant jabs, hooks, and uppercuts. A barrage of combinations, right, left, right, left, and one straight in the face. With each hit, the reverend threw all his body weight in just the correct position to keep us upright. Still, we were getting pounded. Any referee worth his salt would've called the fight, but he wasn't there to save us. We were on our own.

Sheets of ice-cold waves continued to come over the top and hold us down. Kicker Tom and I paddled furiously trying to break their grasp. Finally, she let go and we rode to the top of a crest and held our position. For the first time, we felt a sense of control. That vanished in short order. We somehow drifted left and hung on the right cheek of the a-hole. Kicker Tom noticed this as well and immediately dug in. I followed suit and we started making progress when our momentum pushed us over the crest. As we cruised down its backside I noticed a gigantic wall of water coming from the right. It was enormous. I could barely see the top of it. It was Momma Bear standing on her hind legs waiting to gobble us up. As we begin the surge up its bank, my side of the *Titanic* started to point to the sky. Kicker Tom was now almost directly below me. Farther and farther we climbed up the face when reality began to set in. We were going to flip. As we were about at the apex, the reverend jumped with everything he had to the same spot, half his body hanging over the front right hoping to break through the top and keep us upright. As the reverend's body went forward, mine decided to obey the laws of gravity and go the other way. The force of the wave sent me flying over Kicker

Tom's right shoulder and into the a-hole. Like that, I was gone. CC had me.

As I quickly learned, she was in no hurry to give me back. I guess she wanted to have a word with me in private. So, she took me to her office, which happened to be on the bottom floor. The elevator consisted of a sucking motion down. With each new suck, the water became colder and colder, darker and darker until the light vanished.

I knew I had officially arrived when the sucking motion stopped and was replaced by complete stillness. Absolute silence. Eternal blackness. I floated effortlessly in a sea of nothingness, held into place by forces around me, movement in stillness, stillness in movement. I was facing the unknown, yet felt at perfect peace. This was pure nothingness at its finest. This was zero hertz, the alpha and omega, the beginning and the end. It was familiar. I had been there before with my grandmother and slipped through the door with ease into that world of pure love. Absolute freedom. Now, here I was again at its door, looking into the stillness of the void knowing I didn't have the innocence of my childhood to walk me through. This trip was going to cost me something. The price was my life. Had I not been there before I would've walked away with my tail between my legs. But I'd seen it once and had no choice but to see it again, touch it again, roll around in it one more time.

So I dove in, slipping back through the door, head first into that void, into that stillness, into the abyss. And like that, I was gone. I entered that place where the universe and self vanish into nothing. I became the We looking back at myself that was no longer there.

I guess Kicker Tom was right. That little bastard was downstream.

Now, I don't know if we stayed as one for two seconds or two hours or if in that realm time was relevant. I do know at some point after I vanished into that pure truth I heard a voice say, "Swim."

It was Konka. It was the first time he had spoken to me since he left. Or maybe to be more truthful, it was the first time I had heard him.

"Swim, Pahana. Swim now."

I made a movement with my arms on his command and a pain shot through both ears. The pressure from CC's office was too great. My lungs started to scream at me. They wanted air. They wanted air now. I began to swim to what I hoped was up. I used everything I had left in me. My arms and legs pulled upwards and upwards only to be greeted by more stillness and blackness. *Was I going the wrong way? Was CC not finished talking?* I only had a few more moments in me. I was out of air.

Just before real panic emerged I managed a few more frantic strokes when CC burped and spat me out. My head popped out of the a-hole and into the rushing fury for just enough time to get a gasp of air before it pulled me down again. Luckily, this time I moved forward and not down. I popped up again for a few more seconds, grabbed some more oxygen, and back down I went. CC seemed mad at me, as if I had stolen her virginity and knew I wouldn't call. Maybe she was toying with me, keeping me alive but not ready to let me go just yet. Maybe she still had a point to make. She had opened herself and let me in on a secret, a secret that carried great responsibility. I think she was making sure I was worthy. I guess I was, for she finally let me go.

I popped up again and a hand grabbed the back of my shirt. At first, I thought it was the hand of God. However, after a quick glance, I knew it wasn't him. Even God didn't have a set of teeth like that. Before I knew it, the reverend and his smile pulled me back into the *Titanic*.

As I coughed up water and tried to catch my breath I looked over and Kicker Tom wasn't there.

"Where's Tom?" I barely got out.

The reverend didn't hear me. He paddled like a crazed man against the tide and his head was on a swivel.

"Where's Tom?" I yelled louder.

"He jumped into the a-hole after you," he screamed.

I gathered up my wet noodle of a body with what little

strength I still owned, grabbed a paddle, and tried to help the reverend as best I could. We tried not to lose any ground as we kept our attention on the a-hole waiting for her to release Kicker Tom, but we were losing. I was all but useless and the reverend was running out of gas. Despite our efforts, CC slowly took us downstream. I did a 360 in the raft hoping to see something. Hoping CC had released him. Nothing. I glanced over to the reverend for encouragement. His face told the story. That perpetual smile was no longer present. Reality started to set in. Kicker Tom was gone.

Was that the price to pay for rolling around in the void again? Was Kicker Tom just a sacrifice so I could play in that garden? I was about to scream my useless bloody protest from the top of my lungs at the universe when the reverend started paddling with a fury. I joined in again as we made our way to a large rock on the right side of the river. The reverend bent over and pulled Kicker Tom's black cowboy hat off the side of it. He threw it back to me and started paddling again with purpose. As we made our way around the bend, his smile returned. Up on the left, stretched out on a boulder like a turtle, was a large cowboy taking in the sun.

I don't know if that was the happiest moment of my life but it sure felt like it.

As we paddled up, Kicker Tom pulled a cigar out of a plastic bag from his vest. "One of you boys got a light?" he asked.

"Hell of a place to take a dip," said the reverend.

"Thought I might learn somethin' in that vast pool of knowledge."

"And?"

"Well, for one, never jump into an a-hole."

"Is there a two?" the reverend asked.

"Hell, wasn't there long enough. She crapped me right out."

CHAPTER TWENTY-SIX

Reverend Willy's daughter was waiting for us at the take-out point another forty miles downstream. Then they drove us as close as they could to our starting point. The reverend seemed relieved no one had died on his watch. Before we said our thanks and goodbyes, the reverend looked at me like he wanted to give me some words of wisdom but instead placed his finger just below my sternum, then moved it to my forehead, and of course grinned.

He turned to his Marine brother and gave him a firm hug. No one said a word. Dirt and dust shot into the air as the reverend and his daughter drove off. Kicker Tom and I threw on our back-packs and hiked another few miles back to the Mystery Machine. The day's light was fading and so were we. CC had taken its toll on both of us. We were physically and mentally wiped. We tossed our gear into the van and headed out.

Kicker Tom threw in an eight-track of some band called Three Dog Night, lit up a joint, and took a hit. He passed it toward me. "Want to say hi to Mary?" he asked.

My head motion said no before I had time to say yes. I guess a wiser voice inside knew I needed what focus I had left to concentrate on the road.

I wanted to ask Kicker Tom why he jumped in after me but I

guess I already knew the answer. I also wanted to thank him for the gesture but for some reason couldn't get the words out. Plus, he didn't seem the type who cared much about that sort of thing. So, I kept quiet.

I turned up the AC hoping it would provide some relief to my sunburnt skin. It did.

Kicker Tom and I didn't say a word as we listened to a mix of Three Dog Night and the hum of cold air coming out of the vents. After several more miles Kicker Tom tilted up his cowboy hat away from his eyes and said, "I felt it."

"Felt what?"

"Freedom."

"When?" I asked.

"In the canyon. The day before. I don't know what happened. One moment I'm floating there looking at the canyon wall and then…the sound of the rustling water slowly started to fade. The seconds started to slow and then slow some more. Everything just slowed down and stretched out. At one point I felt that everything around me was about to just stop. I felt like I was in an alternate world. It was as though I was the canyon wall. I was the rock. I was the water. It was me. Then just like that, it was gone again. I haven't felt like that since I was a kid. In fact, I forgot that even existed. Was that the We?"

"Yeah, I think so."

"I want to see him again."

"You will," I said.

"How do you know?"

"Because you're Kicker Tom and you're seeking the We."

He started to chuckle and then howl out loud. "Ah hell, son, how right you are." He kissed Mary again and turned up the sound on the Mystery Machine's kick-ass stereo system as Three Dog Night sang without sorrow or shame.

Twenty more miles passed and I don't remember driving. It was at that moment we passed a sign that read "Las Vegas 37 miles."

Who knew the road to Shambala went through Vegas?

Kicker Tom stole another kiss from Mary. "Ah hell, son, ya think the We likes to gamble?"

CHAPTER TWENTY-SEVEN

L as Vegas, the City of Lights, shouldn't be confused with Paris, the City of Light, though I do believe we drove past the Eiffel tower. Okay, I was the one confused. Paris received its nickname during the Age of Enlightenment because it was the center of new ideas and education. Vegas, on the other hand, didn't seem to be offering any new ideas from what I could tell, but an education and enlightenment were definite possibilities.

According to one of many pieces of free literature handed to us through the van window at every stop, a person could order a one-legged Asian dancer to their room in twenty minutes. Of course, I doubted the accuracy of that claim. I believed they were overly optimistic on the time front.

Kicker Tom called the number as a matter of principle. They informed him the one-legged Asian dancer no longer worked for the company, but a two-legged Asian dancer could be there in forty-five minutes. When they couldn't explain to him how a two-legged dancer would take twenty-five minutes longer to arrive than a one-legged dancer he started having his doubts about the quality and reputation of the company. Regardless, it was all for naught. It seemed they wanted an up-charge for van service and Kicker Tom wasn't willing to pay.

They, whoever that might be, say casinos pump oxygen

through the vents to keep the patrons awake. While that sounds like pure urban legend to me, I have to admit that standing in the middle of it all I became much more alert. The tiredness and exhaustion I'd felt on the ride up were all but gone. Whether that was due to the overwhelming number of flashing lights, the sound of coins hitting metal, the throngs of people rushing by, extra oxygen, or a mere second wind was anyone's guess. Whatever the reason, it worked.

Kicker Tom headed straight to a craps table. After the day's events maybe he felt lucky. Maybe Lady Luck had surfaced and his fate was about to change.

After several hours at the craps, blackjack, and poker tables it appeared my initial thoughts were inaccurate. It seemed Lady Luck was no lady. She kept asking him for more money and he kept giving. This was obviously a one-sided relationship because she didn't have the courtesy or desire to give back. For whatever reason, Kicker Tom didn't seem to mind. He gave freely with what seemed to be not a care in the world. I guess when you're full to the brim with guilt, and whatever is left of your self-esteem is on life support, you think you deserve such treatment.

I don't know how much he donated, but I couldn't watch any longer. I grabbed him by the shoulders and forced him to buy me a beer with what was left in his wallet.

However, we never made it to the bar. A certain roulette wheel caught his attention, and before I could speak he had thrown down another $100 and asked for chips.

"Don't you think you need a break?" I asked.

"You see that?" he asked, pointing to the lit-up board that showed the most recent winning numbers.

"Yes."

"The last six winning numbers were red."

"So?"

"Well, son, odds are in our favor that the next number will be black."

"It doesn't work that way."

"It's got to average out, son."

At that point, I didn't know if he was making the decisions or Mary. "It'll average out, but the previous rolls have no effect on this particular one. Your odds don't change," I said.

Despite that sage advice he put all of his chips on black as the dealer let the ball fly, and to Kicker Tom's delight, it came up thirty-five black. "Ah shit, son. Looky there," he said with a smile.

I decided it best to let it go. It was one of the few victories he'd enjoyed all night, so my being right didn't seem important. Besides, maybe this was the kick in the butt Lady Luck needed to show her appreciation. It took another twenty minutes to realize that wasn't going to be the case. Kicker Tom was down to his last ten dollars in chips. After standing and watching the slow bleed, my exhaustion returned. My mind had given up the fight and took a nap as all thoughts vanished, all sounds disappeared, all activity ceased to exist. As the dealer let the ball fly on its journey around the roulette wheel a single image appeared before me. It was the number eight.

"Number eight," I told Kicker Tom.

He casually put the last of his chips on number eight without hesitation.

"Black eight," yelled the dealer.

Neither Kicker Tom nor I reacted to the win. Several more rolls were made and several more losses for Kicker Tom. As the dealer let another ball fly another image flashed in front of me.

"Twelve," I said to Kicker Tom.

He proceeded to put $100 on it.

"Red twelve," the dealer yelled.

Again, neither Kicker Tom nor I reacted. However, several other people at the table let out a happy scream. I suppose it was loud enough to cause some concern, because a large man in a black suit showed up behind the dealer and watched as she paid Kicker Tom and others at the table. He tapped the girl dealer on the shoulder and she left. I guess her shift had ended. However, lucky for us, a balding older gentleman was standing right there to take over. The man in the black suit must have thought he knew Kicker Tom because he watched him for the next five

153

minutes as Kicker Tom gave a significant amount of his chips back to Lady Luck and the casino. I continued to blankly stare at the roulette wheel as the new dealer let another ball fly.

Again, an image floated up before me. "Thirty-one," I whispered to Kicker Tom.

He put the remainder of his chips on thirty-one. Several other players at the table followed suit.

"Red thirty-one," said the dealer.

Again, we didn't react, but we didn't need to. Our fellow players made up for our apathy. A scream went up so loud it shook me sober. Whatever realm I had visited I now was back in reality's saddle. I looked around and people were high five-ing, dancing, and slapping Kicker Tom on the back. One woman kissed him right smack on the lips. I'd never seen so much joy in a given moment, though I don't think the man in the black suit was having the same experience. His stoic expression never changed. Yet he must not have been all bad. After they paid Kicker Tom all his winnings, he called another man over, who was wearing what seemed to be an identical black suit, and that man offered us a complimentary suite in his hotel. At first, I didn't want to take him up on it. I wanted to move on from that place. However, after our past few days, a hot shower and a clean bed sounded a tad better than the old used mattress in the back of the Mystery Machine.

CHAPTER TWENTY-EIGHT

The man wearing black suit number two must have liked us, because the suite he put us in was larger than my house back home. My room easily held a king-size bed with a fifty-inch television that popped up in front of it with the touch of a button. The bathroom itself could have slept five. Kicker Tom had the same setup on the opposite side. The two rooms connected by a large living room with floor-to-ceiling windows that looked over the Vegas strip.

After a lengthy, hot shower, I made my way into the living room, where Kicker Tom had ordered us up an abundance of room service. He walked over to the well-stocked refrigerator, grabbed two cold beers, and handed one to me. We clicked bottles and both took a long swig. He wheeled over the room service cart next to the couch and placed a large tray of food on the table in front of us. He worked on a cheeseburger with fries while I munched on the fruit plate as we stared out over the millions of lights and moving cars down below.

"So, why did they give us this room?" I asked.

"I suppose they didn't want to see their money leave just yet."

After witnessing Kicker Tom at the tables for the last couple of hours, I'd say it's a good probability it might never.

After stuffing the last half of the cheeseburger into his mouth,

Kicker Tom reached down into a bag on the floor and threw down several stacks of crisp, bound $100 bills between us on the couch.

"There's your half," he said.

"How much is it?"

"After tipping out, almost $35,000. Seventeen somethin' apiece."

I picked up one of the stacks of fresh bills and thumbed through the edges then dropped it back on the pile.

"I don't want it."

"What do you mean you don't want it? It's yours."

"No, it's not," I said.

"Listen, son, I'm not sure what in the hell happened down there, but that was all you."

"I'm not sure what it was either, but I can tell you for a fact it wasn't all me. In fact, it wasn't me at all."

"Well what in the hell do you want me to do with it?"

"Keep it." I pushed the money closer to him. I figured he'd spent the last eight years of his life trying to do what he believed was the right thing for this world and that same world had turned around and destroyed his life. If anyone deserved a gift it was Kicker Tom.

"It's not mine," he said and pushed it back toward me.

I pushed it back. "Give it away, start a college fund for Jacob, do whatever you please, but I don't want it."

"Why not?"

"I'm afraid of it."

"Money?"

"Konka taught me to be careful of it. That's why we lived on very little. While it can buy you a particular type of freedom and experience, it also is the culprit for most of man's evils. One only has to look at our current political situation and see how it's destroying our nation. The problem seems money's ugly cousin is always close by and when they team up usually a lot of bad things happen," I said.

"Ugly cousin?" he asked.

"You know, it's what you talked about the day I picked you

156

up: power. Our past 2,000 years of existence is littered with examples: the Roman Empire, British Empire, Mongol Empire, pretty much any empire, throw in the Catholic Church, Wall Street, Mussolini, Hitler, Franco, Lenin, Stalin, Castro, Hussein, and just about every king, dictator, monarch, and czar who ever lived."

Kicker Tom looked out over the Vegas strip and recited a poem of some sort in his Texas drawl. Something about a poor man and a king. I wasn't familiar with it.

"Chomsky?" I asked.

"Springsteen."

"Is he a poet?" I asked.

"You could say that."

"I'd like to read his stuff."

Kicker Tom put a handful of fries into his fry trap and shook his head.

"Only a person who knows who they are, only a person who is in total control of their faculties, only an honest person can handle both money and power. For whatever reason, it doesn't seem man has learned that skill very well. We keep making the same mistake over and over again. I surely don't possess such skills either. So for now, it's better to walk away from it," I said.

"Holy shit, son, that's a mouthful. Where did you learn all that?"

I took a sip of my beer and peered back out the window. "We read a lot, talked a lot. History, politics, philosophy, everything," I said.

"Your grandfather?"

"Yeah. He made me read the newspaper every morning before school and we would discuss it in the evenings. The front page, editorials, the advice column, nothing was off limits. "

"The advice column?"

"He was fascinated by human nature. We talked about it so much that by the time I was in high school I think I could have written that column. If you get to the core of it, everyone's issue is the same." I turned to look at him. "We tend to make decisions based on emotions. That's why people make so damn many

157

mistakes. Emotions triumph intelligence every time. They control us, our behavior, our fate."

"Just think, son, had Hitler just read Dear Abby maybe it would've saved the world a whole load of bullshit." He took a gulp from his bottle. "So, did he teach you that thang downstairs?"

"He was teaching me to see, to listen with this." I pointed to my heart.

"Is that what Reverend Willy meant with all that *ET* finger stuff?"

"*ET*?" I asked.

"*ET*? The movie *ET!*"

"Never saw it."

"Never saw *ET*?"

"Nope."

"Just plain sad, son."

"Konka used to do that to me when I was a little kid. He'd put his finger on my chest and then on my forehead. He did it anytime I made a wrong decision."

"I don't get it," said Kicker Tom.

"He'd say, 'Listen with your heart.'" I tapped on mine with my finger, and then did the same on my forehead. "Not your head."

"Why?"

"The mind will trick you. The heart doesn't lie."

"How do you know the difference?"

"Practice."

"Practice?"

"We used to play a lot of games. This one game we would mix up a couple of decks of cards and pull out about twenty random ones. He'd concentrate on one and I would try to listen with my heart for the answer."

"But roulette is different. No one knows the number. It hasn't happened yet," he said.

"Time is relative. Einstein proved that."

"Relative?"

I grabbed a grape from the fruit plate and held it up. "The

past." I grabbed another one and held it up. "The present." I grabbed a third grape. "And the future." I threw the grapes in my mouth and began to chew. "All exist…simultaneously."

"Are you saying it already happened?" he asked.

"I'm saying an event that happened at a particular time for you might have happened at a different time for me."

"But we were standing side by side at the same time."

"Only physically. Mentally I was in a different realm, a different space," I said.

"Then who was sending the message?"

"I think the We."

"Damn, son, that little bastard gets around."

"Sure seems that way," I said.

"Could you do it again?"

"I don't know. That's never happened like that before."

CHAPTER TWENTY-NINE

My eyes opened and the City of Lights still illuminated the strip. I'd been asleep for about five hours, but a deep sleep it was. I felt well rested and putting my head back down on the pillow didn't seem like the right move. So I laced up my running shoes and decided to get a long run in before the heat or Kicker Tom awoke. I soon found out one of them had never gone to bed. As I strolled into the living room, the big cowboy was sitting on the couch in front of a tray of half-eaten food and numerous empty beer bottles, staring out into the dark Vegas morning.

"Did you go back downstairs?" I asked.

He didn't answer. He continued to look straight ahead. I went over and sat down next to him. We sat in silence for another five minutes and peered out over the strip.

"Do you think the universe keeps score?" he asked.

"In what way?"

"My son, my wife, my best friend, did I lose them because of the bad things I did over there?"

"You mean karma?" I asked.

"Whatever you wanna call it."

"Yes and no," I said.

He looked at me. His eyes were worn and red.

"I don't believe the universe is in the eye for an eye business if that is what you're asking," I said. "However, I do believe for every action there's a reaction, simple cause and effect."

"What do you mean?"

"What happens when you stop watering a plant?" I asked.

"It dies."

"For anything to grow, including relationships, they need attention. You couldn't pay enough attention to yours because you weren't there. So, it died—cause and effect."

He looked back out the window. "I killed people over there."

Dear Abby had suddenly lost her voice. I searched for words of wisdom but only mustered up a soft and pathetic, "I know."

We sat together frozen in thought when he finally broke the eerie silence. "For a while, I went downstairs for a while."

I was about to ask him if he'd gambled more but I knew the answer. "For a while" was more than enough time to give the man in the black suit all his money back, but I didn't ask that either.

"Can we leave? I hate this place," he said.

I guess I had my answer anyway.

So, under the gauntlet of a billion man-made lights, in the stillness of the morning, propelled by forward motion, Kicker Tom and I slipped the grasp of Lady Luck and back onto the road and into the darkness we went.

CHAPTER THIRTY

Dobie Gray's soulful voice eased out of the speakers as the Mystery Machine pointed in a southwesterly direction, making its way toward San Diego. Kicker Tom had made peace with the old mattress in the back and drifted away. I guess a lack of sleep, two days in the Grand Canyon, a heavy heart, and a long evening in Vegas had sucked every bit of energy out of the big cowboy. He hadn't moved a muscle in the past four-plus hours, which was all right by me. I used that time to reflect on the past week and to see if I could make sense of it all. Despite my best efforts, I couldn't. It was still a large bowl of gumbo that wasn't ready to be eaten. Each time I tried to taste it, life would throw in another ingredient and change its profile. Instead of staring at the pot and waiting for it to be ready, I put the lid back on and gave it more time to cook.

It was almost 10 a.m. and we were outside of Joshua Tree when Kicker Tom awoke and lumbered up front. I guess he was used to not having a full night of sleep. Whatever had tweaked him the evening before, at least for the moment, had disappeared.

"Good to go! Good to go! Good to go!" he said, clapping his hands together. "What in the hell is for breakfast? Can't chase the We on an empty stomach!"

"I have some bananas in the cooler," I said.

"Bananas? Bananas? What in the hell am I gonna do with bananas, son? Steak, eggs, and biscuits. I'm buying."

I guess the man in the black suit had let him keep his credit cards. I found a dive in town and Kicker Tom found his steak and eggs. We sat in a corner booth up against the window that let in the morning sun. I fiddled with my coffee cup on top of the scratched, lime-green Formica table-top as I watched Kicker Tom mix a bottle of beer with orange juice. He took a long swig and said, "Beermosa."

The smell of bacon and coffee permeated the air as the big cowboy covered his breakfast with Tabasco sauce. After several bites he asked, "What do you suppose exactly is this We?"

"I think it's energy. Konka had many names for it: grace, source, Divine, intelligence, the great spirit, the universal mind."

"What does this energy, this intelligence do?"

I took a sip from my coffee mug. "It's the source that holds the universe together. It is the universe. It's the center that contains every bit of information in the history of time. To be in touch with it is to be directly connected to the world, to be at one with everything. See everything. Communicate with everything on a level most humans never experience."

"Like telepathy, clairvoyance, second sight, like that quasi-*Rainman* stuff you did last night?

"*Rainman*?"

"Dustin Hoffman, Tom Cruise."

I shrugged my shoulders.

"Ah no, son. You've never seen that either? Have you seen anything?"

"No."

"You never gone to the movies?"

"No."

"You've never been to the movies!?"

"No."

He sat dumbfounded, trying to figure out how that was possible. When he couldn't come up with an answer he began to attack his plate again.

"But don't let the mystical stuff seduce you. That is only a side product. That's not the carrot," I said.

He stabbed a large piece of steak and lifted up his fork. "So, what's the carrot?"

"It's what we are both searching for. It's what the whole world is longing for. It's what you experienced in the canyon. Freedom. True freedom," I said.

"So, this center is sort of like a big-ass library?" he asked as he put the large piece of meat into his mouth.

"Something like that."

"How does one get a library card?"

I wanted to say near-death experiences like drowning but thought it better not to give him any extra ideas. "There seem to be many ways in, but few have found a permanent path."

"Did your grandfather find that path?"

"He did."

"And you're looking for it as well?"

"It's starting to feel that way."

"Is that why you do it?"

"Do what?"

"Meditate?"

"It's one reason."

"I don't think I could pull that off."

"As my grandfather would say, there's a thousand ways to kneel and kiss the earth; walking, running, gardening, sewing, washing dishes, painting a wall, checking the mail, it can be anything. If done right it's all meditation."

"Done right?"

I picked up the salt shaker and stared at it. "Meditation is just focusing on the here and now. Doing that thing and nothing else. If you're washing dishes, just concentrate on washing dishes and nothing else, if you're changing a tire, just concentrate on changing a tire, if you're walking just walk, if you're gardening just garden." I put down the salt shaker. "But that's not how most people go about their business. Their minds are elsewhere."

"Hell, Tag, not much of a dishwasher." He downed the rest of his beermosa.

"Then do what Buddha did."

"Remind me again. I might've missed school the day we covered great sages of the world."

"He sat under a tree," I said.

"He just sat under a tree?"

"Yep."

"He sat there and found the We?"

"No, the We found him," I said.

"How?"

"The same way it found you in the canyon."

"I wasn't doing anything."

"Neither was Buddha."

"Are you saying do nothing?" he asked.

"Exactly."

"But what happened in the canyon was an accident."

"Well hell, son," I said, "I guess you need to have a few more accidents."

"Damn sure would've been easier if Konka just showed you the way."

I peered back out the window to the lonely roadway out front. "I think he is."

Kicker Tom and I finished breakfast and then pulled into a gas station. We had just begun to fill up when a white VW van with the words "Professor Lightning Bolt" spray-painted on the side pulled up next to us. A man supporting a long, grayish ponytail was inside along with what looked like his daughter.

"Love the van, man," said the professor himself.

"Thanks," I shot back as though I had something to do with it.

This was followed by a long pause where I think we were supposed to reciprocate the same feelings toward his ride but we were too slow on the uptake.

"You guys playing in the Tree today?" asked the girl.

"The Tree?" I asked.

"Joshua Tree. The park."

"No, we're heading through on our way to San Diego," I said.

"You sure you don't want to hang out for a day in the Tree?" she asked.

"And do what?" asked Kicker Tom.

"Sing with the sun, fly with the birds, float in the wind, swim with the angels," said the professor.

Kicker Tom and I looked at each other hoping for a clue. It didn't appear.

"We've got cactus," said the girl with a big smile.

I wasn't sure what cactus was, but by the look on Kicker Tom's face he sure did.

"Ah hell, son, looks like the We is in the Tree! The We is in the Tree! That little bastard's looking for us," said Kicker Tom.

"Sounds like an accident waiting to happen," I said.

CHAPTER THIRTY-ONE

According to my paper placemat menu at the breakfast diner, the yucca palm, palmyra cactus, yucca brevifolia, and the big tree yuccas were all names used to identify the wild-limbed trees of this national park. But it wasn't until the Mormons rolled through during the mid-nineteenth century and named them Joshua that their moniker was set in stone. Supposedly, the limbs of the trees are said to resemble the outstretched arms of Moses's successor Joshua, who led his people to the Promised Land.

Now, I'm not sure of the authenticity of my source being it also misspelled OMLET and COFFE and claimed it was voted best Mexican food three years running by someone named Jack Says. Of course, maybe they had something against too many E's in a word, but I didn't see anything Mexican on their menu, and the owners were from Thailand. Regardless, we followed behind our two new friends as they led us deeper into the Promised Land despite neither of them being named Joshua.

We pulled the van up close to theirs and parked next to a massive rock formation. As we got out I noticed civilization was nowhere in the vicinity, only open land in every direction covered with sandy dirt, the occasional rock formation, and what seemed millions of cartoonish, twisted-limbed trees spread out as far as the eye could see.

Professor Lightning Bolt had obviously been to the Promised Land more than a few times. I say that because not only did he talk about the local terrain with great confidence and passion, but his crazy-intense bug eyes and nonlinear thought process suggested that maybe cactus was part of his regular diet.

My psychic powers of perception were off kilter because Meghan, his daughter, turned out to be Meghan, his girlfriend, despite the twenty-plus-year age difference. They had met at a spiritual conference where the professor was the headline speaker. His claim to fame was that he had invented a holographic light ray that re-engineered atoms at the quantum level. According to his girlfriend and spokesperson, Meghan, this light ray was used to change negative molecules into positive molecules, making something bad, good. A mere forty-five-second zap from this not-yet-FDA approved hand-held mini flashlight could turn the dangerous properties of a milkshake into safe properties, thus making it a healthy drink without destroying its flavor, or it could take all the toxins out of carbon emissions, or make a cancerous mole on your skin non-cancerous. She assured us the potential uses were limitless.

While the professor wasn't ready to sell the product to the public just yet, he was accepting offers for priority positions as a regional distributor for only $20,000. And it so happened to be our good fortune most regions were still available.

"Too rich for my blood," said Kicker Tom.

"Some move forward, some get left behind," replied the professor.

"And some get shot," said Kicker Tom.

"How'd you get the name Lightning?" I asked, trying to change the subject.

"I had the pleasure of receiving it."

"As therapy?" asked Kicker Tom.

"That wouldn't be natural," replied the professor.

"You've been struck by lightning?" I asked.

He looked up to the sky. "Twice."

"Oh, bad luck! What are the odds of that?" asked Kicker Tom.

"When you're looking for it, the odds increase."

"Hot damn, Professor." Kicker Tom slapped him on the back. "That's fantastic."

"You're right, it is. It opens you up to different dimensions. It was only days after my second encounter with all those beautiful electrons that the idea came to me of combining nanotechnology with holograms to change the intensity and polarization of light rays," said the professor.

"The professor's ultimate goal is to use technology to save the planet," Meghan said.

While I admired his ambition, I don't think the planet's chances had improved. "You're a physicist?" I asked.

"I don't like to use labels," he said.

I guess the artwork on the side of his van announcing his presence didn't count. "Where did you go to school?" I asked.

"Like Edison, Mozart, and Zappa I'm self-taught," he said.

"You guys want to go rock climbing?" asked Meghan.

"Is there rain in the forecast?" asked Kicker Tom.

They both looked up to a clear blue sky, not catching the joke.

"The ceremony doesn't start for a few more hours. The others should be here by then," she continued.

"Ceremony?" I asked.

"Peyote is a sacred gift from Mother Earth." The professor kneeled down and grabbed a handful of dirt. "It's a proper way of saying thanks," he said as the dirt fell through his fingers.

"The others?" asked Kicker Tom

"We find it's a better experience with a group," he said.

"You guys go ahead and hit the rocks, I'll hang here and wait for the others," said Kicker Tom.

"I'm going for a run. Maybe I'll catch up with you afterward," I said.

"Waiting and running, running and waiting, protons and electrons, electrons and protons. Opposites attracting," said the professor to no one in particular.

Was he talking about movement and stillness, the alpha and omega? I wanted to ask him his opinion but his left eye started making strange movements on its own toward Kicker Tom while his right eye stayed planted on me. Movement and stillness on perfect display. I let it go.

Professor Electron walked over, jumped inside his van, and disappeared.

Meghan grabbed a water bottle filled with a brownish liquid out of her backpack and handed it to me. "Cactus tea. It'll help you on your run," she said.

"Help me how?" I asked.

"Endurance. Indian runners of Mexico use it."

"What about the professor?" I asked.

"Don't worry. He's getting stoned."

"What about the group experience?" Tom asked.

"You're absolutely right." She grabbed the bottle back, took a big swig, and made an awful face. Then she handed the bottle to Kicker Tom, who didn't blink. He took a large gulp and handed it to me. I hesitated. While I wanted to experience it, everything was happening so fast. I hadn't had a chance to process the past week, and now before I could, life was giving me more. *But wasn't that what I wanted - to seek knowledge? Wasn't that why I was out here—to see, to learn, to discover?*

I couldn't think straight. My head was spinning, my power of focus on hiatus. I wanted to pass to give myself a moment to breathe, but I made the mistake of looking at Meghan, who gave me such a wonderful, easy smile behind a wall of mirrored sunglasses. Before I knew it, I had taken a big drink of the cactus brew. I guess it wasn't the first time in history a female had influenced an outcome. Nor would it be the last.

The second it touched my lips I understood her initial response. It was the worst- tasting stuff I ever put in my mouth. Honey and lemon were trying their best to mask the jolt of the bitter acid dirt sludge. They didn't succeed.

Meghan took one more swig. "That should do the trick," she said.

"I sure hope so," said Kicker Tom. He took another gulp.

I followed, despite my feeling it might not stay down for long.

"Tastes like a sweet cowpie," said Kicker Tom.

I didn't ask. Meghan gave Kicker Tom the rest of the tea, grabbed us both by the shoulders at the same time, and gave a squeeze. "Enjoy your flight, boys," she said with that same smile. She banged the side of the van with her right hand. "Come on, Papa," she yelled.

The side door opened and the professor slid out through a cloud of smoke carrying an assortment of ropes and other climbing gear.

"We'll see you guys later," said Meghan.

We watched them disappear into the distance.

"Two cups full to the brim," yelled Kicker Tom.

"Two cups?" I asked.

"Two cups of crazy that dude."

"If he's freaking you out we can go," I said.

"Ah hell no, the We's around here somewhere and I can't wait to meet the others."

CHAPTER THIRTY-TWO

K icker Tom stayed at camp to greet the rest of the party while I threw on my running shoes and despite my growing nausea headed off into the Tree. I got about five miles in when my stomach started to revolt. It decided both breakfast and the cactus brew were no longer welcome. I spent the next half hour on my hands and knees in the powdery dirt bracing against their exit. Surprisingly, only minutes after my guest left I felt somewhat normal, so I took off running again.

It was a bit before noon and the heat was letting itself be known, but it felt good. It was similar to home yet without the humidity. The next several miles flew by without a whisper from my surroundings. While I knew they were awake, like a drunk recovering from a hangover, communicating would happen slowly, on its terms, if at all.

This place was different both from the hill country in which I grew up and the canyons I had just experienced. The energy here lacked flamboyance. Subtlety was its protective cape. It had no other choice. This land was much harsher, fewer things lived out here, and the ones that did were survivors. They had been through a lot. They were tough, hardened, and didn't open up to strangers, especially ones who threw up on them.

Making friends with your environment was something Konka

taught me early on. It began with the stars on the night he told me about my grandmother. It continued with any and every life form, animate or inanimate, plant, rock, tree, stream, animal. To him there was no difference. "Everything has a soul. Find it," he would say.

Since I found it difficult to find it in kids at school, I spent many hours wandering through the hillside trying to locate it there and make friends. While not any easier, at least the environment was never intentionally mean.

For now, Joshua wasn't ready to talk, which was more than fine by me. I wasn't alone, yet I was able to enjoy absolute solitude. I was free, free to run, free to wander, free to be. So I picked up the pace and ran with the joy of a child through the Promised Land.

About an hour in I had settled into a nice rhythm. Despite the increasing heat, I felt great, better than great. My system now purged, I felt like I could run all day.

With each new mile, the heat seemed to rise another degree though the surroundings hadn't opened up one bit. If anything they tightened and took a step back. Despite Joshua's open arms, he wasn't ready for a hug. So I kept my distance and continued on. Eventually I came upon a set of large rock formations not unlike those where we'd parked. Even though I felt I could run two marathons, I decided to stop in the shade of the rocks, take in some much-needed water, squat for a bit, close my eyes, and do the only thing one can do when looking for answers; shut it and listen.

I found a nice smooth boulder in the shade and did just that. For the first twenty minutes or so no one seemed interested in talking. Both the universe and Joshua were quiet. Then, a slight warm wind appeared and began to kiss the left side of my body and face intermittently. In that wind, I felt his pulse. It was strong yet calm and easy. Joshua was alive and comfortable in his own skin. With each new gust, that strength and serenity entered me until we were on the same wavelength. Joshua had let his guard down and said hello.

I sat still in that greeting and warmth for several more minutes, or what I thought was several more minutes, when my eyes decided they wanted to open. What awaited them was different from what they had witnessed since their arrival. Joshua Tree was open and alive. I jumped to my feet and took a few steps. The rocks that had been cold and dead less than an hour ago now glowed with life. Their surfaces, washed smooth and soft from millions of years of rain, wind, and sand, now had a voice. Everything around me was dancing with color: greens, reds, browns, blues, yellows, and the millions of colors in between streaming all over the place. I jumped on the nearest boulder and climbed to the next one, and the next one, and on and on until I was at least twenty feet high and could see out over the desert floor. The land was radiant, open and free. Joshua's soul was bursting out loud. He had officially welcomed me to the Promised Land.

I had felt the energy in Sedona with ease. I'd made friends with it at home after years of pursuit, but here I saw it. I physically saw the connection, like a spiderweb from one thing to the next. I saw its pattern, from the smallest speck of dirt to as far as my eye could see and everything in between. Universe's blueprint. How real. How perfect. This harsh, closed desert had morphed into an open, beautiful, living interactive being.

But how could it be both? How did that happen? How is that possible? Joshua Tree doesn't have two personalities, or does it?

It occurred to me—the cactus tea, the mescaline martini, the buttons, nubs, tips, half-moons, the big chief, peyote, or whatever you want to call it was doing its thing.

Was I swimming with angels? Was the drug making me see something that wasn't there, or was it always there and I never noticed? Maybe I was the one with two personalities? Maybe there was another me? Maybe this other me, this other personality can always see but doesn't speak or for whatever reason isn't allowed to see. Maybe I have my hands over my other personality's eyes like a jealous boyfriend who doesn't want the other me to have a voice, to be an equal.

Was that what all the meditation was for, all of Konka's

games? Was it a way to help pry that hand away from my other self's eyes?

I guess I was at the point in my education where the hand had widened enough so I could occasionally see through the cracks of the fingers. But the cactus tea removed the hand altogether, and I could see everything, an unobstructed view.

I looked around, and the love, joy, and happiness that permeated my surroundings zoomed through my pores and infiltrated my being. Joshua had me. The universe had me. I was smiling uncontrollably, from ear to ear. I couldn't stop. It was plastered on my mug without any effort from me. I knew that smile well. It was the same one that possessed Konka, Iris, Reverend Willy, Buddha, or anyone who has ever taken a happy pill. Our other self was smiling. Our other self could see. Our other self was free.

I grabbed my water bottle and took off running back the way I'd come through the Promised Land. A different Promised Land than the one I had traveled earlier. It ran with me.

I floated over the desert floor for the next several miles, stopping on occasion to say hello to my new friends along the way and to study the detailed design patterns of energy that connected us all. That's when I heard a voice say, "Pahana."

I looked up and in the distance was a figure on the same trail as me. *Was it Konka? Was he here?*

I took off running as fast as I could toward him. As I got closer my excitement started to dwindle. I knew it wasn't him. Konka was taller. This person was more my height. About fifty yards away I stopped running as I got my first glimpse of this stranger. I couldn't make him out, but he looked familiar. As I got closer I stopped altogether and so did he. The desert was flashing with brilliant colors and parts of it moved, all around me, all around us, though I still couldn't quite make out this stranger's face, his features.

We moved toward each other one step at a time until we were a few feet apart and his face came into full focus. Holy shit! It was me, with a better tan.

Was this some strange reflection or was this pure hallucination? I wasn't sure. But this other me seemed as real as the sandy dirt I was standing on. He put up his hand and smiled as if to say hi. For some reason, I couldn't move.

"Pahana," he said again.

I took another step forward. "Hi," I said.

"Nice to finally meet you," he said back.

"Who are you?" I asked.

"I'm your brother. Some people call me soul," he said.

"You're my soul brother?"

"Matter of speaking, yes," he said.

"Then who am I?"

He smiled. "Pahana, my lost white brother, the white wolf."

"I'm the white wolf?"

"Yes."

I looked directly into him. "Are you real?" I asked.

"Of course I'm real. You just don't know me. You didn't know I existed. But I'm just as real as you. I have to be. I am you. You are me. At least sometimes you are me," he responded.

"Sometimes?" I asked.

"When you meditate deeply, go on a long Zen run, dance like a maniac for hours, take a happy pill, almost die, drink that disgusting brown tea."

"And the rest of the time?" I asked.

He grabbed my hand and put it over his eyes.

"Why do I do that? I asked.

You like to be in charge, in control."

"Me?"

"You. Mankind," he said.

"Why?"

"You started listening to the wrong voice."

"Whose voice is that?"

"The dark wolf's."

"How do I stop?"

"Continue on your journey, your education." He looked down at the dirt and drew a line with his foot from me to him. "Find the way," he said.

I looked back up to him. "The permanent road?" I asked.

"Yes."

"But I'm lost?"

"Not anymore. You found me. Most people go through their whole lives and never know I exist, and the few that do never develop the friendship."

"Why?"

"Because they're afraid?"

"Of what?" I asked.

"Of giving up their power. Unfortunately, that power is driving us all over a cliff."

"That sounds like Konka."

"Because it is Konka."

"You can speak to him?"

"To him, your grandmother, Bodhi, I can communicate with anything and everything."

"How?"

"We all live in the same house, so to speak."

"I want to talk to them."

"They can only communicate with me."

"But Konka spoke to me in the river."

"No, he spoke to me. When you jumped into the void, you disappeared."

"Turn me, into we, be free," I said.

"Yes."

"How do I find you again?"

"Don't worry. I don't live far away."

Before I could ask another question, he gave me a Buddha smile and ran directly into me and his image was gone.

But he was still there. He had to be. Joshua Tree was still ecstatic with energy, colors, and joy. I guess I hadn't put my hands back up over my brother's eyes. I hoped I never would but knew as soon as the martini started wearing off it would happen automatically.

I had made it almost all the way back to where we'd parked when I came across the big cowboy sitting under a Joshua tree. He was staring straight ahead, next to him, the empty bottle that had contained the rest of the tea. I guess he'd gotten thirsty. I took a seat a few feet away. "What are you doing?" I asked.

"Nothing."

"Just like Buddha?"

"Just like Buddha."

"Have you seen the We?" I asked.

"I'm not sure, but George Harrison is here." He looked at me. "For the love of rock and roll, please tell me you know who George Harrison is."

"Of course. But I don't see him."

"He's right there." He pointed to a large rock a few yards away. "His face, it's right there in that rock."

I looked to where he was pointing. The rock itself was glistening. I could see its energy that kept it together and made it whole but could see nothing that looked like the former Beatle. "I don't see him," I said.

"There, Tag. Right there," he pointed again.

I looked closer yet still saw nothing. "The sixties George Harrison or the seventies George Harrison?"

"The later version with the long hair and mustache. You can see him right there. It's as plain as day."

I looked closer. "Oh yeah," I said.

"You missed it. He was singing 'Here Comes the Sun,' and when he hit the chorus, you could see the actual rays of sunlight penetrating everything, everywhere. It looked like waterless rain."

It was official. The other Kicker Tom could see. His smile gave it away.

The wind blew against the sweat on my face and body, which despite the afternoon heat, kept me cool.

"How long did he wait?" asked Kicker Tom.

"Who?"

"Buddha. How long did he sit under that tree before he understood?"

"Forty-nine days."

"Forty-nine days! Hell, son, the ole peyote prince could've saved him forty-eight and a half of those days. Somebody tell the monks to stop meditating, the swamis to stop chanting, the yogis to stop yogi-ing, Catholics and Muslims get off your knees, Jews drop the prayer book. You can all skip the pray, hope, and luck method. Hallelujah and amen, I have not only seen the light, I've seen the palace, the mountaintop. Krishnas keep your hair, your TVs; Baptists do the drunken two-step; Jehovahs grab a thin mint; yo, Amish, the new Cadillac is on sale; filet mignon Fridays at the Vatican, because there's a better and quicker way. Say hello to the Lord Cactus."

He grabbed the empty bottle of cactus tea and held it up to the sky, then brought it back down to his face and took a closer look at it. "Oops. I meant to save the last sip for you." He sat for a moment in his joyous happiness before taking a long look at me. "I'm glad you're alive," he said.

"Me too."

He looked back out into the Tree. "It's beautiful. It's all so beautiful," he said, smiling ear to ear.

"Yes, it is," I said.

He started to giggle to himself.

"What's so funny?"

He let out another chuckle. "The professor and Mary Ann have left the island."

"Mary Ann?" I asked.

"Gilligan's Island." He could see I was clueless. "Ah hell, son, Meghan. The professor and Meghan took off."

"Why?"

"It seems," he said, trying to hold his laughter back, "Professor Two Cups had the wrong date." The wave was building. "Imagine that," he said. Kicker Tom was about to explode. "The others…the others…they're not coming for another week." He burst out into a full-blown laughing tirade, which rolled over me and sucked me right in. We began to flail around in the dirt as the laughing fit took its hold on us, and it wouldn't let go.

Kicker Tom squeezed out, "Then, those two got in a fight."

Tears started to stream down our faces.

"I guess he wasn't too happy with..." he looked at me and moved his eyes in different directions, "...her starting the ceremony without him."

We both erupted again.

I began to laugh as hard as possible. My stomach muscles, sore from their morning purge, were getting another workout. Oxygen became harder to process. At one point, I felt like a rib might break. But I didn't care. They could all break. I didn't want it to end and neither did Kicker Tom. Every moment it thought about fading, a quick look at the other automatically restoked the funny. This cycle continued until time and physical exhaustion brought it to a close. We were empty. We sat in that happy emptiness for several more minutes as Joshua continued to dance all around us.

"They left a while ago," Kicker Tom said.

"How long was I gone?"

"I don't know, four or five hours. I thought you might have gotten lost, so I headed out to look for you. But this tree's arms starting moving, so I figured it best to sit down for a while. Every time my thoughts got sad or I felt a bit of remorse, this damn tree would wrap its limbs around me and hold me like an infant. Isn't that crazy?"

"No, it's not crazy at all."

"Why do you think it did that?"

I looked up and into the tree. "It's trying to save you," I said.

"Why?"

"So you can save it."

He didn't say anything.

"All these trees are slowly dying and the young ones aren't taking their places," I said.

"Why's that?"

I rubbed my hand over the dry, powdery dirt. "The environmental conditions have changed. They can't survive here anymore. If we don't change, they'll perish. Then, we will."

"How do you know that?" he asked.

"It told me."

"Told you."

"I can't explain it. It's like a silent whisper," I said.

I now understood why my surroundings had been so guarded, so distant. The person that had started my run was the enemy. He was the guy responsible for killing them. It wasn't until he left, until he disappeared, that Joshua Tree became an open book. It was my brother they wanted to talk to, to share with. It was my brother who was honest, genuine, and kind, who understood. It was my brother who could communicate with them. It was my brother who could save them. He was a bigger, stronger, wiser, and nicer version of me. But why wasn't he in charge? Why was he in the background hiding? Why didn't he just take over?

I didn't have an answer.

Kicker Tom and I spent the next several hours strolling through the Promised Land, getting to know Joshua better and enjoying our newfound freedom. Then one finger at a time, the hand started to move back into place.

CHAPTER THIRTY-THREE

I t was sometime in the evening when we jumped into the Mystery Machine and left the Tree. Kicker Tom wasn't peyote-free, so I thought it best to take the wheel. No need for him mistaking a light pole, tree, or ditch as an invitation for a hug.

When we got back to the main road I was about to take a right turn when Kicker Tom said, "Wrong direction."

"That's the way to San Diego," I said.

"We're not going to San Diego."

"You said, just south of San Diego."

"That is more precise."

"How far south?" I asked.

Kicker Tom rolled down the window, stuck his head out, and looked into the distance as though he were surveying the trip. He pulled his head back in and said, "About 1,500 miles."

"Mexico?"

"I do believe your calculations are correct," he said.

"Just south?"

"Okay, I might've miscalculated, but I do believe I was under the influence of a very powerful schedule-one narcotic at the time of that statement."

"You're under the influence of a powerful schedule-one narcotic right now."

"Good point."

"In fact, since I've met you when have you not been under the influence of a schedule-one narcotic?"

"Better point."

"Do you think it's a great idea for two gringos in a seventies drug van to drive through Mexico in the middle of the night?"

"Your best point yet. But yes."

"Yes, what?"

He put his hands on the dashboard and looked at it closely. "Yes, I think we should drive this stylish vehicle through Mexico in the middle of the night." He looked over to me. "We have to. We must. We are on a journey, man. A quest. We can't stop now. The We has left the Tree, he's on the run, on the lam, he's getting away, we got to move, we've got to follow him. He's heading south, I can feel him, and I'm pretty sure he's speaking Spanish. *Cum-Pren-Day A-Mee-Go*!?"

I guess when you consider Kicker Tom had spent almost the last decade in two of the most dangerous areas in the world, a little trip through Mexico seemed like a vacation. Besides, if my goal was to discover knowledge that would lead me to the permanent road, the one back to Soul Brother, the one back to the We, hadn't I found the perfect guide? One that wasn't afraid of the outcome, one that didn't hesitate, one that didn't question—one that just did? While I'm sure that philosophy will get you in trouble from time to time, it'll also get you to your goal the quickest. I didn't possess that gear. For that, you needed either confidence or to not give a shit. Kicker Tom had both, and I had neither.

I put my hands back on the steering wheel and said to Tom, "*Sí, mí amigo. Yo comprendo.*"(Yes, my friend. I understand.) I turned the Mystery Machine to the left and back onto the main road. Five hours later, after midnight, we crossed over into Mexico.

CHAPTER THIRTY-FOUR

The brown tea finally left Kicker Tom's system as we headed toward a tiny little fishing village another thousand miles away. A marine buddy had told him about the place, saying if you wanted to escape life, that was the spot.

The eight-track was acting up worse than normal, so we gave it a rest. Kicker Tom played with the radio dial trying to find something worth listening to. The farther we made it into Mexico, the more our options dwindled. It was either different varietals of Mexican music or some preacher from Arizona. He chose the preacher, I believe for the entertainment value.

I'm not sure who was listening to a sermon at three in the morning on a random Tuesday, but it must have been important. It was by far the strongest signal on the dial. However, after a half-hour of listening about Satan's work in the homosexual community, Kicker Tom turned it off. "Makes you want to reconsider First Amendment rights," he said. He rolled down the passenger's side window and put his leg out on its familiar resting spot. The warm night air circulated through the cabin and kept us company as we cruised south on Highway 15D. As Kicker Tom stared into the darkness of the Mexico night he said, "Why not use the word 'God'?"

"What do you mean?"

"You, your grandfather, you don't use the word God, you have other names for it: energy, source, universal mind. Why?"

"God means too many different things to too many people. It's just too polarizing. People are too sensitive to it. I guess when you get to this point in history and we are still killing people in the name of God, isn't it better to use another name, another word, one that doesn't stir up such emotions, one that doesn't trigger the angry button so quick, one that fits better, that better represents the truth?"

"Maybe we should call him Frank. Start all over, give him a new name," said Kicker Tom.

"Sure, why not? If it works."

"Don't think a Southern Baptist would go for it," he said.

"The sad part is God is such a great word," I said.

Kicker Tom tilted up his cowboy hat and looked over. "How so?" he asked.

"The word God at its source is a Sanskrit word that means to invoke, to call upon. It has the same meaning as another great word."

"Which is?"

"Educate. Which at its root in Latin means educe, to evoke, to draw out."

"Draw out what? Invoke what?"

"The answers."

"The answers to what?"

"Everything."

"How's that possible?" he asked.

"You know."

"The big-ass library."

"Exactly."

"So you just have to draw it out, invoke it, call upon?"

"Yes. Educate yourself," I said.

"So, just ask Frank?"

"In a manner of speaking, yes," I said as a gust of wind blew Konka's poem off the rearview mirror and landed it on the dashboard. Kicker Tom picked it up and brought it closer to him. He seemed to be studying it. After several minutes of silence, he hung it back over the rearview mirror. "You were really close to your grandfather, weren't you?"

"He was my best friend."

"How'd he die?"

I paused for a long time.

"Sorry, I've never talked about that night with anyone," I said.

"Hell, son, none of my business," he said, then looked back out the window.

I wanted to tell him but I couldn't get the words out. And truth be told, I wasn't sure how he died. He had started slowing down a few months before. But it wasn't like he was sick. I mean he never went to the doctor, he wasn't coughing or anything like that, there were no visible signs—he just slowed down. His runs in the hills had turned into walks. About a week before, they stopped altogether. He still worked in the garage, tended his garden, and read, but not for long periods. His energy was low. A few times I saw him staring into the world as though he could see something coming his way. The whole time, that smile never left. If anything it got wider, more joyful. I got home late one night, and he was sitting on the front porch waiting for me. We walked into the house and he went over to his desk to show me where he kept all his important papers and pertinent information. I asked him if he was going somewhere and he looked right into me, and in an instant I knew.

"When?" I asked.

"Tonight," he said.

I stayed up with him all night and we talked and laughed. I cried. I tried not to, but the tears had a mind of their own. His breathing started to get a bit slower, then slower. He looked at me one last time, closed his eyes, and his breathing stopped. He sat in his chair, still smiling yet no longer there. He was with the spirit world.

As I stared at the high beams hitting the pavement in front of me I had a sudden urge to go to the back where it was dark, lie down on the bed, and curl up in a little ball. A position I had occupied many nights after his departure.

Before my thoughts had sucked me in, Kicker Tom grabbed an Allman Brothers eight-track and slid it into its proper place in the dash. With the help of a gum wrapper and a small piece of cardboard, he managed to get the kick-ass system up and running smoothly again.

I turned up the volume, knowing the Allman Brothers could sing and play with abandon without the worry of repeating themselves. I soon learned that wouldn't have been such a bad thing. For the next nine hours, the Mystery Machine headed southbound through the middle of Mexico without notice.

CHAPTER THIRTY-FIVE

Kicker Tom took over the wheel sometime well before noon as all my mental abilities had begun to shut down. Somehow he was still going strong, despite staying up to keep me company. I tried to return the favor, but somewhere along the way my head had leaned up against the window for a moment and was seduced into a deep sleep. I woke hours later to a soft-spoken Al Green and a not so soft-spoken Kicker Tom.

"Ah shit, shit, shit, shit, I'm an idiot," he screamed.

"What's wrong?"

"Missed our turn."

"Are you sure?"

"Yep. Don't know how that happened."

"You haven't slept in twenty-four hours, that's how that happened," I said.

"No excuse."

"Get off at the next exit. We need some gas anyway, and I'll take over."

We turned off at the next exit and about five miles in he was at it again.

"Oh, shit, shit, shit mother f'er."

"What?"

"Federales stop up ahead."

I looked up and could see one guy with a machine gun standing next to a large red sign that read "*Alto*."

"Let me handle this. I speak the language," said Kicker Tom. He rolled down the window as we came to a complete alto. "*Que Pasa A Mee Go*," he said confidently with his Texas twang.

The name printed on the soldier's left shirt pocket read "Jesus." He looked like he was about fourteen. He had innocent eyes and a starter mustache. He answered Kicker Tom by poking his machine gun and head into the window to take a look around. "Where are you going and do you have any drugs?" he asked in rapid-fire Spanish.

"*A meee Go, Don da Esta…*"

Jesus repeated his question again before Kicker Tom could finish. Kicker Tom didn't answer. Jesus pointed the gun at him.

"We are going fishing and we don't have any drugs," I said in Spanish.

"Where?" Jesus asked.

"Tom, what's the name of the town?"

"Sayulita."

"Sayulita," I said to Jesus.

"That's in the other direction," he said.

"I know, we missed our turn back there. We needed some gas so we got off the highway," I said.

"Where are your fishing poles?"

"At a friend's house in Sayulita," I said in Spanish.

"*Tengo que revisar su vehículo, las malatas*," he said.

"He wants to search the van. Our bags," I said to Kicker Tom.

"He can't."

"Why not?"

"He might get the wrong idea."

"About what?"

"My backpack."

"What's wrong with your backpack?"

"It might be holding a bag of peyote buttons, an ounce of Mary, a dozen of Sweet Lou's happy pills and eighty thousand in cash."

"Might be?"

"Most probably."

"On a scale of one to ten, how probable?"

"I'd say an eleven."

I looked at Jesus as he held a tight grip on the machine gun pointed toward Kicker Tom. I noticed he was wearing a wedding band. "Señor Jesus, are you married?" I asked.

He looked over to me never taking the gun off of the big cowboy. "Last month," he said.

"Where did you go on your honeymoon?"

"We are still saving."

"It's expensive," I said.

"*Sí*," he replied.

"Listen, we are already a day late and my friend's girlfriend is, let's just say, she's not happy. We promised her we would be there by six tonight and as of now we are behind schedule again. Is it possible we could make a trade?" I asked.

"Trade?"

"*Sí*, we would like to give you a late wedding gift for you and your wife for your honeymoon and you could let me get my friend get back to his girl on time."

"Gift?" he asked.

"Does your wife like music?"

"*Sí*."

"*Perfecto*," I said.

As I grabbed a random tape from the box, I asked Kicker Tom for some money. He slipped it to me and I gave Jesus $200 on top of an eight-track tape of Freddie Fender's greatest hits. As he took the gun away from Kicker Tom's chest, Jesus slid the money into his pants pocket while not taking his eyes off the eight-track. He inspected it from 360 degrees. "This is música?" he asked.

"*Sí*, the best," I said.

He put it up to his ear waiting for the sound to come out.

"It needs batteries," said Kicker Tom.

"*Necesíta baterías*," I said.

"*Sí. Sí.* Batteries, of course," he said.

Fortunately, another car pulled up behind us waiting for inspection. Jesus put the eight-track in his side pocket as he looked back at the other car.

"*Vámonos*," he said as he waved his machine gun forward as a signal for us to continue.

"*Grácias*," I said as we pulled away.

Silence was our passenger for the next few miles, which was fine because it took that long for my heart to get out of my throat.

"Who in the hell is Freddy Fender?" Kicker Tom asked.

"I don't know. Why do you have $80,000 in your backpack?"

"I tried to give it back."

"I thought you lost it all."

"Hell, I tried to. After what you said, I tried to lose it. But the more I tried to lose it, the more I kept winning. I started playing crazy and the more crazy I started playing the more I kept winning. That's why I wanted to get out of that place."

"Because you were winning."

"No, because it was a reminder."

"Of what?"

"That no matter what I seem to want, the exact opposite happens. I want a family, it gets taken away, I try to divorce life, and I kill an innocent fucking deer. I try to win, I lose, I try to lose, I win, I try to show you the Grand Canyon and almost get you killed, and now, I can't seem to even follow simple directions. Try to find a beach and end up in the middle of the fuckin' desert with young Mexican Jesus pointing a machine gun at us. For fuck's sake, what in the hell is going on? It's got-damn opposite day, *Groundhog Day*–style and nobody told Kicker Tom. Tell me there's no Karma, then why in the hell is the universe fuckin' with me? Answer that."

"Groundhog Day?" I asked.

"Ah shit, son!" He slammed his hand down on the steering wheel. "And don't tell me what Konka would say! No, no, no, I take that back, please tell me, please tell me what he'd say. I'd love to fuckin' hear it!"

"He'd say now is not the best time."

"I'd say he was wrong. I think now is the perfect time. Come on, lay it on me, I'm a big boy, I can take it."

I didn't say anything.

"I'm not going to stop talking until you tell me," he said.

I looked forward and kept quiet.

Kicker Tom put his large boot on the gas as our rate of speed dramatically increased. I caught a glimpse of the speedometer as it glided past seventy with no intention of slowing.

"He would say you made some bad decisions," I said.

"No shit!"

"And you're right where you need to be."

"This is where I need to be?"

"Yep."

"This is where I need to be!?"

"Absolutely," I said as the Mystery Machine hit seventy-five.

"Right here, right now, this is where I need to be!?"

"Uh-huh."

"How the hell you figure that?" he asked.

"Because you decided to be here."

"No, I didn't!"

Eighty m.p.h.

"Sure you did. Every decision you've ever made has led you to this point," I said.

"Well, son, he may be right about that last thang, but this here is not where I need to be. Where I need to be right now is in front of a shot glass full of somethin' and if God, Frank, the universe, the source, the light, or whatever the hell else it answers to would listen for a change, then that's where I'd be. But it ain't listenin'! That's why I'm divorcing life. It never listens. How in the hell can you have a relationship with somebody that don't listen? Who does only what they want to do? For fuck's sake, isn't communication supposed to be a got-damn two-way street? It's been a bad partner, and I'm done with it."

Eighty-five.

"Maybe it is listening."

"History begs to differ."

"Well, maybe you haven't made yourself clear."

"Maybe you're right," he said. He rolled down the window. "Maybe I can educate it. Maybe I can invoke, draw out a response." He stuck his head out and started to scream at the sky as the wind rushed into the van. "Hey, Frank, this is your old buddy, Kicker Tom, and I was wonderin' if it was possible you could do me this one little favor. Could you do a brother a solid and find him a damn drink? Don't care what it is or how it gets here, but I need it fast and I need it now. Not asking you to cure cancer, world hunger, or man's stupidity, just my current emotional state of mind. Please and thank you!"

He pulled his head back in. "You think he got the message?" he asked.

Ninety m.p.h.

"It seems so."

"Are you sure?"

"Positive."

"How do you know?"

"There's a town straight ahead," I said.

"So?"

Ninety-five m.p.h.

"It's named Tequila."

He took his boot off the gas pedal.

CHAPTER THIRTY-SIX

There are two types of people in the world; those that drink Tequila and those that don't. And the ones that don't, did until they had that one they shouldn't and ended up swearing on their mothers' lives that they never would again, and they never did. They kept their promise. They all do, for once you've been on the wrong side of the agave juice, you never return. Just a whiff of big blue brings you back to the exact moment you held the cold, round porcelain with tender love wanting your Mexican vacation to end.

Fortunately for me, I never crossed that line, mostly out of pure respect. I'd seen the señorita do her dirty work on those with weaker wills and wanted no part of that. Besides, I loved the way she made me feel. The warmth that rode up my backside and finished in my neck. It was a warm blanket on a cold night.

The first time she entered me I was fourteen. It's what Eddie drank, that and beer: simple, straightforward, and to the point. He taught me the correct way, without training wheels. No salt. No lime. Just pure, straight tequila. Then sit back and let the magic mescal do its thing.

Tequila opened up the world a bit. I didn't know it at the time, but it was a sure-fire way to relax the hand over my brother's eyes, a way to see.

I hoped she was about to do the same for Kicker Tom but he seemed nervous, agitated, and angry. Was this PTSD rearing its ugly head? If it was, my advice-column degree was of no use. Only a true professional could help him, and in lieu of that, copious amounts of the señorita would have to do. If that were the case, at least he wouldn't have to go far when it came time to pray. The old bar we found ourselves in was named *La Capilla* (The Chapel).

As we sat waiting for our first round, it occurred to me; maybe this was more about distance. We were a few hundred miles away from Kicker Tom's ultimate destination. He was getting close to his divorce papers, too close. His first day of school was here, and maybe he didn't want to go.

"You don't have to do it," I said.

"Do what?"

"Divorce life."

"Sometimes you got to know when to cut bait," he said.

"So you're done fishing?"

"Yep."

"So, why are you divorcing life in a fishing village?"

"Bad metaphor."

"Ironic metaphor."

"Shit, Tag, I can't even get my metaphors straight. I'm all screwed up, son. Ya wanna' know the truth? I love to fish. That's the reason I wanted to come down here in the first place. I just want to wake up each morning, jump in my boat, and go fishin'. That's it. I don't want to do anything else. I don't want to think about anything else. I don't want to be responsible for anything else. I just want to fish and be left alone."

Kicker Tom looked up at a large crucifix with Jesus hanging on the wall as Mexican music played in the background. "See what happens when you get involved? Your ass gets strung up and made an example of, pure and simple. Poor bastard never had a chance," he said.

"It did make him the most famous person in history."

"He had a pretty damn good PR firm. Besides, I don't want to be famous."

"I know. You want to be free."

"Is that too much to ask?"

"No, it's the only thing to ask. That's why we're here. We are looking for freedom. We are looking for the We. And you've seen him. You know what he feels like, you know what he looks like, you know that he exists. You know it's possible," I said.

"For moments, maybe. But that little bastard is elusive, he never stays still, he's just a tease. He doesn't want permanent company, and I don't want to spend the rest of my life chasing after him. That's what everyone else does, always chasing, always striving, for what? For a few moments of freedom, for a few crumbs, and then we all crawl back into our cubicle, our prison for another fifty miserable weeks of hell."

The owner of the bar dropped off two shots of his finest house tequila and two cold beers on the old carved-up wooden table where we sat.

"*Dos más, señor,*" said Kicker Tom as the owner walked away.

I was sure that request wouldn't be an issue. We were the only patrons at one in the afternoon.

"Well, here's to your last day as a married man," I said as I picked up my shot glass full of tequila.

"Hell, I'll drink to that."

We clicked shot glasses and slammed the Mexican juice straight down. Kicker Tom followed it up with half his beer.

"Ah hell, Tag, now that's what I'm talking about. A little lube, a little grease. Hell, son, a few more and that little bastard the We might even show up at this fine old establishment."

That was the beauty of tequila. No need to wait, it was instant. Its powers had kicked right in and loosened the vise grip over Kicker Tom.

For the next hour, I nursed my beer as Kicker Tom continued to grease his wheels with señorita agave. Perhaps a little too much grease. As the owner dropped off another round Kicker Tom said, "Mr. Señor, how come you named your bar after a chapel?"

"It used to be one."

"No shit!"

"No shit, Mr. Señor," said the owner.

"Hell, then, how about dos más tequilas so we can give proper thanks inside the house of the lord."

"You see that," said the owner as he pointed to a faded-out painting on the ceiling of a stretched-out arm with the finger of the hand pointing toward the door.

"I do," said Kicker Tom.

"That finger is pointing to the east, which also happens to be the exit."

"*POR QUE* (Why)?"

"*Porque* (Because) when one can no longer hold their water. It's time to leave." He looked right at Kicker Tom. "Comprende."

"Mucho," said Kicker Tom.

The owner walked away as I looked back up at the painting, then out toward the exit to the east. As my thoughts were fixated in that direction, Kicker Tom said, "Ah hell, no service, how about yours?" He looked up from his phone and over to me. "I want to check the map."

"I don't have one," I said.

"Don't have one. What do you mean you don't have one?"

"I don't own one."

"You don't have a phone?"

"No."

"Why?"

"Never needed one."

"Sometimes it's a want."

"Never wanted one."

"I don't get it."

"What's to get?"

"You've never seen a movie. You don't own a phone. Next thing you're going to tell me is that you didn't have a computer or TV."

I didn't say anything as I sat my beer down next to a carved-out heart with an arrow through it. For an instant, I thought of El.

"Holy shit son. You don't know how to use a computer?"

"Of course I do. We just didn't have one at home."

"Did Konka have something against technology?"

"No. He loved technology, but I think he was wary of it."

"Why?"

"Ultimately, I think he believed it can keep us separated," I said.

"From what?"

I looked up to Jesus hanging on the wall next to a neon Dos Equis sign. "From the We, the universal mind, from Frank."

"How?"

I wanted to explain it to him but didn't have it fully worked out myself. "Still working on that part."

"Well hell, son, send me a smoke signal and let me know when you're done deciphering."

"I do know society is addicted to technology, and that you can't have an experience like you had in the canyon while you're texting, watching TV, or surfing the net," I said.

"I'll remember not to take my fifty-inch flat screen with me next time down the rapids."

"But that's the point."

"What's the point?"

"You didn't take it with you. That's how you found the We, or how it found you. You were in it, completely in it, completely relaxed, completely focused, without any distractions, and the We magically appeared. I don't think it's the We that is so elusive. It's us. I think the We is always around, it's us who are always moving."

He finished off the last of his beer. "Moving from what?"

"Konka said that society has become afraid of silence, of still-ness. 'Find peace in the silence,' he would say."

"Why are we afraid of silence, stillness?" he asked.

"I'm not sure."

He looked down at his empty shot glass and seemed lost in thought. He looked back up and said, "So society is addicted to technology."

"We all are in some capacity."

"Hell, I'm not."

"Sure you are."

"Nope, son, you're wrong."

"Well, son, I beg to differ." I picked his phone up off the table. "Why do you have a phone?"

"In case I need to get in contact with someone."

"I thought you were divorcing life. I thought you wanted to be free. I thought you wanted to be left alone."

He hadn't seen that coming and didn't have an answer, so he stared at me. I stared back. Like a seasoned poker pro, I had called his bluff. Yet he still had one more card to play. He took the phone from my hand, got up from the table, followed directions from the painting above, walked outside, threw his phone halfway down the street, walked back inside, sat down, let out a giant exhale, and said, "Feels good to be single."

I guess I'd underestimated his hand and he'd overestimated my point.

Kicker Tom looked over to the owner and yelled, *"Dos más,* mi ameee go...Hell, Tag, maybe that little bastard the We likes to fish."

"I'm sure he does."

"Well, why don't we find out? Maybe we should call upon Frank to be sure, to give us the answer, to set us straight. No need to fly blind." He looked up to the roof. "Hey there, it's your old amigo Kicker Tom again."

"I don't think it works like that."

He looked back at me. "Sure it does, it worked before." He looked back up to the roof. "Hey, Frankie, just wanted to thank you for the libations and I do appreciate your generosity. However, I was hoping for one more favor, if possible. Could you please tell us if our good friend the We is a fisherman? I'd surely be mucho grateful for any sign you may bestow upon us in this hour of our great need." He looked back at me. "You just got to know how to invoke properly."

"So, you guys are on speaking terms again?"

"Shhhh. Focus, son, Frank might be trying to give us a signal." Kicker Tom started looking around the room for a sign as the owner dropped off what looked like two cokes with salt on the rim.

"Casa especial," he said. He pulled out a large knife from his back pocket and stirred both drinks to help properly mix up the Coke, lime, and tequila.

"Looks like a Mexican Cuba Libre," said Kicker Tom.

"We call it El Batanga," said the owner.

"El Batanga! I'll drink to that," Kicker Tom yelled as he lifted his glass and took a big gulp.

"What does it mean?" I asked in Spanish.

"When one is in bliss or ecstasy, like when one is drunk or getting drunk." He looked over at Kicker Tom.

"My friends say, 'he *es en el agua*.'"

"On the water," I said.

"Yes. *Batanga* is a type of boat. Its shape looks like this glass," he said as he held up my drink.

As I inspected the tall, slender vessel, I asked, "What kind of boat?"

"They use them mostly for fishing," he said in Spanish.

"What did he say?" asked Kicker Tom.

"He said the We likes to fish."

"Ah hell, son, I knew that little bastard was an angler."

I don't know if that was luck, pure coincidence, or if Frank had spoken. But I knew when I awoke that next morning it would be to the sounds of the Pacific Ocean.

CHAPTER THIRTY-SEVEN

Millions of years ago the relatives of whales, dolphins, and porpoises began making their way back into the sea and calling it home. That process took over twelve million years to complete. Talk about patience and persistence. Scientist can't say for sure why this happened, though natural selection seems to offer the most common explanation: adapt or die. I believe it was something much simpler. I'm convinced those former land dwellers were seduced by the ocean's perfume, a briny, tangy, salty, sea-weedy aroma with a hint of black truffle that intoxicates the soul. Like a spring morning, it's the promise of a new beginning.

I understood why Kicker Tom wanted to begin his new life here. Each breath filled my lungs with this rarified air, and that, anyone could get used to.

After an hour and a half of this infusion, my eyes opened through the tequila haze of the previous evening and I was greeted by the early morning rays of the sun as they bounced off the Pacific.

I looked over at my backpack, which was lying next to me in the cool sand. The package Konka had left me to open after graduation peeked out of the unzipped top. I suppose he had caught a whiff of the glorious air as well and wanted to check it out for himself. I had wanted to open it sooner, but the universe, like a black hole, had swallowed and stolen the necessary time since my departure. Maybe it knew I wasn't ready. Or maybe I was afraid to learn what was in it.

My mind, quiet and still only a few minutes before, was now racing with anticipation. Like a six-year-old on Christmas morning, I wanted to rip open the package like a wild animal, but instead, unfixed the clasp with a stoic hand and pulled back the flap of the envelope. I guess I was trying to give the moment the respect it deserved.

Inside was a red-covered notebook. An Indian chief stenciled in black covered the front. It appropriately called itself Big Chief Tablet.

I opened to the first page and in the middle of it Konka had written the words *La danse de l'esprit*. I flipped to the next page, which was blank, as was the next, and the next. In fact, there wasn't another word written anywhere else in it.

I turned back to the first page and reread the title.

"La danse de l'esprit."

"The Spirit Dance," I said out loud, which I believed was correct if my French translation was to be counted on. I took another look through the notebook to make sure I hadn't missed anything. Surely, those three words weren't the only message? There had to be more.

I sat silent for another minute and began to chuckle and then laugh. Of course, there wasn't more. It was Konka giving me one last riddle to solve on my own. But what did it mean?

As I held the notebook, I noticed Sama's bracelet on my wrist smiling at me. "Dance."

It all seemed to be right there, right in front of me, begging me to know its truth. Yet my mind was as blank as *La danse de l'esprit's* pages.

A sound from the ocean released me from my trance, and I looked up to find a fast-approaching Mexican boy standing with his back toward me on his surfboard. He had ridden to about ten feet in front of me, jumped, and turned 180 degrees just in time before landing on shore. I watched him and the other horde of surfers catching perfectly groomed waves that ran on forever. While all seemed to be having a good time, none could match this little boy's joy, passion, and focus. He wouldn't need twelve million years. The sea was already his home.

And for the next hour, it would be mine as well. She called me, and not wanting to be rude to my host I jumped in. The warm, salty water cleansed my body and soul of the previous day's sweat and sins. I felt pure and knew I would have a love affair with her for the rest of my life. Like a baby surrounded by its mother's protective liquid, I was safe. I was alive. Here not even one on the white road can hide. Nature is on you, physically on you. The illusion of separateness is impossible to ignore. Maybe that's the real reason those animals made it back to the water. They were losing their connection to nature, to the universal mind. They, like us now, were headed in the wrong direction. And before they lost it completely, they transformed back into the water where its tactile form was a daily reminder of oneness.

As I floated in the warm, wet snug I wasn't sure of my next move. I had done what I had come here to do—drop off Kicker Tom. Movement was wanting to jump back on the road and continue our journey while stillness wasn't ready to leave our new friend. But if the past week had taught me anything I knew it was a decision I wouldn't have to make. Just keep my senses awake and a path would appear. And it did, right over me.

"*Pardon, señor!*" screamed the little Mexican boy as his surf-board zoomed across my floating body. He jumped off in time just as the large fin underneath scraped my side.

"I'm sorry, mister, I didn't see you. I was facing the other way," he yelled in Spanish as soon as he resurfaced.

"It's okay. I'm all right, only a slight scrape," I said back in Spanish.

He grabbed my arm and walked me out of the water to inspect my injury firsthand. After a few moments of surveying my super-ficial wound, he said in Spanish, "You're right. It is okay."

He pulled his board, which was more than double his size,

from the water. His name was Raul. He was ten years old, but his small frame suggested much younger.

"*Buenos días*," I said.

"*Buenos días*," he replied back. "Do you speak English?" he asked in Spanish.

"Yes, do you?"

"No, I don't know how," he said in Spanish.

"Do you want to?" I asked.

"*Sí*."

"I'll teach you if you want."

"I'd like that," he said.

"*Bueno*, good," I said.

"Why were you sitting here with your eyes closed earlier?" he asked.

"The same reason you surf," I said.

"*No comprendo* (I don't understand)."

"I'm becoming one with the world," I said.

Which of course is a stupid thing to say to a ten-year-old. One look on his bewildered face was confirmation of that.

"Like you, becoming one with the wave, together as one," I said as I clasped my hands together.

"Maybe you should surf instead. It's more fun than sitting."

"I'm sure it is, but I don't know how."

He lifted up his board. "I'll teach you if you want," he said.

"I'd like that."

"*Bueno*, good," he said.

Just like that we both had a teacher, and I had another reason to stay.

CHAPTER THIRTY-EIGHT

After the first week of sleeping on the sand, I guess Kicker Tom decided if he was going to divorce life he was going to do it in style, so he rented us a casita set up high amongst a blanket of trees less than a block from the beach. It looked out over the town's main square to the east and the Pacific Ocean to the west. We soon found out we weren't the only ones who called it home. Lucy and Ricky, a pair of iguanas—one red, one brown—that hung out on our back balcony and the overhanging tree weren't shy about strolling through the premises at any given moment. And Raul. When he wasn't on his board, he was hanging around our place, and our couch became his second bed. His mother worked at one of the resorts in Puerto Vallarta and would stay there during her work week versus taking the hour-long bus ride back and forth.

Kicker Tom managed to make friends with the many fishing-boat captains that left early every morning to take tourists fishing or snorkeling. It didn't take long for him to learn the area and the customs of the local fishing trade, though he didn't have any interest in competing for their business. He wanted the knowledge for his edification. He then bought one of their old *bantangas* so he could do what he came here to do: divorce life, fish, and be alone. Despite his best intentions, though, his personality wouldn't allow the alone part, at least not completely. Within a week he was on a first-name basis with about everyone in town and in return had received the nickname *Vaquero Blanco*, or white cowboy.

Vaquero Blanco's fishing boat was small, yet you could still make him and his cowboy hat out from a mile away. Despite the boat's size, there was still enough room for two other people and supplies, though he wouldn't have many passengers in the near future. It was off-season here in Sayulita. Temperatures were hot and only going to get hotter. During the day the beaches received some action from neighboring Puerto Vallarta, but at night it was just a mixture of locals, expats who had left the rat race many decades ago, and a smattering of tourists, mostly surfers, who endured the heat for the cheap accommodations and the perfect wave. The full-time population couldn't have been more than a thousand or so, spread out over the mile and a half of beachfront, the small dirt road town, and the lush, green jungle that surrounded it.

A month passed by in quick order, and I slipped into a simple routine: meditate with the rising sun; learn to surf and teach Raul English afterwards; long Zen runs through the jungle in the afternoons; out on the boat with the *Vaquero Blanco* in the early evenings, when he wanted company; and go to the stars at night waiting for a clue.

Kicker Tom spent all his mornings and afternoons en *el agua*. Every day he seemed to stay on his boat for longer and longer and usually by himself. Except for helping the local bar owners pay their rent in the evenings, Kicker Tom was slowly checking out. I didn't know if the divorce was final, but nothing about his actions suggested reconciliation was in the works. I wanted to ask him about it but a silent peacefulness had appeared to enter his being. At least I hoped that's what it was. Regardless, I didn't want to mess with it, so I left it alone.

Raul was picking up the English language at a much faster rate than I was the surfing. But to be fair, Raul's teaching method lacked instruction. He didn't know how he did what he did, so how was he going to tell me? For him, it was like walking. He didn't remember how he did it, he just did it.

"Watch and repeat," he would yell, as I bobbed up and down out in the Pacific Ocean, while he took off paddling in front of a wave and easily popped up on his feet as though he had casually stood up from a chair.

I was good at the watching part, though the repeating part was still a work in progress. But Raul was well on his way. Mistakes didn't bother him the least. In fact, he seemed to thrive on them. "Oh well, Mr. Tag, I say it again," he said anytime he mispronounced something.

To be fair, his mistakes were on a slightly less aggressive feedback system than mine. Mis-conjugating a verb never resulted in being thrown headfirst over a surfboard and slapped viciously by the wave that just threw you there, followed by a body slam, facial scrub, and thirty-second timeout on the ocean floor.

Early one morning I found out that wouldn't have made a difference. As we sat on our boards in between the morning swells, Raul repeatedly popped himself up on his board into a headstand before eventually falling over and into the water. Each time he resurfaced he would giggle with joy. This activity continued between sets for the next hour. As the morning swell was about to give way, we both caught a large wave in unison. As I struggled to get to my feet, I lost my balance and fell back down on my stomach, an insurance move to keep me from eating another mouthful of water. As I rode down the side of the wave on my stomach, I looked over to Raul, who after making a few cuts up and down suddenly popped up on his hands and did a handstand as the wave was in full gear. With tremendous speed, his board began to shoot down the face at a steep angle while his feet pointed to the sky. As the wave began to close out, his body slipped past parallel and the momentum was too great for it to stop. Within a flash, the back of his body and head slammed onto his board, and then the wave closed and ate them both. I slipped off my board and dived down to where he had crashed. The currents underneath tossed me around like a pair of socks until they subsided and I came up for air. By the time I pulled my leash, grabbed my board, and slid back on, Raul was already back on his.

I paddled over and was met with more hysterical giggling. "Did you see that, Mr. Tag?"

"Are you okay?" I asked.

"Of course, Mr. Tag," he said as he continued his giggle fit. "I'll get it next time," he said before paddling back out past the break.

Watching Raul was like watching someone without the hand over his brother's eyes. He wasn't surfing, his soul brother was, the better brother. That's who was the one in charge. It was obvious. His grin gave it away.

As the weeks passed, I began to realize that was how Raul treated life. As a game. Not to be won but to be played. He played at surfing. He played at learning English. He played at strolling down the beach. And in that play, he possessed the same quality Konka owned—he disappeared.

Maybe that was what Raul was here to teach me. To be a child again, to just play.

Or as Konka would say, "Be a child without being childish. To have the awareness of an innocent child combined with the maturity of an adult minus the adult cancer of self-consciousness that sees the world of wonder through the prism of fear and boredom."

That was Konka in a nutshell. He was afraid of nothing and never bored. And right in front of me every morning, sitting on a surfboard, was a ten-year-old boy who treated life the same, afraid of nothing and never bored.

Was that the permeant path to freedom, to live without fear and boredom? I wasn't sure. And even if I was, how do you do that?

CHAPTER THIRTY-NINE

Two more months passed and my patience started to wear thin. Not as much as a sprinkle or drop more of insight into Pahana, Soul Brother, the red road, the white road, the dark wolf, the white wolf, the universal mind, the We, freedom, the permanent path, fear, boredom, or what my next move should be. Nothing was coming to me. No one was speaking. No images, no insights, no revelations, nothing, nada. I was beginning to wonder if staying here was a mistake, if moving on would've been the better move. Movement had produced results. Stillness was being shy.

Konka would say, "Sometimes in order to find something you need to get lost."

So that was exactly what I planned to do. I laced up the sneakers, purposely veered away from my normal routes, and ran with reckless abandon through the jungle with no destination in mind. Each mile a new path appeared and splintered off in another direction, and without worry I instinctively followed. It was as though the jungle was pulling me in, leading me toward something it wanted to show me. It made the decisions, not I. Farther and farther I flowed into the belly of the jungle without the slightest idea of where I was or how I was going to get back.

I put over ten miles behind me in the hundred-degree heat and felt another ten was in my grasp, yet a quick glance at my water bottle suggested that might be a mistake. It was on E. Considering I had no idea where I was or how to get back, my legs decided to stop motoring. It was the wise choice. The probability of finding more water out here was low and if I did, local knowledge suggested the probability of a monsoon in my shorts would increase soon after.

As I looked around, I found myself in the middle of a deep, lush, green natural arboretum. The heat hung on me like a wool coat. I took the last sip from my water bottle. As my breath found its way to normal I walked back on the trail I'd come on. This system was working fine until I came upon a split path. I stared at both trails hoping one would cough, snort, or wink as an indication of which one was mine. Neither made a sound or move. Common sense told me to take the one on the left for no other reason than it looked wider. After about a mile in on it I had the distinct feeling that common sense had never been a Boy Scout. I came upon a large opening that housed several old buildings that looked like they hadn't been lived in for several decades, buildings I hadn't passed on the way in. I had started my way back to the other trail when I stopped and took a longer look. This must be one of the old coconut farms Raul had told me about during one of our surfing sessions. It had been the local trade business in the area many years ago before falling on hard times.

As I stood in the midst of hundreds of coconut trees, I picked up a coconut that lay at my feet and looked at it carefully. Its outer shell was hard as a rock.

I turned it over and inspected it closer. I noticed three small holes on one end resembled two eyes and a mouth. As we looked at each other with keen interest I heard it say, "*Hola.*"

Did a coconut just speak to me?

I wanted to reply, but what does one say to a coconut? Before I had time to figure an appropriate response, it spoke again. "*Aquí.*"

I turned around and in front of me stood a short, thin, and much older Mexican man wearing little more than a smile that held a single tooth. In his left hand, he loosely held a bottle of beer and in his right a tightly-held machete.

How come everyone I meet in the middle of nowhere is carrying a large blade?

"*Aquí,*" he said again.

He put his beer in the pocket of his tattered shorts and looked down at the coconut in my hand. "*Aquí,*" he said one more time.

I tossed the coconut to him.

He too looked at it and pointed to the holes I was just inspecting. "*Cara,*" he said.

"Sí, *cara*, face," I replied back.

He rubbed the matted hair on top of the coconut. "*Pelo,*" he said.

"Sí, *pelo*, hair," I replied.

He kept rubbing the *pelo* with his fingers as though it was a family pet, then, with his knuckle, he gave it a good rap on top. "*Cerebro,*" he said with his one tooth smiling at me.

"Sí, *cerebro*, brain," I replied as I pointed to my head.

"Sí, *cerebro*," he repeated, looking at me with a big smile. In one quick motion, he lifted up the coconut *cerebro* and smashed it down the middle with his machete into perfect two halves. Before I had time to panic and run, he dropped his machete to the ground and raised his left hand with half of the coconut. "*El lado izquierdo* (the left side)," he yelled. He raised his right hand with the other half of the coconut. "*El lado derecho* (the right side)," he yelled.

I stood in silence as a weird déjà vu moment flooded into my being. He handed me the left side of the coconut. "*Bebes* (drink)," he said.

I followed his request and drank the coconut water from the left side as he did the same from the right side. We switched coconut halves and drank from the other's half. We kept alternating until all the water was gone.

He took both halves. "*El lado izquierdo.*" He again held up his left hand with half the coconut in it. "*El lado derecho.*" He did the same with the right. "*Ahora, son amigos* (now, they are friends)," he said and put the two halves back together as one. He looked at me. "*Y nostros también* (and so are we)."

"*Si, y nosotros también,*" I said.

I learned that Manuel Rafael Fuentes had spent all his life on this land. The rest of the family had moved away for work several decades before. He had stayed and was planning to restore it to its former glory. He was going to be the coconut king of Mexico.

He dropped the coconut in his hand, picked up his machete, gave me his best smile with the one tooth, and invited me inside one of the old structures, a place he called home, for a warm beer and to let me in on the rest of his plans.

I wanted to say yes, but the skies had begun to darken and the wind pricked up its ears. A tropical rainstorm that passed through about every other day was on the way, so I decided to move on before it opened up.

My new friend filled up my plastic bottle with coconut water, gave me directions, and sent me on my way.

As I ran back through the jungle, the raindrops began to fall and cool me and my surroundings. The wind gusts became more intense, and a coconut fell from a tree and landed in front of me.

As I stared at it on the ground, I thought about the simple sight of a falling apple that had spurred Sir Isaac Newton's theory of gravity. Contrary to popular belief, Granny Smith didn't slap Newton upside his head, though it makes for a better read. It's just a little hot sauce on the dog, a little spice, a better visual for the viewing audience.

But Golden Delicious did have a part. It sparked a flash of brilliance into Newton's *cerebro*. And that's how it usually happens, when you're not looking for it, not consciously thinking about it, and out of thin air, like magic, the universe supplies the answer.

Konka said, "The answer was always there. You couldn't see, hear, feel, taste, or smell it, not because it was elusive, but because you weren't prepared to receive it."

However, the universe being ever so diligent and giving, continues to throw apples at you until you're ready. Your mental abilities and state of awareness are what determine how long that takes. For Konka or Newton, that time was short. Washington State wouldn't notice any drop in its inventory. For most of us, however, it might take a bushel or two to get the message, and for others, an apple pie in the face wouldn't do the trick.

I took a step forward, and it's lucky I did. Another coconut fell from high above and missed my coconut by a few feet. Maybe a direct hit in the noggin would have done the trick, though I doubt it. Lying unconscious in a Mexican jungle isn't usually a recipe for evolutionary insights, despite making for a better story.

I picked up the universe's latest arrow from the ground and took another look as the warm rain continued its deluge. *Cerebro.* The brain. Split in two. *El lado derecho*—the right side. *El lado izquierdo*—the left side.

The brain. It has two sides. If my Texas high-school anatomy book was correct, what runs down the middle and connects those two sides is the corpus callosum, the nerve center, CC, Corpus Colorado. Right side, left side, the two hemispheres make up our brain, noggin, calculator, bean, melon, our coconut, the most powerful tool in the woodshed, the greatest computer ever devised.

Was the answer right in front of me, or, to be more precise, right inside me?

The purpose of almost every exercise, game, puzzle, or talk with Konka, was to develop and enrich that processor, my mental motor. He believed that was the key to everything, the cultivation of our mental abilities.

With my free hand, I picked up another coconut from the ground.

I began to move the coconuts in my hands up and down like Manuel, my arms acting as a scale. Right side. Left side. Right side. Left side.

Was that what Reverend Willy and Manuel were saying? That the two sides of our peanut need balancing?

As I stood in the howling wind and pouring rain I looked up at the coconut tree that had thrown the *cerebro* at my feet. She was receiving the worst of it, bending and swaying with each punch of nature's glove. Yet despite what seemed like punishment, the old girl moved in perfect rhythm and beat with each new offering. She was giving, she was taking. She was in perfect step with her partner, and I swear with each torrent of water and each gale of air that consumed her she laughed with delight.

There it was. Perfect unity. Perfect harmony. Perfect balance. Oneness. The We on full display.

Had I just witnessed La danse de l'esprit? Was that nature's version of The Spirit Dance? Is that what it looks like?

I looked back at the two coconuts in my hands as the rain poured over them.

Are we out of balance with nature and each other because our cerebros are out of balance?

I continued moving the coconuts up and down when the heavier of the two slipped out of my left hand. As I watched it roll away a voice in my head said, "Control it, or it will control you."

I looked at all of the fallen coconuts on the ground, then looked up at its hundreds of cousins hanging in the trees. All those *cerebros* blowing aimlessly in the wind.

"Control it, or it will control you," reverberated again through my gourd.

Before I could figure out who was doing the talking, a beam of sunlight landed on my face as the wind and rain that had suddenly appeared just as suddenly stopped. The storm had passed, and the sun made its way back out. So did the sounds of the jungle's inhabitants, which replaced the sound of the voice in my head.

I looked down at the coconut in my right hand, grabbed my water bottle out of my pocket with my left, and began running back toward the ocean.

CHAPTER FORTY

I got to the edge of the forest and could make out the beach that lay about a mile south of town. It's where I always started and finished my Zen runs. It was my sanctuary. It was always empty, nothing but sand and surf, cordoned off and protected by the vastness of the jungle. I'd spent many nights using her soft blanket of sand as a mattress as I meditated on the stars above.

I made it halfway to the water's edge and began my afternoon ritual: shoes, shirt, water bottle, and, today, coconut, all flung in no particular direction, then a mad dash into Mother's cooling embrace. I closed my eyes and floated in the nothingness as time slipped away.

"Ah hell, forgot my harpoon!"

My eyes opened to *Vaquero Blanco* looking down at me from his *bantanga*.

"Damn, son, did I interrupt your nap?"

"Aren't you out a little early for your evening fish?" I asked.

"Goin' snorkelin' first, wanna come?" he asked as he held up masks and fins.

We gathered my stuff from the beach and headed out to a small remote island about fifteen miles away and spent some time in its crystal-clear waters exploring the surrounding coral reefs and their inhabitants. It was Kicker Tom's favorite spot. If he wasn't fishing, he was here. I got the feeling that if he could, he would make this little island his home so that he could distance himself even further from life.

After our swim with the underworld, we docked the *bantanga* on the beach in the lagoon, grabbed Kicker Tom's well-stocked cooler, and pulled it into the shade under some palm trees, at which point he looked at the invisible watch on his wrist and shouted, "Ah hell, son, looky there. If I'm not mistaken, happy hour just started."

He pulled out two ice-cold beers, tossed one to me, and we proceeded to wash away our thirst.

"Ahhh. Better than the backside of a rib-eye," he said after finishing his first and before opening a second.

For the next several minutes not a word was spoken as the sounds of the Pacific and wildlife kept us company. I wanted to tell him about Manuel and the coconuts but before I had a chance to get it out, he said, "Well damn, son, it's been fun, really has. However, it's time to move on."

"Where we going?" I asked.

"We're not going anywhere."

"Where are you going?"

"I'm not," he said.

"Okay, where am I going?"

He took another gulp from his bottle. "Forward. I'm holding you back, Tag. It's time for you to leave."

"What do you mean?" I asked.

"The We, your journey, freedom, is not here, it's out there." He looked out into the distance as the voice of seagulls took up the empty space.

He put his hand on my shoulder and looked at me. "This is where I need to be for a while, this is where I need to make peace with myself, with the world."

I sat down on a large piece of driftwood and looked into the still water of the lagoon.

"Are you dumping me?" I asked.

"More like releasing you," he said.

"From?"

"From the bondage of responsibility," he said

I looked up at him. "I don't feel responsible for you."

"Sure you do, but hell, it's not your fault. It's human nature to feel attached to those who you've saved. Trust me, son, I know all about it."

"Saved? I think you're overestimating the situation," I said.

"Overestimatin'! Overestimatin'! Shit, son, Napoleon overestimated. Hitler overestimated. Japan overestimated. Custer, McNamara, and Rumsfield overestimated. Amelia Earhart, Evil Knievel, Apollo Creed, the vice-president of the math club who asked out the prom queen, they all overestimated. But I'm pretty damn sure I got this just about right."

"Apollo Creed?" I asked.

"Shit, son, I need to get you a VCR."

"I don't think they make those anymore," I said as I looked back into the lagoon.

"Tag, I was as good as dead when you found me in that ditch. I'd given up, I was done, toast. While my flesh was alive and well, my soul was barely hanging on. It was on life support, but the vultures were circling, the priest was called into the room, the plug was working its way out of the wall, Kevorkian was driving over for a visit, dead man walking, son. But you got there first. And somehow your skinny butt was able to pump some adrenaline into my heart to keep it going, to keep it beating just long enough for a few rays of sunshine to slip in. Shit, son, while it's not by any means out of the woods just yet, it's out of intensive care and breathing on its own." He took another swig of beer. "Thank you. But hell, you don't have to worry about me, and you sure the hell don't have to take care of me, I'm going to be fine."

"I know," I said as I fiddled with the sand between my feet.

"Then go, damn it. Go. Go out there into the unknown, live there, someplace you don't know. Here, it's safe. You've gotten too damn comfortable."

"Maybe I'm not ready yet," I said.

He squatted down next to me like a catcher waiting for the

next pitch. "You know, I spent nine years with bullets flying over my head, sleeping close enough to the enemy that any night he wanted to, he could have snuck in and finished my ass. I walked through blind passages, roads littered with bombs, dark houses, impassable mountain ranges, and every step, every move could've been my last. Yet not once did I feel anxious, nervous, uneasy, not once could I not sleep. Hell, I could sit in a foxhole, lean up against a tree, lay down in the bushes, all for hours at a time without a care in the world. Be calm and still as a slug in glue. But when I got home, for some reason, all that changed, the only way to find even a hint of peace was after a gallon or two of this." He made a gesture with his bottle of beer.

"For almost three months now, I've been sitting in that boat." He pointed to the old, beaten-up wooden vessel that sat motionless in the shallow clear blue water. "And every day I still have this overwhelming feeling to move, like I have to do something, go somewhere, like I'm missing out on somethin', like wherever I am, I need to be someplace else. It's the most uncomfortable thing I've ever experienced. Shit, son, it's like..." he pointed to his head, "...someone up in here is nervous, like he knows something bad is about to happen, like he's waiting in line for an ass beatin' or an execution."

"So why do you keep doing it?" I asked.

"It's time to face it."

"What?"

"The fear."

"Fear of what?"

"You know," he said.

I thought about it for a second, yet for some reason nothing was coming, so I took a long swig of beer, buying myself some time. It didn't help. I stared at the bottle hoping it might give me the answer. Turns out, he was drawing a blank as well. "I don't," I said.

"Sure you do. Stillness. Silence. Didn't Konka say find peace in the silence? That's what I'm doing, son, that's what I'm looking for. Peace in the silence. In the stillness. And the best place I can do it is in that boat."

"Why?"

He stood up and walked over to it and slapped the side with his hand. "It's the perfect teacher. It keeps me in check. I can't go nowhere. Damn water won't let me. I'm surrounded. I'm trapped. So I sit there, big bad Kicker Tom petrified of a freakin' ghost. A grown-ass man who can't sit still, who will do anything to avoid that silence, that stillness." He picked up two fishing poles out of the boat. "I start fiddlin' with my fishing poles, my lines." He dropped the poles and picked up the tackle box. "I go through the tackle box. I rearrange it." He dropped it back down. "I count the number of sardines in the bait well, the number of seagulls, the number of ripples in the water, the number of beers left in the cooler. Damn, son, anything to avoid him, anything to keep him away, but out here there's no away, I can't hide. That little bastard's in my space or maybe I'm in his. But regardless of whose turf it is, I'm forced to face him head on."

"How's it going?" I asked.

He walked back over and sat down on the ice chest. "At first, not very well, not very well at all. At one point I wanted to wrap that anchor around my leg and take a dive. But shit, son, I don't have that luxury, though I thought about it a lot. I imagined sitting on the bottom of the ocean with nowhere to go, no place to be, just sitting like one of those reefs out there, and that's when it hit me. What in the hell was the difference, sitting in this boat versus down there? And I realized, for some reason time doesn't seem to exist down there, but up here it's alive and kickin'. It's all around, always pulling at you to do something. That's when it occurred to me. Time doesn't exist for stillness. He doesn't have a word for it in his vocabulary, and that seems to be his secret. That seems to be the field on which we could coexist, on which we could one day play."

"Where time doesn't exist?" I asked.

"Yeah. Sometimes I'm able to slip into that place, and stillness will ease his ass into my boat and he and I come to an understanding. Sometimes he stays for just a little while, sometimes he stays a bit longer. In those moments, Kicker Tom doesn't seem to exist. He's gone. Kicker Tom is dead and I'm alive. Anyway, don't have much control over it, but hell, it's a start."

He stood up and took another gulp of beer. "And shit, Tag, that's what you need to do."

"Face it head on?" I asked.

"I can't stay still out of fear. Maybe you're not moving on because of it."

I attempted a large gulp of beer, but my bottle was empty. So was Kicker Tom's. He reached out his hand, and I gave him my bottle.

"Pahana, you're ready," he said.

He tossed my bottle with the other empties into the cooler, then loaded everything back into the boat.

Happy hour was over.

CHAPTER FORTY-ONE

The smile on Raul's face was absent, letting me know he wasn't too happy about my travel plans. I knew the feeling well, and yet here I was doling it out to my little friend, my little brother, just like I had done to El only a few months before. Life has a weird sense of irony and humor, though I wasn't smiling either.

This would be our last surf together, at least until I made it back here one day.

"Mister Tag?"

"Yes?" I said, sitting on my surfboard a few feet away waiting for the next wave.

"Maybe you stay a little longer."

"I would like that, Raul, but I can't."

"Why?"

"Sometimes, it is time to move," I said.

"I don't understand."

"It's like surfing. Sometimes you must be patient like us now, waiting, being still until the next wave comes, but when it gets here sometimes you let it pass because it's not the right wave. But when it is the right wave, if you want to ride it you have to move, you have to start paddling, and if you don't, then you miss it and you'll never have that same opportunity again. That wave. Lost forever."

"Your wave is here?" he asked

"Yes, my wave is here."

His eyes stayed transfixed on the wax that covered his board on which he sat. "Maybe it's the wrong wave. Maybe you should wait for another wave."

"It's the right wave," I said.

"How do you know?"

"How do you know when it's the right wave?" I asked.

"I'm not sure, I just know. Like someone whispers in my ear or something, but I don't actually hear it."

"You feel it," I said.

"Yes, I feel it."

About twenty yards from our position I could see the next wave build upwards as the reefs below slowed the rush of water. Without looking up and without apparent thought, Raul moved into position with a few easy strokes. I followed suit.

I still needed a lot more practice, but surfing every day for the past several months had sharpened my abilities. Which is a nice way of saying I was now spending more time on top of my board than underneath it.

We moved at the perfect time and the force of the wave had us in its teeth. At the top of the crest, with the nose pointed south, we popped to our feet and slid down the face with ease. Raul took a quick peek back to see if I was still upright. I was. His Buddha smile had returned as he cut back and forth, in and out, and up and down. I followed him as close as I could, though with much less activity or fluidity.

The wave was in charge, and the second you didn't respect that fact was the one right before eating it. I had learned that lesson the hard way over and over.

As I flew over the wall of water I tried to concentrate on the rolling motion of energy under my feet pushing against my board. It was there success or failure lived.

"Listen with your feet," Raul would say. "They'll tell you everything you need to know."

Raul's feet had big ears. They were so in tune with what the ocean was saying, so willing to follow its instruction, that he and his surfboard melded into the water and became nothing more than an extension, an expression of nature itself. It was a simple reminder that nature has the answers, that nature is willing to share those answers for anyone willing to listen. At that moment, it was telling me to be still, so I obeyed. I stood motionless as I glided with joy over the smooth water, motion and stillness, the alpha and omega, all on hand in perfect unity.

The moment didn't end. It became another and another all wrapped up in one. A wide grin from ear to ear had taken up camp on my face as well. My soul brother was surfing too.

I noticed Raul was right next to me as the wave was propelling us toward the shore. He stepped off his board and onto mine without mine noticing. As the wave began to lose a touch of its muster, Raul put his arms around my waist and gave me a hug. He dove off into the water as the wave ended its life and dissolved onshore.

We stayed in the water longer than usual, long after the swell had died down from its morning push. Neither of us ready to let go, ready to move on.

CHAPTER FORTY-TWO

Ricky and Lucy had made their way onto the deck to forage for leftovers now that the crowd had disappeared. They carefully lumbered past scraps of fish tacos, pork enchiladas, shrimp ceviche, grilled blue-fin marlin, and numerous desserts dropped from the plates and mouths of the many surfers, fishermen, locals, and just about anyone else who was in town that night. The pair finally found refuge near a turned-over bowl of salad.

Kicker Tom had insisted on throwing me a going-away party. A party I didn't want, but by the time I relayed that piece of information to him it was too late. Invitations had already been sent, and by invitations I mean he had asked a few people, which in a town this size meant asking them all. However, it was a fun night despite having to answer the question, "Where are you going?" over and over. An answer I didn't have. I settled on Tierra del Fuego for no other reason than I liked how it rolled off my tongue.

As Raul and I lay in the middle of the deck on our backs looking up at the stars, Kicker Tom had his feet up in a nearby hammock smoking a Cuban. Despite the overabundance of food, Raul was eating a multicolored Mexican cereal out of a box.

"You know you're eating mosquito bait," said Kicker Tom.

"Maybe so, *Señor Vaquero Blanco*, but it's good mosquito bait."

Kicker Tom took another draw off his stogie as the night creatures from the surrounding jungle serenaded us.

"That's a lot of stars, Mr. Tag," Raul said.

"Yes it is," I said.

"Where did they all come from? How did they get there? How did we get here?" he asked.

"C'mon, Galileo, enlighten us," said Kicker Tom.

"Well, at a single point in time there was nothing. No houses, no cars, no trees, no earth, no sun, no moon, no galaxy, no energy, no matter, no space, no time or what we think of as time, and definitely no red, orange, and green cereal. Just potential. Then, for some reason that no one can explain with absolute authority, in a nanosecond this itty-bitty nothing we now call the universe started to swell. A few minutes after that atoms began to form, and several billion years after that galaxies formed, and about ten million years later in one of those galaxies a planet formed. Only a short fourteen billion years or so later people evolved on that planet, who eventually developed the wheel, the hammer, the compass, the printing press, the telephone, the light bulb, the telescope, the computer, and a certain chemical that attracts mosquitos that make up a food preservative which keeps your cereal fresh."

"Wow," he said as he put another handful of cereal past his multicolored lips.

"Yes, wow," I said. "They call that beginning el estallido grande en espacio."

"The big bang in space," Raul said.

"Yes, but it wasn't really a big bang and it didn't happen in space. It was more like an exhale that created that space, that created time and slowly started to expand like a balloon with everything in it. But, of course, that might not be totally right either. It's possible the bang or exhale came from a rebound of a previous universe that was already enormous and then started to collapse with everything in it and when it got too small, too itty bitty, when the whole of the cosmos was eventually compressed into something smaller than a grain of sand, the pressure, intensity, and heat of that point erupted or rebounded into a new bang, a new exhale, our big bang, our big exhale that is now our universe."

Raul turned to me.

"So our universe is like a big beating heart, going in then back out again. It's alive."

I turned to look at him. Our faces only a foot apart. "Yes, Raul, it's alive."

"Cool," he said.

"Yeah. Cool."

We looked back up to the beauty above. I don't know how much time passed, but the stars and universe invaded my reality, a reality I stayed connected to until I heard, "Where in the hell did you go?"

Kicker Tom's words broke my connection. He stood above me with cigar dangling from his mouth.

"Just thinking," I said.

"Think any louder and you'll wake up Junior."

I looked over to an empty cereal box lying next to a motionless Raul.

"Looks like my little burrito has had enough," said Kicker Tom.

He leaned over, picked up Raul like a sack of flour, put him up on his shoulder, carried him inside, and laid him down on the couch. A few minutes later Kicker Tom leaned his head out of the doorway and looked down at me.

"Watch after him," I said.

"Are you so sure Frank didn't send him to watch after me?"

I smiled. He smiled back.

There was a long pause.

It took me a second, but I realized this was it. The moment. Neither of us said a word. Either we didn't know how to say goodbye or didn't want to. Probably both.

So we didn't.

CHAPTER FORTY-THREE

I tried to sleep, but my coconut was having none of it. I guess he wasn't too happy with leaving his newest family. It was getting close to five, and I knew if I stayed any longer I'd run into Kicker Tom as he was heading out for his morning catch. We didn't need to not say goodbye again.

The Mystery Machine was already loaded, so I easily slipped out of my summer bungalow in the trees without any commotion. I rolled down the window on the driver's side and took one last inhale of that delicious salty air. And just like that, I was moving again and just like that I was alone.

I decided to head south for no other reason than it was in the opposite direction of the way I came, moving forwards not backwards physically and metaphorically.

Several hundred miles passed and my focus never left the road in front of me. A constant yet unpredictable rhythm coming from the tires bouncing out of missing pavement was my only companion, a quick reminder from the universe I wasn't truly alone.

It wasn't the only reminder.

As I reached behind the seat and grabbed an eight-track by a guy named Led, I realized I had company. Kicker Tom's cowboy hat was sitting on the bed in the back.

I pulled the Mystery Machine over to the side of the road and walked to the back for a closer look. Tucked inside the band of his hat were three perfectly rolled joints nestled next to a folded piece of paper with the number eighteen on the front of it. I pulled the paper out of the band and opened it. It read, "Shit, son, didn't know I'd been cavorting with a minor all this time."

I guess he had seen my passport lying around.

"Knew you had an allergy to money so I got you a get-out-of-jail-free card instead. It's sitting in the rim."

I looked inside his hat and pulled out what looked like a gift certificate of some sort from an airline. I went back to the note.

"It should get you to almost anywhere in the world—first class.

Happy early birthday.

Also, Mary thought you might want some company. Who was I to say no?

Keep the hat. Turns out I don't need it anymore.

Hope you catch the We.

Your friend,

Tom"

On its own a smile took over my face. I grabbed his big cowboy hat, slid it on, walked back to the driver's seat, and put my butt in it. I took a look at my pet coconut on the dashboard and rubbed his raggedy *pelo* hanging over his eyes and mouth.

I slid Mr. Zeppelin into the dashboard with the help of Kicker Tom's engineering maneuvers and a wadded-up piece of paper, turned on the Mystery Machine, rolled down the window, slipped my left leg out of it, placed it on the side mirror, sparked up one of the three sisters known as Mary, took a giant Kicker Tom hit, let it out, and released an appropriate Kicker Tom yell as I cranked up the sound, put the Mystery Machine into forward motion, and rambled on.

CHAPTER FORTY-FOUR

A week passed as Kicker Tom's cowboy hat, the coconut, the Big Chief Tablet, the Mystery Machine, and I made a slow crawl through Guatemala, El Salvador, Honduras, Nicaragua, Costa Rica, and Panama. Other than border guards, and the occasional policeman who all insisted I pay the local tariff, I didn't speak to anyone.

I continued south but soon discovered traveling into South America would have its challenges. Apparently, no passable road existed between Panama and Columbia.

About a half hour from Panama City I passed a family of six on the side of the road standing next to a beat-up, broken-down pickup truck. I pulled over to offer my services, though I wasn't sure exactly what those would include. However, after one peek at the engine I knew instantly. Taxi. Señor Felix Rivera, his wife, four kids, and two chickens were on their way to see family when the engine called it quits. That tends to happen to an engine after 300,000 miles. They not only thanked me for the ride but offered one of the chickens as payment. When I refused they insisted on helping me find a way to South America.

Since I had decided not to use my get-out-of-jail-free card yet, I would need to catch a ride on a boat or hike. Señor Felix informed me the hiking trail was a jungle known as the Darien Gap. It was famous for jaguars, poisonous snakes, drug traffickers, and kidnappings. I opted for the boat, which of course meant finding one. Luckily enough, after several phone calls, Señor Rivera got in touch with a nephew who worked at one of the many marinas in Panama City.

By the time we showed up, his nephew was waiting for us. He had a friend who worked on a cargo ship that was leaving in the next few hours, and he had made arrangements for me to catch a ride.

It was time to say goodbye to the last thing that was familiar to me, the last of my family. I grabbed Konka's poem off the rearview mirror, the camping gear, my one bag of clothes, the Big Chief Tablet, my new cowboy hat, and the coconut from the inside of the Mystery Machine and paused. I didn't know if the pause was more about paying her respect for getting me this far or not wanting to let go, but Konka had taught me that in order to evolve, to move forward, you can't hold on to the past.

I said goodbye to the Mystery Machine and handed the keys to the person who needed her most, though that transaction had its moments. At first, Señor Rivera's pride wouldn't allow it. It seemed he wouldn't accept unless I took both chickens as payment. After some tough negotiations, he agreed. By negotiations, I mean telling him I was vegetarian and accepting kisses, hugs, a prayer and several blessings from the Mrs., and one chicken. To be honest, I think he had protested a bit too much. I was sure I had caught him eyeballing the kick-ass stereo system on the trip up. Regardless, we both had rides.

CHAPTER FORTY-FIVE

The *Get Action Be Sane* was a fifty-one-foot cargo boat of steel and rust helmed by a hardened seaman from Slovenia named Teddy, though from what I could gather that wasn't his real name. It's what his crew called him for his love of our twenty-sixth president, but I soon found out he didn't speak softly and I was hoping not to find out about the big stick.

Despite his ranting and yelling at his all-Spanish-speaking crew, they seemed to respect his leadership and abilities as captain. Besides, he paid a fair and timely wage. From what I was told, in this part of the world that wasn't always the case. And I could attest to the fair part. He agreed to take me as far as he could for a few bucks and one nervous chicken.

The Panama Canal was the greatest engineering achievement of its time, yet not many noticed when it officially opened in the early 1900s. That can happen when the world is watching Germany march through Europe and sit on the doorstep of Paris. And if I remember my history correctly, they hadn't come for the cafes.

Despite the Germans stealing its glory, the canal achieved something the Germans couldn't. Success. Though it took two tries to get it right. Maybe the Germans had drawn some inspiration from the canal's can-do attitude and its second attempt. They too decided to give it another go many years later, though their results remained the same. Hopefully, they never buy into the third time's a charm thing.

Depending on who you talk to, the canal was created either to help speed up trade between east and west or as a naval military advantage for the United States in case of war. Whatever the reason, Mr. Roosevelt was dead set on making it a reality. When negotiations with Columbia weren't going the way he envisioned, he created a new country, called it Panama, and negotiated a better deal. I don't know about the sane part, but that is the definition of action.

After moving through two sets of locks, we coasted into an artificial channel and were on our way to the Caribbean Sea. I sat toward the bow of the boat on a pile of life jackets as the rays of the sun penetrated its warmth through me. I was silent, I was still as the *Get Action Be Sane* moved forward, inching closer and closer, moment by moment, toward the east. Movement and stillness on full display.

As the occasional mist of water hit my face, I felt Konka's presence. I took out the Big Chief Tablet and a pen from my backpack and began to write down memories of him and our time together. I wasn't sure why but my pen began to flow, and pages began to fill. So, I let it.

A half hour before entering the last lock that separated us from the Caribbean, Captain Teddy appeared on deck. He squinted into the distance as though he was looking for a lost object, then took the last puff off the nub of what looked like a Marlboro, which he flicked into the canal. Right after lighting up another, he offered me a cup of coffee from a thermos that looked like it was the only one he had ever owned. How could I resist? Though I should have. Unless, of course, you like the taste of cold burnt coffee with notes of diesel and cigarettes. Only good manners and a certain charm about the situation helped me get it down.

"Awful young to be out here on your own," Teddy said with an indistinguishable accent.

I wanted to tell him I wasn't, but he carried a look that suggested he wasn't in the mood for a metaphysical discussion.

"Got to face life at some point. Might as well do it sooner than later," I replied.

That put a half smile on his heavily bearded face. I looked back down and continued writing in my Big Chief Tablet.

"I see kids all the time traveling through here maybe a few years older than you, and they just don't get it. They have no plan. Just riding along by the seat of their pants until the next thing appears. Recipe for disaster."

"Maybe they're trying to figure it out," I said as I continued to write.

"Nothing to figure out. Simple math. Either you do, or you die."

I think your arithmetic is off, is what my mind wanted to say. Luckily, my mouth got there first.

"Hell is to drift. Heaven is to steer," I said to no one in particular.

"You got that right. Hell is to drift. Who said that?"

I looked up from underneath my new cowboy hat. "Shaw."

"Never heard of him."

"George Bernard Shaw."

"President?"

"Irish playwright," I said.

"What in the hell does he know?" he scoffed and took a large sip of coffee from an old, beat-up tin cup.

I wasn't sure if it was an Irish thing or he had something against the theater. I closed the Big Chief Tablet and put it into my backpack. "Get action, be sane," I said to get back on firm ground.

"Now, Mr. Roosevelt had it right," he said, pointing his tin cup toward me. "You want to get on in this world you need to create, make, do. To get the best out of man, he needs action, movement, it's how we were created, it's how we have survived, it's how we have thrived. The moment you stop, the moment you slow, disease sets up shop, takes over, and eventually destroys. You

233

know the shortest road to unhappiness, to insanity?" He paused and looked at me again.

Enough time passed where I wasn't sure if he was looking for an answer or setting up his own.

"Idleness," he finally said. "Quickest way to the grave? Retirement."

I would have voted for a bullet or perhaps guillotine, but Teddy was giving his best parental advice to a young man, and I knew in these situations a discussion or debate wasn't what he wanted. It was his speech, and he didn't want to share the stage.

As we passed a large tanker going the other direction, he said, "Idle mind is the devil's playground. Says it right in your ole Bible."

I didn't have the heart to tell him he might be mistaken about that last fact.

"And I don't even own a Bible," he continued.

I tried not to smile.

"You know why? Got no time for it, got no use for it, no use for the devil, or God for that matter. Both just get in the way. Both just slow ya down. Both are just excuses, crutches when life isn't going as planned. Man needs justification for what they can't explain or can't deal with. They need a reason. They all need a reason. Well, sometimes there ain't no reason." He looked back over the railing and into the canal. "Sometimes the water is rough. Sometimes it's not. God nor the devil got nothing to do with it."

"My grandfather said 'a busy mind is fool's gold,'" came blurting out before I could pull it back by the tail.

"How the hell so?"

I sat up straight from my reclining position on the life jackets. "He said a busy mind doesn't allow you to make peace with silence, with stillness."

"Man's not made for stillness. You've got to get on with it. And that's up to you. That's what my generation did. We got on with it. We worked. We worked hard, and because of it, we didn't need to lie on a couch and talk about our problems to get through the day. We didn't need pills to cope," he said as he took another drag from his cigarette. "Didn't have time for problems, didn't have time to question, we only had time to act, and we were better off for it, everyone was better off for it."

I licked the cold coffee off of my finger that had been stirring in my cup. "Maybe we've created the devil's playground because we are always on the move, always busy."

"It's what has kept us alive," he said. "We used to sit in a cave shivering to death hoping not to be eaten and now we are top of the food chain."

I suddenly thought of the white road sitting on top of the red road moving farther and farther from it.

"Yes, but to evolve further maybe we have to move beyond our basic instinct for survival."

He looked down into what was left in his coffee cup, then slowly poured it out over the side. "I don't know about all that, but what I do know is it's worked pretty damn good up till now."

"True, but what if survival is in a losing battle with itself? What if it is caught in a real-life catch 22, its motor in direct opposition with what could save it?"

"We've evolved by doing," he said.

"And in the process, maybe we've lost our capacity for being."

"So."

"Maybe that's holding us back. Maybe it's preventing us from becoming the human beings we could be. Maybe we are just a horrible version of ourselves."

He paused as he studied his dying cigarette. He looked back up. "Man's not ready."

Teddy continued on for a while but his day job would cut his pull-yourself-up-by-your-bootstraps speech short. Duty called as we approached the last lock. He stepped off the stage and became Captain Teddy again, but not before he managed to fill up my cup with more coffee, despite my objections.

As thousands of gallons of water pumped out of the last lock, the *Get Action Be Sane* was lowered to the same level as the

Caribbean Sea. As I sat holding a cold, smoky cup of diesel-inspired coffee, we made it through the last lock, settled down into the Caribbean, and headed toward the San Blas Islands to unload Teddy's cargo.

The chain of islands sat off Panama on the way to Colombia and was a stopover point for many travelers heading to Central and South America. There, Teddy assured me, I'd be able to find a ride the rest of the way, though after a look into the eyes of the Caribbean Sea I didn't know if there would be a rest of the way. She was gorgeous. The most beautiful thing I had ever seen. While I had fallen in love with the Pacific, it was a motherly love. This was a whole new ball game. This was that exotic woman you couldn't take your eyes off of. A woman you dreamed about, fantasized about, yet knew, in your heart, she would never be yours, which of course makes you want her more. And while her physical appearance is the bait, it's her ease, her warmth, her kindness that makes you feel special, like you're the only one in the room, that she only has eyes for you. It's seduction at its finest. A seduction, as I would find out, that didn't escape anyone in her presence.

It was Ellie in a few years. The only difference was Miss Caribbean's eyes were a mystical blue. My mind wanted to stay with my green-eyed beauty, but I wouldn't let it. In order to get over one love, sometimes you need another. So I stared deeply into the clear blue and let her help me let go of my emerald past.

Several days and many stops came and went as we dropped off everything from fresh water to televisions. A subtle reminder that the tentacles of technology have room to grow.

The *Get Action Be Sane* eventually unloaded its last piece of cargo—me. That process was carried out with less care than in the previous days. Teddy was on a schedule and didn't have time to dock, which was fine because this island didn't have one. So he got as close as he could, and I was assured of a soft landing in the chest-deep water. I was able to keep all the essentials dry with the help of the crew, who lowered all my belongings to my outstretched arms. As I looked back up to the boat, Teddy kneeled down from the bow. "Be careful what you're looking for."

"Why?"

"You might find it." He stood back up and walked away.

Before I had time to make it to shore, Teddy reversed course and was again, along with his crew and sanity, on the move.

CHAPTER FORTY-SIX

If you were asked to walk the plank anywhere in the world, I can't imagine a better spot. I'm sure other postcard-perfect, sugar, white-sand beaches with warm, crystal-clear blue water exist, but do they come with a formal greeting by two bikini-clad Danish girls and a shot of rum all before one has time to drop his bags?

At least, I think they were Danish. It seems they had imbibed their fair share of the local product, which had their speech patterns all screwed up. Maybe they were Russian. I soon learned everyone on the small island was in a similar state, which made perfect sense. It was noon.

As I walked by a game of drunken volleyball, I kept thinking I needed to keep my senses about me. I needed to stay focused. I was on a mission. I was seeking freedom, Soul Brother, the We. I was looking for a permanent path.

Seven hours later, as the sun was about to disappear, I found myself standing a couple of stories above the water on top of a mast looking down at twenty people below screaming, "Jump." Also, for some reason, I wasn't wearing any clothes, if, of course, you don't count an oversized cowboy hat.

I blame the rum.

But it somehow helped procure a ride on a twenty-five-foot

catamaran named *Follow the Sun*. I say that because that is where I woke up the next morning, shorts tied to the mesh trampoline near the bow of the boat as we sailed over smooth seas. I guess I had found my clothes, though on closer inspection, the shorts didn't belong to me.

When my eyelids peeled themselves open, I became aware I hated the world in a way I didn't know existed. Now, I don't know if that was all the rum's fault or if the constant melodic up and down motion of the boat as we moved forward had more to do with it. Regardless of who was to blame, everything hurt. Seeing hurt, listening hurt, smelling hurt, even my hair hurt. Yet it didn't hold a candle to the nausea that was brewing in my gut.

As I looked at the rope keeping me in place, I couldn't decide if it was there to keep me from accidentally falling overboard last night or for intentionally ending it all as I came to that morning.

As I began freeing myself I noticed I wasn't the only thing bound to the boat. My belongings, a few feet away, were in the same predicament, though they didn't seem to be in any rush for freedom. Which was a good thing. They wouldn't have gotten far. Before I had time to piece together events of the previous day a voice rang out, "Pahana."

I suppose the rum had made me a bit chatty. As I shuffled to the back of the boat like a drunk one-year-old learning to walk, I was put on high alert that the contents of my stomach were making emergency plans for their escape. Before they made a run for it, I caught a vision through the tiny slits surrounding my eyes. It was of a tan-skinned, dark-haired woman wearing a yellow bandana and steering the boat. I knew her face, but the rum and whatever else I had ingested the previous day had robbed my memory bank of any more details.

"Come on, love," she said with a wonderful English accent. "I need to rouse the pilot."

Before I knew what was happening, I was at the helm with steering wheel in hand.

"Light grip and keep us pointed toward the sun," she said right before disappearing below.

The wind was blowing from the southeast and hitting the sails above at the appropriate right angle to propel us in a forward motion. Despite my instructions, my grip on the wheel became firmer, which produced an even stronger mental grip on our direction.

For the next half hour whatever energy and focus were left in me did their all to keep us in a straight line as we indeed followed the sun. There was also another effect. That green feeling began to fade and disappear altogether as did any urge to jump overboard. With each minute that passed my senses started to come back. A feeling of normalcy was beginning to enter my skull as the occasional spray of water splashed my face.

I began to wonder why anyone would give up complete control of their boat to a young, tired, hungover stranger with no sailing experience.

"Like you're holding a dove," said the woman who reappeared from below.

I loosened my grip. "I don't remem--"

"Annabel," she said before I could finish.

"I'm sorry. I was a bit over-served yesterday."

"You and Woody," she said.

"Woody?"

"Woodstock. The pilot."

Must be his spirit name. "Did he tie me up?"

"Safety precaution."

"Are these his shorts?"

"You somehow lost yours."

I put my head down in shame.

"It's okay. You're in the Caribbean. She doesn't care."

That information didn't make me feel any better.

"Why did you guys give me a ride?"

"Because you needed one and who were we to get in the way of anyone's road to freedom?"

Obviously, someone had done a lot of gossiping without my permission. "Just to let you know, I've never sailed in my life," I said as I looked at my hands that gripped the wheel.

"I know," she said.

"Then why am I..."

"Always good to have a set of eyes just in case," she said.

I let go of the helm and watched it bounce back and forth all by itself as we continued to sail in a perfect line.

"Automatic pilot?" I asked.

"The wonders of technology," she said.

A few seconds after my hands relaxed, so did my mind. That was its cue to inform the rest of me it was time to pay the piper. In an instant, I found myself hanging over the back of the boat mudding up the beautiful blue with copious amounts of island spirits from the previous day.

I wanted to apologize to my exotic blue beauty for my assault of her virgin water but couldn't muster up any words. I was limp with exhaustion. I had nothing left. My canteen was empty. As I lay silent and the clear blue water passed through the fingers of my hand, I thought about the guys I'd drive home from Scooter's after a fight. Was the emptiness that I was experiencing at that moment the same as what they so craved, what they so longed for: momentary peace, the momentary freedom that came after getting it all out and leaving nothing?

I guess emptiness can be an easy friend if you're full to the brim with hate, anger, doubt, jealousy, or ample amounts of rum.

I peeked back to find Annabel had disappeared again. Who could blame her? I guess watching me chum the waters wasn't a spectator sport. But how had I gotten to that point? I had violated the "excess is the enemy" rule. But how had it happened and why? I knew my limits. I knew where the line was, yet I had still crossed it. By a wide margin. This wasn't my normal mode of operation. I had dropped my guard for a moment, and someone not only took over but drank so much I'm not sure what he did or didn't do.

Grand theft right before my eyes, and I'd seen nothing. How had Houdini managed to pull that off? Who had ordered the drinks? Who was driving the bus? Who was in charge?

I stared at the steering wheel as it took direction from the automatic pilot and began to wonder if I was fooling myself. *Do I have control of my actions, of my direction in life? Do I indeed have a choice? Does humanity? Do we have a say in this thing? Or are we all sailing on autopilot, following a course predetermined by evolution and circumstance?* I didn't have the answer. After everything Konka had taught me, here I was, not sure who was running my life. Was I in control of my coconut, or was it in control of me? And more important, who was me, the real me? *Is it Pahana, is it Soul Brother, or is it something else?*

One night of debauchery and I was lost. More lost than I had ever been.

I had flung my hand back in the water and begun to stare at the letters painted on the back side of the boat when a cold bottle of water came into view. I looked back to find Woodstock had risen, though the swollen bags hanging underneath his lids suggested that might have been a mistake.

"Why follow the sun?" I asked.

"Because you can never catch it," he said.

CHAPTER FORTY-SEVEN

Woodstock looked like he might once have played lead guitar in a seventies rock band, and he loved to substitute first names for more generic monikers like dude, bud, champ, boss, dawg, slick, killer, Holmes, Tex, man, and handsome, to name a few. I wasn't sure if it was my story or because we had a similar head of hair, but for some reason, he had taken a liking to me. So much so that he insisted on getting me a ride once we got to Colombia. He supposedly knew a guy. Though getting there was going to take some time. Pilot Woody wasn't in too much of a hurry. Wherever he was was where he needed to be. I guess that's why I liked him. Like Konka, he was at peace in the moment.

Inside the *Follow the Sun*, I was sitting at the kitchen table under a light, writing in my Big Chief Tablet when I heard the sound of the bell from above. Which, of course, meant one thing. It was time to get wet.

Every evening around midnight, or when the moon found its highest point in the sky, Woody rang a large bell that hung near his captain's chair, alerting those on board or nearby it was time to go for an evening swim. Every night the routine was the same. Woodstock turned up the music on his kick-ass stereo system (it wasn't an eight-track), and played songs from an old favorite record. Everyone took a hit from Annabel's peace pipe, or a sip from one of her homemade concoctions, or both, then dove into the warm waters of the Caribbean and swam until the music stopped. Clothing was optional. A cast of characters from other boats would usually find us to join in on the nightly dip. On any given evening, you could find fifteen to twenty nude people floating around Woody's boat. For whatever reason, tonight it was just the three of us.

And for whatever reason, I stayed away from the pipe and Annabel's concoctions, and stayed close to my shorts. I guess until I figured out who was making the decisions in my head I wanted to keep it clear. Wasn't sure about the shorts.

As I walked up on deck Woody and Annabel smiled at me.

"What?" I asked.

Woody disappeared below to start the music portion of the evening. Annabel grabbed what looked like wine inside a glass carafe with a unique spout. She put the spout up to her lips and as she began to pour moved it farther away from her face. A thin, continuous stream of wine shot out of its tip and directly into her mouth. She moved the carafe back closer to her face and tilted it to its original position as the stream of wine suddenly cut off without a drop hitting the deck. As she lifted the carafe up toward me, I asked, "What is it?"

"Sangria."

"What's sangria?"

She poured herself another small stream, walked over to me, came in close, put her soft lips on mine, and gave me a taste. I didn't want to do it, but when a beautiful older woman presses her lips up against yours while looking deeply into your eyes, you let her. Before I knew it, she was standing five feet away, and a continuous stream of sangria was flowing into my mouth. She slowly walked toward me again, and as she cut off the sangria's flow, she pressed her lips on mine again, and kissed me. She put down the carafe of sangria, took off her top, slid off her skirt, reached down and loosened my shorts. "Drop 'em," she said.

For some reason I paused.

Woodstock appeared back on deck and stepped out of his shorts. "Freedom wears no clothes, boss man."

As the music made its way through the speakers, my shorts hit the deck. Pilot Woody slapped my bare ass and jumped into the water. The bass beat of the song began to pound like that of a beating heart. I could feel my heart beating too. Annabel grabbed my hand and we dove in. For the first hour, we swam in total freedom in the warm waters as some dude named Pink Floyd invaded my reality.

I believe if I read him right, Mr. Floyd had stumbled upon the problem of modern man, though his overall conclusion seemed a bit pessimistic. He had no answers, no solutions, just the observation that no matter what path man takes, no matter what direction he walks, in the end, we all end up in the same place: disappointed and disillusioned by the insanity of it all.

As I floated by Woodstock, I wanted to ask him his thoughts, but the music and the moment didn't want verbal company. So I kept quiet until I noticed that the moon, for some reason, began to move through the sky as if it were being chased and the stars started to dance to the music, then explode like fireworks on the Fourth of July.

"Annabel?" I said.

She swam over. "Yes, love?"

"What's happening to the sky?"

"It's moving with the music," she said.

"I know, but why?"

"Because it's alive."

I smiled and looked back up at the sky and said, "Yes, it is alive."

As I floated in peace in the warm waters, my body began to drift upwards toward the billion dancing stars, then raced past them until they became a blur of white light all around, and eventually outran them into total darkness to that single moment in time when there was nothing. Only potential. As I hung in the eternal nothingness, everything became crystal clear. I could see behind the curtain. In that single moment of nothingness, there was something, and it was that something that spanked life into our universe. Konka called it the grandfather or the creator, but that was just a name, a label, a made-up metaphorical figure to give our brains something to wrap their minds around. The grandfather didn't have intentions, beliefs, or any grand plan, it just was. An infinite principle living in a self-contained finite world, which happens to encompass us and our universe. And in that universe, in our world, it is our energy, our consciousness, the intelligence of everything that ever existed that makes up the universal mind, the Divine, the big-ass library, Frank. And like our universe, it is just as alive. The substance in that big-ass library keeps growing as we grow, keeps expanding as we expand, keeps changing as we change. We are one and the same. We are not only made of the same stuff as the universe. We are the universe. And the universe is us.

"Tag. Tag. Tag."

The sound of my name propelled me backward away from the nothingness, away from the potential, faster and faster back through the blurred white light, back through the dancing stars, eventually settling somewhere between the warm seas and the sky above. I turned to see Annabel floating next to me.

"What was in that sangria?" I asked.

"The truth," she said.

We floated together in the truth until the stars' dance began to slow. Eventually we made it back onto the boat. Annabel went underneath as Woody and I dried off. I put my shorts back on. Woody continued to be free as Mr. Floyd repeated himself again against the silence of a motionless sea.

"So, is this Mr. Floyd right? There's no way out?" I asked.

Woody sat down on the side of the boat and let his feet and other appendages dangle over the edge in the warm night air. "Well, dawg, a long list of philosophers over the centuries have come to the same conclusion. And an even longer list of artists and poets took their lives when they couldn't find a way around it. Hell, man, even my generation attempted to tackle the problem by dropping out and not participating in the madness, but we eventually learned the same lesson. No matter how hard you try, you can't escape it, man. Our movement faded away, dawg, while never producing the ultimate results it was striving for because we didn't know what we were up against, bud. We were fighting and rebelling against the wrong enemy. We were fighting the results of the enemy, the byproduct, the garbage, the spew, man." He looked up from the water and straight into the distance. "Capitalism wasn't the enemy, money and materialism weren't the enemy. The government, the rules weren't the enemy. Technology wasn't the enemy. The real enemy was what was producing all those things, dawg. We didn't fight the virus. Instead we fought the fever, Tex. And that fever made us mad. Crazy mad. So damn mad we lost sight of our core values, man, our core principles. Peace and love, dawg. Peace and love. And we replaced them with hate and anger. We began fighting fire with fire, man. We became part of what we despised, dawg. We became no different than the machine we were trying to escape. It had sucked us right in, man, and we didn't even know it, one moment free love and a hit of acid while dancing with the daisies and the next vandalism, violence, and spitting on Vietnam vets. We too had caught the virus, man. We had been infected, boss, all because we were fighting the wrong enemy. The enemy wasn't out there, man. It was inside." He stopped and listened to a few lyrics that bounced off the water and hung in the air. "Even the Floyd had known this. The real lunatic is in our head, dawg."

"In our head?" I asked.

"Ego, man."

"Ego?"

"Yeah, dawg, that's the enemy. He's the lunatic, man. And you want to know why?"

At that point, I didn't think I had a choice. "Sure, dawg," I said.

"Because the problem with the ego, man…" he turned and looked at me. "He has an ego. And that little fucker is a nasty dude. Hell, dawg, he even got the better of Jesus. Who do you think ran into the temple that fateful day flipping over the tables of food vendors and money changers while crying out loud, "Not in my house!" That was pure ego, brother. The Romans didn't put Jesus on the cross. It was ego."

He turned and flipped his legs back into the boat and faced me. "Look, Tex, every problem, every social and planetary ill, is a problem of me. A problem of ego. When someone is cut off in traffic, it's ego that gives the finger, man. When a photo of a politician's manhood goes viral, not only did ego snap the shot, he also sent the text. When a man with the wrong skin color was hanging from a tree, it was ego who tightened the noose. When a woman is forced to have sex without her consent, it's ego who holds her down. When kids get gunned down at school, it's ego who pulls the trigger, it's ego who doesn't do anything about it, it's ego who stands up to protect the gun and the bullets, and it's ego who lets it happen again and again, man."

I suppose his speech was gaining momentum because he suddenly stood up.

"Listen, bud, when the ice sheets in Antarctica start disappearing, when the sea levels rise, when the coral reefs vanish, when the forests go away, when the ozone layer is gone, when cities become part of the sea, when millions have no place to live, or food to eat, when temperatures become too hot or too cold to survive in, it was ego who didn't believe the science, man. Ego built the fence, the wall, the castle, the church, and the bomb, bud. And for good measure ego dropped not one but two of those bombs. You know why, Tex?"

"Because ego has an ego."

"Damn straight, dawg! Ego jailed the activist, the artist, and the immigrant. Ego burned the witch, the sinner, and the scientist. He gassed the Jews, the Kurds, and the Ethiopians. He slaughtered the Cambodians, the Tibetans, the Rwandans. He stole land from the Indians, the Scots, the South Africans, the Mexicans, oh hell, Tex, he's stolen land from everyone. Every war: ego; every argument: ego. Every slap, hit, punch, fight was ego, all of it, nothing more than ego, nothing more than me, me, me, me, man. Anything in the history of time that was bad, evil, stupid, moronic, or unfair, ego had a hand in it, ego was in charge, ego was there on his horse with his shirt off posing for a picture, man," he said standing in front of me buck naked.

I looked over at Kicker Tom's cowboy hat sitting to my left and spotted the last of Mary sitting in the brim. I thought that after Woody's fine speech it was more than appropriate to offer my host a taste. I grabbed the joint and held it up to him as a gesture of good will.

He took it from my hand, lit it, took a hit, and let the smoke release through his nostrils. "This was our problem," he said while looking at Mary. "Drugs were a gateway, man, but not the answer. They let us see the concert, but then the band walked off stage. They showed us the kingdom, man, but not the road to the kingdom. That was the dilemma we couldn't figure out, the joint we didn't know how to pass, the shower we ultimately didn't want to take. We never found an alternative, dawg, and I guess we never really looked. But why would we? All we had to do was pop a pill, lick a dot, or smoke a pipe, man. It was quick, it was easy, it was direct. That was our path, man, our road. And while the road of excess may lead to the palace of wisdom, it'll also lead to the mansion of hell if you miss your exit. And we missed our exit, bud. When the drugs finally wore off for my generation, the enemy kept truckin' on. Fifty years later he is still truckin' on and we are still on the hamster wheel, man, the only difference, the hamster wheel is now going faster. The madness still ensues, dawg, despite our rebellion in the sixties and the Floyd's warning in the seventies."

Woody paused and looked out over the sea. "You want freedom, man? True freedom. You got to look deep, deep inside, Tex. You have to face the dog, dawg. You have to find out what makes him tick, what he likes to eat, his nature, his resolve, you need to understand him, you need to watch him closely, man, and the only way to do that is to get that little fucker's ass out of bed and have a chat."

"Where does he live?"

He smiled and said, "On the dark side of the moon."

"Have you been there?"

"Nope," he said. He took another hit from Mary and handed her back to me. "I made peace with this side of the moon."

"How'd you manage that?"

He released the smoke through his nostrils again. "I live out here." He looked up to the stars.

It was either his monologue, the swim, or Mary, maybe all three, but Woodstock was done for the evening. I say that because he had no words left. Neither did I. He disappeared below, and I was left with the white side of the moon hovering over the motionless sea.

I looked over the side of the boat and caught my reflection in the water from the light of the moon above as the sounds of Mr. Floyd were replaced by the silence of the nighttime sea. Several minutes passed as I looked and looked until the person looking back was unrecognizable. I penetrated past my skin and bones, through my eyes, deep into myself, deep into my being when the reflection began to change. I don't know how long it took, but my morphed image was now complete. I say that because staring back at me was the white wolf. Neither of us blinked. There he was. The problem child. The lost white brother. Pahana. The Ego. The Me. The part of my coconut that was in charge, in control. I continued to look deep into his eyes when he slowly transformed from white to gray and then smiled just enough to show me his vicious set of teeth. My heart began to pound out of my chest when suddenly I closed my eyes and he disappeared.

I suppose I wasn't completely ready to face the other side of the coin.

I don't know if my imagination had run amok or if this was just another side effect of Annabel's special concoction, but it all seemed real.

I sat up and looked over at Mary, who was still between my

fingers. I brought her up close to my face, took a long look as smoke escaped her tip, then tossed her overboard. I watched as she slowly floated away, blacked out, and disappeared into the night.

I lay back on some cushions, looked up to the stars, and did the same.

CHAPTER FORTY-EIGHT

Woody, Annabel, and I spent the next several weeks traveling around the islands. Eventually though, with the help of the automatic pilot, the *Follow the Sun* found its way to Cartagena, where it picked up two wealthy older clients for a trip back to Panama and dropped off one poor young one.

After hugs, kisses, and thank-yous, the *Follow the Sun* headed back in the direction it came, and I headed out to find a guy.

I kept the shorts.

The guy's name was Melvin, an expat who owned what looked like a combination junkyard and auto shop. He had known Woody for over a decade and made sure that the *Follow the Sun* could continue doing just that.

Woody swore he was a magician with motors and could help me pick up a second-hand auto on the cheap. The problem was, my cheap and his didn't go to the same school. Yet Melvin the magician was still able to pull a rabbit out of his hat, or, to be more precise, a horse. From the back of his shop, he wheeled out an old beat-up motorcycle with a faded-red gas tank where someone had hand-painted the words *el caballo*, the horse in Spanish.

She wasn't a beauty by any means but was in working order

and wallet friendly. The only real issue at that point...despite my Texas heritage, I'd never ridden a horse before, four-legged, two-wheeled, or otherwise. Turns out, neither had Melvin. But he was kind enough to let me stay at the shop until I figured it out. After a couple of days of figuring, I had the ability to start, usually, and stop, usually, and manage to change gears in between those two acts.

Melvin gave me a map, gloves, an old helmet, and some rope to help me tie my belongings on the back of the old horse. Despite my feeling it might not be anywhere near my best idea, I saddled up and headed out of town.

The two-lane country road we found ourselves on reminded me a lot of the ones I knew back in Texas. Maybe that was what gave me a false sense of security as I rode el caballo with confidence through the flat countryside. As the wind hit us both in the face, the mandala hanging around my neck began bouncing off my chest. I grabbed it with my left hand and ran my thumb over the front of it. Konka had said, "To change your outside world, travel inwards."

I guess I needed to go deeper, to where the dark wolf lived. But maybe Captain Teddy was right. Maybe man wasn't ready. Maybe I wasn't ready. Maybe I should have minded my own business, stayed in Texas, gone to college, gotten a degree, a job, settled down, cashed the check, and not strayed my crayon outside the lines, not beaten the drum, and been a good boy and followed the cow ahead of me right into the slaughterhouse. Dead or crazy, those can't be the only options. I guess it was too late to turn back now. So, if crazy was my fate, bring on the padded room.

I needed to face the music, and if that meant heading further down the dark side of the moon, then so be it. In order to catch the We, I would have to first face the dark side of the Me. The dark wolf needed taming, so I decided to find a nice quiet spot where he and I could get better acquainted. That tactic seemed to work for mystics and monks. Their remedy relied on solitude, meditation, and reflection. And that same formula seemed to be working for Kicker Tom. And I know that Konka spent more than his fair share of time in isolation during his journey and it seems my great-great-grandfather spent most of his time that way. Hell, I read that even the Beatles spent some time in isolation on their spiritual journey. And while I don't know if they ever confronted or tamed the dark wolf, their music certainly improved. Of course, that could have just been the drugs.

Regardless, I headed south into the mountains riding high on my horse toward a date with the enemy. Many hours later I wasn't riding quite so high. I discovered both el caballo and its rider were in way over their heads. It wasn't the twisting mountain roads so much as the huge trucks carrying heavy loads that occupied their space.

El caballo and I learned early on we had few rights. We were just another road bump between the trucks and their destination. We did our best not to make any major mistakes even as the obligatory rocks would fire without warning between the back tires of the big trucks and roadway and ricochet off my helmet, her tank, and both our bodies.

The old horse did her best but coughed and sputtered on the uphill portions of the ride. It didn't help matters that I hadn't quite mastered the changing of the gears. Yet it was traveling downhill that opened up our perspective. Being sandwiched between two large rigs as gravity and momentum sucked us all down the roadway at an ever-increasing pace with little to no room to maneuver, el caballo and I were at the mercy of the convoy. I hoped everyone had their brakes in working order.

The higher we rose into the mountains, the colder it became, and the more I realized I might be a tad underdressed. I say that because I began to lose the feeling in my hands and feet as the up-and-down shifting started to become even more problematic. Then, on cue, the fog rolled in, along with his friend fear, to let us know we were officially in a pickle. They washed over the road, the trucks, the trees, the pavement, and us in such quick order I had no choice but to accept both.

High into the mountains with no place to exit, pull over, or stop, and a roadway that offered the water in the air a place to lie down, it occurred to me that rider and horse might not care for how this would all end. Yet with each corner and curve, each flash of the brakes ahead and the sound of others close behind, my eyesight became clearer, my hearing more acute, and the feeling of the pavement underneath more nuanced, all giving orders to whoever was controlling the reins of el caballo to make sure we kept upright.

I spent the next few hours hugging the back end of a trailer and its one working brake light while hoping the lumber truck behind could see mine as well.

The fog was still present, yet it seemed his friend fear had left. Maybe they weren't friends after all. Or maybe that was me ignoring him.

As total darkness appeared so did a small village, and I was able to veer off and glide into the local gas station as the convoy behind motored on. I'd been in the saddle for over ten hours and yet when I came to a complete stop, I jumped off my ride as easily as I had hopped on. An energy I'd never been privy to was coursing through my veins, an energy that felt incredible, an energy I could get used to. I felt as though I could fly. The world seemed open, free, and easily caught. I was alive. As alive as I'd felt since the start of my journey.

As I looked around, the wave of adrenaline that had been keeping me company for the last few hours began to disappear. I say that because my fingers and hands started to tremble. I suppose fear hadn't left after all.

Several minutes had passed when the shaking was replaced by a weird sense of calm, peace, and serenity. Fear had saddled up next to me real close for the bone-jarring ride down and now that it was all over he was walking away without as much as a wave goodbye.

I had an urge to jump back on my horse and keep going, keep moving, yet someone inside automatically made a better decision, to wait until the morning when the light would be on my side and the fog long gone.

I had planned on sleeping under the stars, but the fog covered their eyes and wouldn't let them speak. After taking a long look at the wet tent tied up on the back of my horse, I could tell he wasn't in the mood. So, I found a cheap room above the gas station and slept as good a night's sleep as I ever had.

CHAPTER FORTY-NINE

I woke up the next morning to find a local kid had given el caballo a bath. I suppose it wasn't the first time around here a gringo had found his motorbike in such condition. The kid knew his business and how to separate his clientele from a few dollars. I was happy to contribute to the local economy. Besides, the kid reminded me a little bit of Raul. I hoped he and Kicker Tom were doing well. I missed them both but knew my journey was forward.

I filled up both my tank and el caballo's with some fuel and put our focus back on the road. We made it to Medellin without issue and on to Cali where the flat farmland and lush green countryside were a welcome change from the crazy and unpredictable mountain roads. I was able to purchase some warmer clothes, as I knew my destiny with the mountains and the dark wolf were not far off.

We eventually crossed into Ecuador and back up high through the Andes, riding above the clouds along more pretzeled mountain roads. The air was crisp and had a freshness, a newness, unlike anything I had ever experienced, as though each breath of oxygen was created just for me. El caballo, on the other hand, wasn't enjoying the same experience. The higher we rose, the more he coughed, the more he showed his age.

At any point I could have stopped and gotten lost in those mountains, yet for some reason I wasn't ready. Something was calling me, telling me to keep moving forward, or maybe it was the simple fact I was having a blast, enjoying my horse, my ride, my surroundings, the freedom of it all, and wasn't ready to let it end. So, for the moment, I didn't. Instead, I decided to move back down toward the flatlands and catch up with the Andes and the dark wolf farther down the road. Sure, maybe I was just making a convenient excuse. Maybe I wasn't ready to face him yet, and this was a case of avoidance at its finest. Whatever the reason, my horse and the road shouted at me to keep going so I followed the voices speaking the loudest.

El caballo and I finally made it back down to earth and the warmer weather. There we slipped into Peru. A country that, if my map was to be believed, was divided up by mountains, desert, and the Amazon rainforest. Yet as we cruised over its coastal highway and away from the Andes, nothing indicated a forest of any kind was in our near future.

We headed into what looked like nowhere, surrounded by enormous sand dunes and rocky gray wastelands I can only describe as a place where Alan Shepard might once have teed it up. For the next half hour, el caballo and I rode with reckless abandon down a stretch of deserted highway. I was beginning to love el caballo and the road as much as my time gliding with the waves in the ocean. I guess it made perfect sense. Both made the connection with nature automatic. A connection impossible to escape. A connection that infiltrated my being and filled me up. But it was something else they shared in common that I was after. Energy. Flying down the road at eighty miles an hour created an incredible abundance of energy, the same energy I had felt coursing through me the previous night riding el caballo, the same energy that appeared when I thought I was going to flip over Woody's boat, I suppose the same energy Kicker Tom felt on the battlefield, the same energy our leaders got sending him there, and the same energy that kept both Teddys on the move.

Get action, be sane. But was it? Sane?

I wasn't a hundred percent sure, so I continued to give it a test drive. I pulled off the paved road onto a dirt trail. The deeper I traveled, the harder I rode. I began taking each corner a little sharper, a little faster. And with each turn, my focus became more laser like, and I could feel the energy coursing through me. An energy that felt good. So good I kept pushing el caballo and my luck to the edge, to the breaking point. I hit the throttle harder as I rounded a turn and the back tire began to slip out from under me. I noticed the gap between me and the ground was narrowing at a rapid pace. Just before I lost my horse and kissed that same ground someone turned the wheel slightly and adjusted my weight, which reversed my momentum and somehow kept my horse and me upright as we flew down a narrow path at break-neck speed.

But who was that someone? Was is it Soul Brother? Was it Pahana?

I gave el caballo all she had and was barely hanging on as the world flew by.

Had I fallen so drunk in love with this new-found energy I didn't care about the outcome, or had I finally realized what I was up against and knew the exact outcome?

As the warm wind pushed hard against my body and threatened to displace me, el caballo pressed on at full volume not seeming to notice or care.

Do we feed off of this energy? Are we addicted to it?

I felt the heat from the overworked manifold and exhaust burning near my leg, yet my hand wouldn't let up on the gas. *Is that why we are always on the move, why we can't stay still? Why we have a hard time sitting in silence, in stillness?* The front tire began to wobble and my numb hands were in a losing battle with the vibrating handle bars. *Is it our drug?* I was no longer in control of my horse. *Is that what is driving us over the cliff?*

My pathway began to narrow, then disappeared. *We are heading in the wrong direction!* I looked up and saw a cliff, a real one, approaching quickly. I let up on the accelerator and slammed on the brakes as the dust storm from our sliding stop engulfed us. With my heart pumping and adrenaline racing, I jumped off el caballo, tossed my helmet, ran through the dust screen to the edge of the cliff, and took a long look at my surroundings. I was overcome by absolute silence and met with equal force by the energy from the stillness in this barren land. There it was. Plain and simple. Two separate energy sources on direct display. One that needs to be manufactured, the other that is always there. One that feeds Pahana, ego, the me. The other Soul Brother.

As my heartbeat began to slow, I noticed a falcon floating with the currents of the wind through the valley with ease and eloquence, cutting through the air without bruising the sky, leaving no animosity. Movement and stillness, steering and drifting, doing and being, both at the same time. All heaven. No hell.

Did the universe just toss another coconut?

CHAPTER FIFTY

El caballo and I made it back to the black strip of highway and continued toward our eventual date with the dark wolf. As we headed farther into the stillness of this land, forms of life didn't exist or at least had yet to rear their heads. No plants, animals, or people, just el caballo, Pahana, and endless miles of black road.

A few more miles in and I let up on the reins of my horse, and she began to slow. This land of void was calling me to take a closer look. Following orders, I coasted to a complete stop in the middle of the road, turned the key, and let el caballo rest. I took off my helmet and set it on the red gas tank as my body slid off.

There, for the next half hour, I found myself standing on the moonscape alone. My surroundings didn't seem to care or have an opinion. No sound, no movement, nothing, at least nothing I could detect with my everyday senses.

As I walked over the black roadway, I found a small crack that divided the two sides. Inside was a tiny, cactus-like flower about half the size of my pinky. As far as I could tell, it was the only form of life here on the moonscape. I sat down and softly touched her with my finger. I wasn't sure why. Maybe to let her know she wasn't alone or perhaps to remind myself I wasn't.

I looked around the place and wondered if this was what

Earth would look like after we get through with it: a barren scape of nothingness. Earth another uninhabited moon after we consume and destroy its every resource.

I looked back at the little cactus flower and had an overwhelming urge to protect her from humanity, which, of course, made her laugh. Not sure what tickled her so much, me as savior or the fact the ones needing saving from humanity were humanity.

I sat for another half hour with her in that barren land. Yet I felt no separation, no conflict, no fear, no boredom. Like her, I was at complete peace. I was a fly on the wall, or to be more precise a small cactus flower in the desert observing the world around me without judgment, without mental chatter, without words. I just was.

Konka said, "The man who can sit in the universe alone isn't." Out in nature, I wasn't. I never would be. Konka had made sure of that. Out here, I could sit in the silence, in the stillness. I didn't feel the need to move, the need for excitement, for action. Out here the dark wolf wasn't around, at least for me. But where was he?

I jumped up and looked at the long road headed south that disappeared into the distance and screamed, "Where are you!?" Then I turned back from the direction in which I came and screamed, "Where are you!?" I repeated this action to the east, to the west, and finally to the sky.

He didn't reply.

I squatted back down and picked up a pinch of sandy dirt that surrounded my little cactus flower and brought it up to my face. I rubbed the tiny grains between my thumb and forefinger, and as they fell to the ground I whispered, "Where are you?"

I peered back out over the barren plane. It was empty, and no one was coming. I sat still on the desolate moon, but it wasn't the dark side. Nor would be the mountains or any other place where nature was my guide.

I suppose the lost white brother was still lost.

And I suppose facing the dark wolf would have to wait.

My eyes found their way back to the little cactus flower. She was looking back. Her sun-bleached petals and bright-green stem reminded me of El. I visualized that perfect cactus flower nestled into El's sandy-blonde hair as she smiled at me with those translucent green eyes. I smiled back, grabbed some water from my jacket, and gave the little cactus flower a drink. The water vanished into the cracked earth as soon as it hit her lips.

I walked back to my beat-up, dusty old horse, put on my helmet, and slid back on. I didn't have a clue to my next move but knew the universe would eventually supply the answer. It just so happened that answer came sooner than later.

I turned the key and jumped on the kick-starter, but el caballo wouldn't respond. For fifteen minutes I did everything I could to get the old girl to wake up. She tried but her faint coughing, wheezing, and sputtering sounds went silent. My horse was dead.

I took off my gloves and helmet, thanked her for our time together, slid off, and looked out over the deserted plain. Laughter began to erupt from inside, a conscious recognition of the universe's sense of humor.

Several minutes had passed when the laughter gave way to the thought of, *Now what?* I looked back at the long road I had just traveled, then turned and looked at the one I had yet to.

I grabbed Kicker Tom's cowboy hat from the back of el caballo, put it on, pointed myself in the direction of the road not yet traveled, and said, "Ah hell, son, walk."

So, for the next eleven days, the left foot, the right foot, Pahana, Soul Brother, the Big Chief Tablet, the coconut, Kicker Tom's cowboy hat, and the rest of my belongings, did just that.

CHAPTER FIFTY-ONE

I f you don't count La Capilla bar in Mexico, the last time I had
entered a church was when my mom was baptized by her new
beau along with a slew of other folks during a hot evening on a
random Wednesday at the Church of Jesus Christ and the Holy
Rollers.

To be honest, "J.C. and the Holy Rollers" wasn't exactly a
church. I say that because not counting a few hours on
Wednesday nights and a few more on Sunday mornings, the rest
of the time you could order beer, chicken wings, and knock off a
few frames if you were so inclined. Proprietor, ex-semi-profes-
sional bowler, and newly-minted preacher Jimmy Love had
turned an out-of-the-way bar and twelve-lane bowling alley into
an out-of-the-way bar and eight-lane bowling alley complete with
altar and organ.

My mother's new flavor of the month had been reborn and so
would she. However, that particular flavor only lasted a few
weeks, and it seemed her commitment to the good Lord and used
bowling shoes was not much longer than that.

As I stood in front of the Church of San Pedro Postal in the
small Peruvian town of Andahuaylillas, a touch tired, dirty, and
dazed from my hike through the Andean mountainside, no part
of me was thinking about going inside, unless, of course, what

they were offering was a shower. However, by the looks of its modest-looking mud stucco building, nothing suggested running water was within its walls.

As I began to motor on, a voice rang out from a little boy who was holding brochures in his hand. "Señor?"

"Sí," I said.

"You're going in the wrong direction," he said in Spanish.

"I am?"

"Sí, the most beautiful church in the world is right in front of you."

I took a peek back at the simple whitewashed building. "That's the most beautiful church in the world?"

"Sí, everyone says so."

"So, how much does it cost to see the most beautiful church in the world?"

"I can get you a ticket for only five dollars."

I looked around. Other than a few strolling tourists and a couple of locals selling their crafts, not much seemed to be happening in this one-horse town.

"Thank you, maybe later," I said, and continued on my way.

"But señor, there's the most beautiful painting from a very famous artist, there are two roads..."

I stopped. "Two roads?"

"Sí, his painting of two roads, one that leads to hell and the other road that leads to heaven. And señor, that road," he pointed to the one I was planning on walking, "is not the right road."

"Let me guess. Your name is Jesus?"

"No, señor, Raul," he said.

Of course it was. Moments later, I walked into the Church of San Pedro Postal with a four-dollar ticket that cost me five.

I don't know if it was the most beautiful church in the world, but it was spectacular. No need for mind-altering drugs. There were extremely bright and impressive colored murals, geometric-painted walls and ceiling, gold leaf and flakes that sparkled everywhere, a magnificent piano, and two functional organs that would have made Jimmy Love proud, though they seem to have passed on the bowling option.

According to the literature, the Spanish built the most beautiful church in the world sometime in the early 1600s after their conquest of the Incas. I guess to conquer a people you need to take more than their land.

I looked over and spotted the mural of the two roads Raul had spoken of. On the left, a wide road that led to hell and on the right, a narrow road that led to heaven. I couldn't help but notice some of the similarities with the Hopi white and red roads. The white road or wide road, the one most people were traveling, the one headed for destruction or hell, and the red road or narrow road, where few people still travel, the road of harmony with nature and each other, the pathway to heaven, to glory, to Frank.

Were those two paintings saying the same thing, just using different terminology, different interpretations? That humankind was walking down the wrong path, living the ego-led life and that life was leading us toward hell and destruction?

The one significant difference was this mural didn't seem to have an option or path from the white road back to the red road. Looking at it more closely, I realized the artist had painted it on the wall of an entrance. The doors of those walls divided the two roads. At that moment those doors flung open as people walked in and you could see another road, an actual road straight ahead. Was this an accident, or had the artist chosen this wall for that reason? Had he given it a hidden third option, another road, a road between the left and the right, between technology and nature, between ego and soul? Was he being clever or was I making up my own art?

As I was lost in thought, I heard a voice ask, "Have you seen the original?"

I turned to an older woman standing next to me.

"Original?" I asked.

"Michelangelo's version."

"Michelangelo?"

"Yes. Michelangelo. *The Last Judgement.*"

"No. I've never seen it."

She put her hand on my arm, gave it a squeeze, looked into my eyes, and said, "You should go. You should really go. It's illuminating."

Before I could get out "go where?" the women had walked away.

The church was becoming crowded as more tourists made their way in. I followed a small tour group to another portion of the church when a beam of sunlight from a hole high in an adjacent wall landed on me. It reminded me of my great-great-grandfather's cave and the hole in the ceiling with the sun shining through and the painting of the Indian on the rock ceiling with the rays of sun permeating through him.

I looked up at the ceiling and pictured my great-great-grandfather hanging high above painting his message for future generations to see. As I thought about him painting the ceiling of his cave, Raul strolled up next to me. "Señor, was I right? It's the most beautiful church in the world."

"Yes, Raul, it is beautiful."

"Why else would they call it La Capilla Sixtina?" he asked.

"La Capilla Sixtina? I asked.

"Sí, señor. The Sistine Chapel of the Americas. That is its nickname."

The universe had tossed another coconut.

And it was pointing to the east, to Rome.

CHAPTER FIFTY-TWO

My get-out-of-jail-free card had not only allowed me to move on from South America, it also introduced me to champagne. I didn't even know if I liked champagne, but they kept bringing it, so I was able to make a more than fair assessment, though about the time I did some real assessing I no longer possessed that skill.

By happenstance or some strange quantum physics invoking voodoo by Kicker Tom, it was my birthday. At first glance, I had appreciated the kind gesture of the free bubbly celebrating my eighteenth by the ladies in the light-gray, matching polyester suits. Though on closer inspection, I wasn't the only passenger receiving the same treatment. I decided the reason wasn't all that important.

As I gazed out the window at 40,000 feet into the blackness of night and took my last sip of champagne, I began to wonder what the Sistine Chapel had to do with any of this, if it indeed held some sort of message, some sort of clue. Or had coincidence and imagination teamed up to show me the cool lake in the middle of the hot desert?

It was around four in the morning when the sparkling stuff forced my lids to open and suggested a visit to the facilities. I stood up, but before proceeding forward decided to take a peek behind the curtain in the aisle. I suppose curiosity wanted to know. What curiosity found was a mass of humanity stuffed into an area meant for less. And no one was drinking free champagne. A bee colony had better quarters. It was a school of tuna stuffed inside a home aquarium. There was little movement. Sleep, the only escape from the temporary prison.

I understood why Kicker Tom had insisted on the grand gesture of a first-class ticket. He wanted my birthday to be happy. From what I was witnessing, nothing behind the curtain was suggesting any form of cheer.

I took a closer look at the curtain in my hand. What was its reason, its purpose? How ironic that Orville and Wilbur's flying machine, which brought so many people together, now came with a curtain. Another reminder of separation.

I'm sure Ego put it up.

My head was getting lighter. Maybe I'd had one too many freebies. I headed to the bathroom.

I left the curtain open.

CHAPTER FIFTY-THREE

Rome

While an early-morning rain is an easy excuse to stay in bed, it's also an invitation to have the streets to yourself. An invitation I had rarely passed up.

My soaked sneakers did their best not to skid or slip on the ancient cobblestones. While they preferred the easier going in the park of the Villa Borghese or the path next to the Tiber for the morning run, it was the twisted, mangled side streets and lanes of the historic district and its old neighborhoods that spoke to me. Where a connection to humankind's potential filled up my pores at every turn, like knowledge slipping into your cells after a long, slow stroll through an old museum.

There was no escaping it. It was all around. A maze of monuments, statues, fountains, squares, ruins, temples, and cathedrals showing the way as I cruised and darted in and out, over and around.

Every morning my route was different, another chance to get lost and see something new, another chance to soak up energy from the morning stillness and the ghost of wisdom's past.

The rain began to lighten up a bit as I made my way past the Forum, and then a couple of loops around the Colosseum, before picking up the pace as I hit Circus Maximus. As I ran around the same track of the famous chariot races, it occurred to me that perhaps the Romans were one of the first large-scale societies that had to deal with a young ego. The recipe they came up with was oddly familiar. Keep him busy. Games, races, and fights to the death pitting man against man, man against animal, and animal against animal, where death becomes entertainment. Just keep the masses focused on other things besides their own plight, for bored egos make for a dangerous society and a nervous government. Yet doesn't that strategy always end with the last gladiator? When the games eventually died, so did the empire, while young-man ego was still alive and kicking and none the better.

As rain gave way to a sunny sky, I made my way back to the studio I occupied before the espresso machines awakened the hordes and the city's other energy source, which would prevail from its morning slumber to its eventual late-evening crescendo. It was a different kind of energy, one that I'd never experienced before. It was kinetic, chaotic, and high volume. Millions of bustling amoebas bouncing off each other, hands flying, mouths yelling, creating more movement, more energy, everyone getting higher and higher on the drug of motion as the day progressed.

Unless, of course, you couldn't connect, couldn't plug in, and were lost, alone, and didn't fit. But here anyone could fit. Rome wasn't prejudiced; it didn't care who you were, what you did, where you came from, or what you looked like. If you wanted to join the club, you didn't need a card, badge, pass, or permission, though a well-tailored suit didn't hurt. Either way, dive in and become part of the big ole electric pizza pie. It was up to you.

So I did as the Italians did. Jumped in. Head first. It felt good, really good. It was magnetic, and I loved it. The energy, the language, the people. Whatever was left of the serious, stoic, and disciplined Romans of yesteryear was no longer evident. The people here didn't seem to have a care in the world despite all the shouting. They loved the moment. They loved life. The only thing they wanted to conquer was a good time. And while maybe they weren't the only society in the world to pursue that goal, they made an art form of it. How one could be bored in this place, how one could feel alone, how one could feel separate, was beyond me.

As the days passed, I came to terms with the fact that the dark wolf might not live here either. Rome was a lot of things, but the dark side of the moon didn't seem to be one of them.

I got back to the studio a few ticks past eight. Enough time to finish my ice-cold shower in the sink. My current home, if you wanted to call it that, consisted of a beat-up old couch surrounded by easels, canvases, and the aroma of wet paint, cigarettes, and chemicals. The amenities included a toilet, a sink, and a battered espresso machine covered with every hue in the rainbow. Throw in a cowboy hat, a coconut, and a beat-up bag with the rest of my belongings, and I had about everything one would need to make do.

The space belonged to Don Alessandro Pascuzzi, a local artist I'd met on a small square my first night in town. D'scuzzi, as people referred to him, had made a living selling his work to tourists for the past ten years on the famous Piazza Navona, but had recently decided he had painted his last Colosseum, Forum, Pantheon, St. Peters, and the like, and was now solely putting all his time and effort into the art he wanted to create. His old motto, "*due per loro, uno per me*" (two for them, one for me) was now "*solo per me*" (only for me).

While that courageous and bold decision had freed his spirit and reignited his passion, it had left him a touch lighter in the wallet, which explained my new sleeping quarters.

Our arrangement consisted of him having the studio from nine in the morning until seven at night, when it became my crash pad.

Every morning was the same. Up early to meditate, then leave to go for a long run and return to get ready for my day out, but not before we had our morning coffee. On the mornings he wasn't ready to face the canvas, Don Alessandro wouldn't stop talking, and on others, he would barely speak, knowing some creative urge was about to explode, and he didn't want to lose it to small talk. On those mornings, I'd take the cue and leave in short order. Today wasn't one of those mornings. In fact, I hadn't experienced one of those mornings since he'd begun his new project.

"*Bello*," he said as he handed me a cup of espresso.

Any time he called me Bello, I knew he was about to launch into a monologue and my participation wouldn't be necessary. In the last week, I had listened to verbal dissertations on the mysteries of meatloaf, the ecstasy of not wearing underwear, the glory of napping in the park, the importance of a quality shoe, and why Shakespeare was really an Italian.

Today's topic was why monkeys would make better drivers than most of his countrymen. I believe his main point was that monkeys had bigger brains, but I could be wrong. I could only make out part of his rapid-fire Italian.

It was around the second or third cup of coffee that he would wrap up his rant, light up a cigarette, and walk over and stand in front of an empty canvas. For days, not as much as a drop of paint would find its way onto its surface. He would walk around his medium from different angles, as though he was searching for a way in. He would stop and eye it carefully as though he was waiting for it to speak. The only art produced was a sculpture of ash and butts on top of a plate that acted as an ashtray. Nights later I'd arrive home to discover both canvas and D'scuzzi covered in paint with the canvas looking like it had gotten the better end of the deal.

His current work consisted of a vast, blank white canvas he had been surveying and pondering for the last week. For whatever reason, it was giving him trouble.

"*Ciccio* (buddy)," he said, waving me over while not taking his eyes off the canvas.

I walked over and stood next to him.

"What do you see?" he asked in a heavy Italian accent as a lit cigarette dangled in his mouth.

"A blank canvas," I said.

"No, no, no. It only looks like a blank canvas. But inside, somewhere inside, is a masterpiece."

"How do you know?"

He blew out a large puff of smoke over the cigarette still in his mouth. "The first time I laid my eyes on it I started to get nervous, afraid-a. I could barely look at it. Every part of me wanted to avoid it, wanted to run, wanted to do something else, wanted to be someplace else. Mediocrity never intimidates. But that…" he pointed to the canvas with his cigarette, "…scares the shit-a out of me."

I stared at the blank canvas. "So, how do you face it?"

"Let's just say, I'm-a comfortable, with being uncomfortable," he said.

I took a sip of my espresso. "When do you start?"

"Start? I've been working on it for a week."

"I mean when do you grab a brush?"

"When she tells me."

"She?" I asked.

"The muse, the spirit, whatever you want to call her."

"She talks to you?"

"She becomes me."

"How?"

"I don't-a know."

"When?" I asked.

He drifted deep into the canvas and recited a poem over his Italian inflection.

"The impulse strikes, she knows-a no time or place.
She has no conscience. She wears no face.
She makes-a no promises of good or bad.
Today, a vision of joy, maybe sad.
Never judge her or control her mind-a.
Let her take over and beauty you'll find-a.
For when you feel her blood in your veins
The mind will free from its protective chains.
Ah! This is it. This is what life ought to be.
The high you get as your soul-a is-a set-a free

274

As it dances with confidence from brush to da page.
Strokes of genius from an ancient old-a sage.
She's wild, dangerous, and sings-a without fear.
Then like a frightened turtle in a pond suddenly disappears.
Images that were rampant in my mind-a
As hard as I search I can no longer find-a.
Where did my lady run to, why did she go away?
No one is talking and she didn't say.
Yet I guess that's why I love her because you never know-a.
When she'll come and when she'll go-a."

He took a sip of espresso and another drag off his cigarette. "I don't-a know. I've never been able to figure out her schedule. But if I show up, so will she. So I wait."

I wanted to ask him more about this process but noticed his gaze and focus had gone back to the canvas and silence had come over the room. As D'scuzzi slipped into his daily meditation, I knew it was my cue to leave. Painting was a solo sport. I grabbed my backpack and headed out to face another day and night of the energy that was Rome.

As the universe would have it, the Sistine Chapel wasn't available for a viewing for another week. I was told it was being prepared for the throngs of holiday travelers. I wasn't sure who was doing the preparing. As far as I knew, Michelangelo had retired. What made matters worse, getting a golden ticket in to see his masterpiece once it did open was about impossible during the month of December, unless of course you did some proper planning or knew someone. I was out of luck on the first option, but it so happened D'scuzzi had an associate. Associate of what, I did not know, but I was assured he was reliable as long as he stayed away from booze, women, and the racetrack. When I asked the odds of that happening, D'scuzzi smiled and said, "A small-a chans-a."

To make that small-a chans-a even smaller, I was informed that if his associate came through it would happen with little notice, which of course became a problem since I didn't possess a phone. But D'scuzzi did. In fact, he owned three. One for family and friends, one for business, and one in case something happened to either of the first two. From what I had learned, that wasn't uncommon for Italians. They loved their phones, which made perfect sense. They loved to talk. And talk they did. If they weren't talking to someone in person, they were talking to someone on their phones. And if they weren't talking to someone on their phones, they were talking to themselves. Silence, stillness was not the Italian way. Movement, action was king, at least verbally, anyway. And I, on some level, was about to become a part. D'scuzzi loaned me his backup cell phone in case the small-a chans-a cam-a a-callin'.

CHAPTER FIFTY-FOUR

As the days passed, Rome began to catch the fever that was the holiday spirit. Another excuse for the locals to add a little more energy to its already explosive grid. Lights sprung from every archway, bagpipes bellowed, musicians played, carolers sang, chestnuts roasted, and on every other corner a nativity scene, or so it seemed. Little reminders, in case one forgot Jesus's birthday was around the corner.

Despite all the activity, neither D'scuzzi's muse nor his associate had made a move. I suppose a pair of Ferragamos with legs, a bottle of chianti, or a first-timer bred for the turf had side-tracked the associate, though I wasn't sure of the muse's excuse. Either way, we were both still waiting.

And I have to admit D'scuzzi was handling it with grace. Day after day he sat and looked, contemplated and paced, wondered and thought, yet the large canvas hadn't opened up. Ten to twelve hours on end he would face it in silence, and at the end of the day whisper, "*Forse futturo* (maybe tomorrow)."

But every day he was there. Every day he would show up. Patience and persistence on full display. Then one morning after our coffee, he walked over and took a long look at the speechless canvas and then back at me.

"*Ciccio,* let's go for a walk," he said.

With that, we grabbed our coats, and were out the door and into a cold, overcast, and misty morning.

I followed him as he walked in and out of alleyways and side streets while barely coming up for breath as he rambled on about the incessant corruption of his government and the necessity of a good hand lotion. Or was it the necessity of a good government and the incessant corruption of hand lotion? I wasn't sure. We ended up on a dead-end path that led us behind a broken-down stairway where we entered through a faded-red door. There he ordered two lemon-and-sage gelatos.

I didn't know gelato was a breakfast item.

"It might-a change your life," he said as he handed one to me.

While that might have been a bit of an overstatement, I have to admit it was one the best things I'd ever put into my pie hole.

We worked on the lemon and sage as we made our way to the open market of Campo de' Fiori and gazed over its fruits, vegetables, flowers, and tourist trinkets.

"Why did you want to leave today?" I asked.

"Sometimes you have to make her jealous."

"How do you do that?"

"Just pay attention to something else. For some reason, she loves to speak to me the farther away I am from the brush." He stopped and finished his gelato near a large and ominous statue that guarded the square.

I looked up through the light mist against the gray sky. "Who's that?"

"Giordano Bruno."

"What did he do?"

"He supported ideas of Copernicus that the sun was indeed the center of the universe, not the earth as the Church preached."

"So they gave him a statue."

"No, they burned him alive," he said as he took his last bite of gelato.

"Mighty Christian of them," I said.

"The church wasn't fond of being told they and their book were wrong."

I suppose only Ego could write a story where the whole universe revolves around himself.

"What about Galileo?" I asked.

"No flames for him. Friends in high places."

"God," I said.

"Bigger. The Pope."

I took another look up at the statue above. "Killed for science."

"No, no, no. He was killed because he couldn't keep his big-a mouth shut. A free thinker, yes, but his big problem, he was a free talker. You don't walk around-da callin' Jesus a street magician or say Mary had a healthy sex life. True, maybe, but not-a smart."

"Bruno was a freethinker?" I asked.

"Yes."

Bruno was like the German intellectuals who had founded my tiny town in Texas. Did another coconut just drop?

"Why did he get a statue?" I asked as I finished my gelato.

"Because he was looking to find the truth, not what was taught as the truth. The statue is a symbol of freedom of thought. It faces the Vatican as a reminder to not blindly follow someone else."

D'scuzzi looked up at Bruno and then over to the Vatican. "Have you been?" he asked.

"Not yet."

He began walking in that direction and farther away from his brush.

CHAPTER FIFTY-FIVE

Other than running around its two-mile border, I had yet to enter the hallowed grounds. I told myself I was waiting until my time with the Sistine Chapel to see it all, but maybe that was an excuse. It was one thing to stroll through a small chapel in Peru or hang out with Jimmy Love and the Holy Rollers in South Texas. It was quite another to enter Vatican City. It was its own country, with its own laws, and with its own particular set of rules. And while they no longer burned people at the stake, the Department of the Inquisition, though the PR department had issued them a new name, was still open for business. What kind of business wasn't clear, but my beliefs, while not statue-worthy, were enough to make me a tad nervous and enough for me to keep them to myself. As Konka said, "An opinion doesn't always need a voice."

D'scuzzi had never gotten that memo. As we zig-zagged in and out of tourists and the faithful on a wet St. Peter's Square, he was expounding on why baloney should be outlawed. By the time he finished his diatribe we stood in the middle of St. Peter's Basilica under its massive dome.

"Taka look. A long-a look," he said.

I did a three-sixty to try to take it all in, which was impossible. The enormity of the place was mind-bending, the artwork majestic: such beauty, such grace. Everywhere you looked, massive amounts of bronze, gold, marble, and paint molded, sculpted, and occupied every inch of its insides. The idea that man was able to create such a structure left me speechless, left me in awe, and at the same time the place left me as hollow as its cavernous and ominous insides. For some reason, I felt as far away from nature and the universe as I ever had.

"*Tutta la mente* (the whole mind)," said D'scuzzi as he looked up at the dome above. "Art-a and-a science melded together in perfect unison, in perfect harmony, in perfect balance."

"Like a good gelato," I said as I gazed closely at the dome's structure and the hundreds of mosaics that lined its walls.

"Yes. Yes. Like a good gelato. For Renaissance artists and other men like our friend Bruno, they learned to use all of their mind. Intellect, true intellect, was both-a analytical and-a intuitive. A scientist and an artist. The known and the unknown. Words and images. Movement and stillness."

I took my eyes off the dome above and looked at him. "Movement and stillness?"

"Science is a doing thing. It's movement, it solves things. Art is a being thing. It's stillness. It evokes things. Men of the Renaissance had the capacity for both. They knew the value of both. They had learned a proper balance," he said.

Movement. Stillness. Balance. It's raining coconuts from the universe!

"They knew when to use one." He held up his left hand. "And when to use the other." He held up his right hand. "And when to use them both." He raised both arms high in the air similar to the way Manuel had done in the Sayulita jungle.

He dropped his arms to his side and looked at me. "That was the path to the truth. They balanced the swing-a."

"The swing?" I asked.

He looked up at the ten-story-high bronze canopy that we stood next to. "Since the Greeks, Western thought has swung back-a and forth-a between the rational and the intuitive, until the Renaissance, where there was an attempt at a balance. The

Romantics tilted it a bit back toward the intuitive for a little while." He looked at me. "I believe-a you Americans tried a similar experiment in the '60s but science, technology, and rational thought has pretty much-a ruled with an iron hand since the time of the Renaissance."

The path my great-great-grandfather had warned against.

"But didn't Bruno and the other freethinkers advocate rational thought?"

"They used rational thought as a way to the truth. But what they were fighting, what they were truly rebelling against was authority, tradition, and dogmatic thought. Yet like-a anything, some took it too far. Some made rational thought the gold standard. Some made it the only way to think, the only path-a to the truth. Eventually, they became the authority, the tradition. They became-a what they had rebelled against. They were now in power, and like-a the ones before them, didn't want to give it up. Whatever didn't fit their new model or wasn't proven correct by their new standards was shunned, ridiculed, and wrong-a."

"So, rational thought isn't the problem?" I asked.

"No, no, no. It's using it as your only tool. It's using it at the expense of intuition."

"How do we balance the swing again?" I asked.

He thought about it for a second, spun around, and again was on the move. I followed him as we headed back in the direction from which we had come. After walking the length of a football field, we stepped into a chapel on the left side before the famous holy door. I don't know for a fact if the door in question was famous or holy, but a man standing next to it thought so. He was telling his children it represented Christ, the Savior, who, according to the Apostle John, said of himself, "I am the door: by me if any man enters he shall be saved."

I was out of luck. It was locked. However, I got to see the man himself, his limp body lying across his mother's open arms.

"Everything you need to know-a about the Renaissance, about-a balance, is in this five-foot-eight piece of chiseled marble.

Stillness and movement in perfect balance. In perfect unison," D'scuzzi said as we walked closer to it.

I had never seen anything like it. Despite it being made of solid marble, despite Jesus's limp, dead, still body, you could see movement in it. Movement and stillness. I don't know how, but you could. The folds of Mary's clothes, the skin, bones, and muscles of Jesus—it was alive. This beautiful statue moved. Motion, energy, vibration flowed. Unlike on the river with Reverend Willy where it was underwater and invisible to the eye, here you could not only see it but feel it. "What does it mean?" I asked.

For the first time, D'scuzzi didn't have an opinion. "I don't-a know, but I'm sure he does," he said, looking at the statue.

Surely, he wasn't talking about Jesus. And if he was, Jesus didn't look like he was in the mood for a conversation. "Who?" I asked.

"The same guy who designed the dome," he said as he pointed to an inscription on the sash across Mary's chest.

I took a closer look. It read, "Michelangelo Buonarroti made this."

I suppose the Muse's jealousy must have had enough, because D'scuzzi looked up and was lost in thought for a good minute. He then smiled and said, "I gotta go."

He then walked away. I guess the brush was calling. I hoped D'scuzzi's associate would too. I needed to have a chat with Michelangelo, the architect and artist.

He had the answers I was looking for. And those answers, I was now sure, hid somewhere inside the Sistine Chapel.

CHAPTER FIFTY-SIX

It was after 9:30 a.m., and the inside of St. Peter's was now bustling. The tour groups had been allowed in, and despite the fact that the Statue of Liberty could lie down inside with room to spare, I was starting to get a touch claustrophobic. Don Alessandro had gotten out in time. It was now wall-to-wall people, all eager and hungry to see the grand shrine. I passed the holy door and escaped through one that was open—one that made no promises of redemption.

I dodged in and out of the masses to the ticket office of the Sistine Chapel to see if by some weird stroke of luck they might have a cancellation or a ticket in the near future. They didn't. I hung outside and asked people waiting to get in if anyone had an extra ticket to sell. After hearing no from what seemed like every accent in the world, I made my way back into the Square and stood on the steps looking out at the throngs of humanity. Despite the dampness and cold, the Square too had morphed into a sea of people. It looked like a colony of ants after a foot crashed into its castle. Maybe one of them had an extra ticket?

I began to make my way through the madness as the zombies, buried in their cell phones, talking, texting, tweeting, and taking pictures of themselves, glided by, around and through me, as though I wasn't there. I stopped to try to take it all in, to slow down, to make contact, but it was too late. I wasn't in their world. I was a ghost. I was as invisible and unimportant as the cloud of mist that covered us all. I suppose the universe wasn't ready for me to see the Sistine Chapel. I took the hint and got out of there.

A half hour later I stood in a neighborhood bar working on my second espresso as I watched the well-dressed locals motor in and out after a quick shot of the bean. I was as still as possible as the well-organized chaos danced around me. Everybody was on the move. Everybody had a place to go, yet the same energy they ran on, the same energy they exuded, was for some reason no longer available to me. I could watch it. I could see it. I could hear it. I just couldn't feel it. For some reason, I could no longer plug in.

I spent the next several hours roaming the city to see if I could get it back, to see if I could tap back in and get a charge, but it wasn't working.

I found a small cafe overlooking a piazza and grabbed a plate of pasta. I took out my Big Chief Tablet and was hoping to write down my thoughts, but nothing was coming. I was blank. Blank as D'scuzzi's large canvas.

So I watched people in the piazza. Friends laughing together. Couples holding hands, kissing. Families enjoying the holiday air as I sat by myself under a sky of gray. I looked over at a boy and his little dog with big brown eyes, scruffy black hair, gray mohawk, four white paws, and matching white face and chest. He looked like Bodhi, my first friend.

The dog stopped in front of me for a second, and we caught each other's eyes. He gave me the same look Bodhi had the first day we met.

As they passed, a string of holiday lights that hung overhead caught my attention. The third one from the left was flickering at the same pace as one from my front porch back home. Konka had put them up for our first Christmas together because that is what my grandma had done.

A knot slowly began to form in my gut.

I left the cafe and continued to roam around the city in an attempt to reconnect to it and its people. I crisscrossed the city and attended what felt like every Christmas market and festival in town throughout the rest of the day and evening. Despite the frenetic energy that reverberated through my ears from the hordes of holiday crowds, the visual onslaught on my pupils from the holiday lights, and the assault of aromas on my nostrils from fresh pastries, mulled wine, and pine and cedar from the plethora of Christmas trees, I still could not connect. I was on the outside looking in as the moment somehow slipped farther and farther away from my grasp.

I thought about going back to the studio and hiding until the next day, but for some reason kept on wandering. Around midnight I stumbled upon a large outdoor ice rink. In defiance of the time and the cold mist that fell, the rink was still doing a brisk business.

I decided if the city and its people wouldn't join me, then I would join them. I laced up a pair of skates and jumped onto the ice even though I had never seen a frozen lake, pond, or rink. It wasn't my best idea.

When my blades hit the ice, it felt like I had just stepped on a pile of banana peels sitting on top of Vaseline. A second later I was on my butt. I picked myself up and attempted to give it another go. A second later, I was back on my butt. This process continued for another half hour until I nearly took down a few other people with me. They were not pleased. I know this for a fact because they unleashed a barrage of colorfully laced obscenities and insults. Obscenities and insults I knew well. Minus the colorful Italian flare.

Looking up from the ice I saw a hundred pairs of legs that moved in all directions with no particular cadence or rhythm as they glided past me as though I was part of the rink. The laughing, talking, screaming that flowed around me in that stew of movement was the same that had been carried out every day in the halls of my school and cafeteria back home. Sounds I could hear but never be a part of.

I tried to get up from the ice but the talking, the laughing, the shouting, the dull blades of skates carving through the ice, and the Christmas music shooting out the overhead speakers, began to get louder and louder, all mixed in a giant blender swirling around my head, and kept me in my place.

I crawled over the chipped ice to the railing and pulled myself up and eventually made it back to my shoes and firm ground. A half hour later I sat in a dive bar and ordered a shot of tequila and beer. I wasn't sure if I was looking for some liquid courage or just escaping.

I soon found out escaping would not be an option. The universe had other ideas.

Several hours passed as I listened to an eclectic selection of American music that came from the jukebox. I tried to make small talk with the bartender, but he was too busy helping others. The couple next to me only had eyes for each other. The rest of the patrons had already formed their groups and cliques, and from their laughter and contentment didn't seem as if they were looking for a new member. There was a single guy at the other end of the bar, but the look on his face suggested he might have been there for a while. I knew that look. I knew it well. And despite my current mental state, I wasn't up for the Italian version of the man love-stare.

I had another shot of tequila and stayed put. At the same time the heat from my Mexican friend began its trip into my shoulder blades, Willie Nelson's voice began its trip out through the speakers.

As the song played, what was left of the crowd went about their business. I, on the other hand, was hypnotized by Willie's soulful voice and the song's sad melody. I slipped further and further into my past. By the end of the song, I was transported back home, back to Scooter's bar with my other family. I looked up from my empty beer glass and around the room to all the strangers, but it was neither Georgia or any of them on my mind.

The knot in my gut began to tighten. I wasn't sure what was happening, what was going on. I started to slip further down the rattlesnake hole. I needed to talk to someone, someone I knew.

Without thinking, I pulled D'scuzzi's spare phone out of my

pocket, walked out of the bar, and called another one, 6,000 miles away. It was Friday evening back home, and the place should have been jumping. It was.

"Scooter's," said a voice on the other end of the phone. A voice I didn't recognize over the loud music and crowd noise.

"Is Eddie there?" I asked.

"He can't come to the phone right now."

"Who's this?" I asked.

"Bobby."

A name I didn't know. "Bobby, is the mayor there?"

"He's here somewhere. Must be takin' a leak or out watching the band. Something I can do for ya?" he asked.

"Can you tell Eddie that Tag called?"

"Who?"

"Tag!"

"I'm sorry. Who?"

"I'll call back later," I said.

"Come on down. The place is rockin'. I gotta run," he said as he hung up the phone.

Life in Sisterdale had moved on without me. I'd known it would, yet knowing it didn't make it any easier. Especially today. I put the technology back into my pocket. But it was too late. The seal was broken. I had eaten the first potato chip, and though it didn't taste good, I was about to eat another.

I told myself no matter what, I wouldn't do it. It wouldn't be right. It would only make things worse. Despite that wisdom and, so far, the fortitude to follow it, someone slipped his hand back into my pocket and took out the phone again. He defied the agreed-to game plan and went rogue. He called El.

She answered on the first ring. "Hello?" she said as if questioning the strange number.

For some reason, I froze. The sound of her voice brought it all back. Her hair. Her skin. Her smell. Those eyes. *Why did I leave?*

"Hello?" she said again.

"Merry Christmas, beautiful," I said as I watched the heavy

mist glide past the Christmas lights hanging in the plaza in which I stood.

There was a long pause. As if she had heard a voice from the dead. "Tag."

"El," I said.

Again. Another long pause.

"El. You okay?"

"Yeah. Yeah. I'm uh...where are you?"

"Rome," I said.

"Rhome, Texas?"

"There's a Rome in Texas?"

"Somewhere," she said.

"The more famous one," I said.

That's when I heard another voice ask her, "Who is it?"

"Give me a minute," she said to the voice.

I heard a car door slam.

"Sorry," she said to me.

"Did I catch you at a bad time?" I asked.

"No. No. Yes. Yes. Kinda. I mean. I'm going to a party."

"With?" I asked.

Again. Another long, uncomfortable pause. Long enough to know the answer.

"It's okay, El. You don't need to answer that. I'll let you go."

"No, no. I want to talk to you but...but..."

"But what?" I asked.

She started to cry. "I met...I met someone...in school...and I..."

"Hey. Hey. It's okay. Really, it's okay, I understand," I said.

The crying became louder then melted into a full-blown sob. Neither of us spoke as I could hear the tears roll off her cheeks. I stood still as a group of drunk people staggered passed me.

"I miss you," I finally said.

No response.

"I just wanted to say... I love you," I said.

"I, I...can't talk right now. I'm sorry. I'm so sorry. I have to go," she said.

The line went dead.

The person who had taken the phone out of my pocket wanted to play the three-year-old and slam it to the ground, but it wasn't the arrow's fault. It was the Indian. I should never have called.

I suddenly couldn't breathe as the world continued around me, a world that paid no attention, a world that did not care. I looked back at the phone. It was no help. I was out of bullets. I had no one else to call. And even if I did, I no longer wanted to talk.

I looked up to nature, hoping for a ladder, but the sun wasn't shining, the wind wasn't blowing, and the rest of the sky was looking elsewhere as the mist turned to snow and began to fall at a more rapid pace.

Through the falling flakes at a window several floors above me, I caught the eyes of a woman smoking a cigarette. At four in the morning in a city of nearly three million people, it was now only us. Her eyes were familiar. They were thinking, pondering, wanting to help, wanting to make things right, and then they passed through me as though I wasn't there. As smoke clouded the window, the woman disappeared as the curtain shut, and she walked away, never to return.

The snow became heavier, and I was now alone.

My eyes fell to a small garden near my feet, and they stared at the wet dirt between the holiday plants. I grabbed a handful and held its coldness tight.

Then all of the tall old buildings that surrounded me in the square began to inch closer and swallowed up the streets and alleyways, which left no place for escape. I tried to make a move, but a large cape made of lead dropped over my shoulders and kept me in place. A vise began to crank around my heart, squeezing out its last bits of oxygen as my surroundings had transformed into a picture screen in which I was no longer a part.

It was official. I was standing on the dark side of the moon. I knew this to be true because all I could smell was fear.

I closed my eyes and took as big a breath as I could muster and held it. It released itself and took another breath in. Automatically this process continued on and on until Konka's words rang in my ear, "The only way to truly destroy an enemy is to make him your friend."

It was time to face the canvas, time to get comfortable with being uncomfortable, time to have a little chat with the dark wolf and let the taming begin.

I slowly opened my eyes, let the dirt go from my hand, put one foot in front of the other, and began to roam around the city facing that part of myself I hadn't come to terms with, hadn't dealt with.

Like a gladiator about to do battle with a hungry tiger, I stared the dark wolf right in the face, and we walked and walked, and I wasn't going to stop until we came to an understanding. Several hours later, we were still walking. The dark wolf was stubborn. He wouldn't let go of the reins. So I continued to walk and walk until the sun came up and it was time for my morning run. Though that morning I didn't.

I was done running.

CHAPTER FIFTY-SEVEN

I found my way back to the studio for a shower and a change to dry clothes before heading back out. I never made it to the sink. It seems I wasn't the only one who hadn't made it home last night. On the couch smoking a cigarette, covered head to toe with paint, sat a motionless and silent Don Alessandro. Other than a long stream of smoke that escaped his lips when I first laid eyes on him, nothing moved.

I took a look over my shoulder at the big blank canvas. It was no longer blank. I walked over and stood in front of it. Instantly, I was sucked in and became a part. I slipped into the void and was lost. I was as empty as the artist on the couch.

Without warning, tears flowed from of my eyes, yet no sorrow existed in their wetness. I knew nothing about art, but I now knew what an artist was. D'scuzzi had become the vessel that created what was in front of me. The Divine, Frank, that big-ass library in the sky had flowed right through him and poured genius onto the canvas. An abstract of thousands of strokes mixed and matched in different directions in a rainbow of colors placed in the perfect area without conscious thought.

From a rational or scientific point of view, I couldn't prove what was on the canvas was art, or beautiful, or extraordinary. But it was. True as gravity. I just couldn't produce the math.

I looked back at Don Alessandro on the couch. He was vacant. Gone. Like Konka, D'scuzzi had disappeared. The Me had turned into We.

I'm not sure how long I stood there, and time wasn't keeping score. Then Don Alessandro made a move, and my concentration broke. He got up from the couch and walked over. I wanted to express what I felt as I stood in front of his masterpiece, but my vocabulary wasn't up to speed. It didn't matter. He already knew. He grabbed me by the shoulders, looked through the water in my eyes, and gave me a big kiss right on the lips. He smiled, put on his coat and hat, and slipped out the door.

A smile of my own took over the room as I stood alone in his studio. We both had spent the day in the condition of aloneness. While I was drowning in the crowd, he swam in the solitude. I the prisoner and he, the free man.

The technology in my pocket began to vibrate. I pulled it out and took a look. Christmas had come a few days early.

It was the associate.

CHAPTER FIFTY-EIGHT

The associate's text would lead me right back to the lion's den, but at that hour of the morning, the masses were gone. The claustrophobia and chaos of yesterday had been taken over by solitude and peace. St. Peter's Square was quiet and a white blanket of clean snow had replaced the cold, damp mist.

But it wouldn't have mattered. I was in a different place. While my cape hadn't disappeared, it was untied, and I knew it would take some time for it to slide off my shoulders and hit the ground for good. I suppose it took a while to put it on and it would take a while for it to fall off, but at least it no longer could choke me.

I now knew what he looked like, what he felt like. The dark wolf and I had spent a whole evening together, and I was no longer afraid. I now understood him. We weren't friends yet, but he would never again be in control.

As I stood next to an outside wall of the Sistine Chapel, I heard a voice say, "Don't stand too close."

In front of me was a movie-star-attractive Italian man, who looked like he had just left a cocktail party. I should have known he was there. His cologne had showed up a good minute before he did.

"Why?" I asked him.

"You see those stained-glass windows?" The man pointed overhead.

"Yes," I said, looking up.

"They have special holes in them."

"What for?"

"To pour hot tar out of," he said.

"Why would they do that?"

"To keep armies from overtaking the building."

"I don't have an army," I said.

"I guess you're safe."

The associate had arrived.

"Merry Christmas," he said as he handed me a pass for a semi-private tour of the chapel.

I tried to give him money but he said D'scuzzi and he had an arrangement. I didn't ask. One of his lady friends worked for the tour company and had secured my pass. I suppose they had an arrangement as well. Before I could thank him, he turned and was gone. A minute later so was his cologne.

CHAPTER FIFTY-NINE

On a busy day, 35,000 people pass through the Sistine Chapel. If you get a good twenty-minute view before they shuttle the cattle out the door, you've seen and experienced more than most, or so I'm told.

I, on the other hand, was blessed with a full hour and only had to share the space with a few guides and about thirty other people. Not sure the price of admission, but I was grateful for the arrangements.

The excitement and anticipation that were running through me escaped as soon as we stepped inside. I took a look up and knew I was in trouble. The magnitude, scope, and details, while beyond magnificent and breathtaking, were plain overwhelming. If Michelangelo had left some clue or message above, an hour wasn't going to be enough time to find it, much less figure it out.

Our guide took quick control of our group and peppered us with facts and history as he guided us through every panel and wall. My focus never left the ceiling as it scanned each fresco, each figure, each color, looking for something, anything, that could answer my quest.

After forty-five minutes of constant information and inspection, I was no closer to what I had come here for: an answer. The only thing apparent to me was that Michelangelo was one, a genius, and two, a big fan of muscular, nude men.

Maybe I am wrong. Maybe what I've been looking for doesn't exist. Did I misinterpret a clue from the universe along the way? Did I make up a story that wasn't there? Did the crafty Ego lead me astray? Have I been on the wrong path?

Those thoughts flowed through my noggin as we were freed to roam the chapel on our own. The majority of the patrons' curiosity and interest must have been satisfied because only a handful of us were left.

I had no idea what I was looking for, and none of the nude men on the walls were talking.

I took a deep inhale of the musty air that smelled as old as the chapel itself, pulled my mandala necklace from beneath my shirt, and took a long look. I tried to remember every image and detail from my great-great-grandfather's cave, hoping I could somehow connect his room with this one. Despite my best efforts, it wasn't working. I took one last look around hoping something might catch my eye, but nothing did. As my luck and time ran out, I put the mandala back under my shirt as a security guard passed by and said, "Smaller than the one above."

"What?" I asked

"Your mandala. It's smaller than the one above."

I looked up at the ceiling. "Where?"

"The ceiling," he said.

I looked back up and took the whole ceiling in as one. "Holy shit," I said to myself.

The ceiling as a canvas for his masterpiece was divided up into geometrical patterns similar to my mandala. Michelangelo had painted his masterpiece within a gigantic mandala. Talk about not being able to see the forest for the trees.

"Why paint within a mandala?" I asked.

"The mandala is a symbol of balance and harmony. Maybe Michelangelo was trying to tell us something?" he smiled and walked away.

I hurried close to the center of the chapel, like I had in my great-great-grandfather's cave, took a seat, and looked back up, hoping to find another clue. Unfortunately, there were no wolves and no Indian chief with light coming out of his chest. However, almost directly above was the most famous of Michelangelo's panels: the creation of Adam, where God stretches out his finger toward Adam's finger and sparks life into him. Our group had seemed to spend the most time on this one, yet nothing had sparked in me other than I had seen a partial version of that image back in the chapel bar in Mexico.

Two panels back, Adam and Eve ate the forbidden fruit from the tree of knowledge of good and evil. I don't know if there were any hidden messages, but if that was where humanity first became conscious, first became aware, then that was the moment Ego was born. The immature baby Ego, alone, separate, and naked. He had split off, no longer one, for the first time not feeling part of nature. Was that the evil?

Our guide said Michelangelo had used the more traditional story as his guide and thus painted a fig tree instead of an apple tree—the same kind of tree Buddha had meditated under to receive enlightenment. Was that the good? I don't know, but it was more than interesting that Buddha tamed his ego at the same place it was born.

I pulled out my Big Chief Tablet and a pen and had begun to write a thought down when I felt a presence close to me. Had the Inquisition found its guilty party, or was security back to tell me to get my butt off the floor? Before I had time to look up I heard a female voice ask, "American Indian?" as a body plopped down right next to me.

Shoulder to shoulder I sat next to a fair-skinned, dark-haired, blue-eyed girl with a raspy French accent and a seductive perfume.

"What?" I asked as though I hadn't heard the question.

"Are you American Indian?"

"Partially," I said.

She looked deep into my eyes and studied my face. "I thought so."

"Is it the hair?" I asked.

"Cheekbones," she said. She touched my face with her hand as if to make sure. "High cheekbones." As she took away her hand she asked, "Left-handed?"

I looked at the pen in my left hand. "I write with both, but yes."

"You're in good company. Da Vinci, Raphael, Michelangelo, the three greatest artists of their time, all left-handed. A lot of artists are."

"I'm not an artist."

"Everyone's an artist," she said. "Both hands?"

"My grandfather insisted."

"Why?"

"You ask a lot of questions."

"That's how you find the answers," she said.

For some reason, I instantly liked her. "Balance," I said.

"Are you?" she asked.

"Am I what?"

"Balanced?"

"Working on it. And you?"

"Almost never," she said.

"Nicole," said a voice from a few yards away.

Standing above us was a man and what looked to be the rest of the family.

"Nous serons à l'extérieur (We'll be outside)," he said.

"Oui, Papa (Yes, Father)," she replied.

As they left, I noticed we were the only two left from the groups.

"Ta famille? (Your family?)" I asked.

"Oui. Tu parles français? (Yes. You speak French?)"

"Un peu (A little)," I said.

For some reason that made the fair skin on her cheeks turn the shade of a pale raspberry. "Where's your family?" she asked.

"They're not here."

"They didn't want to see the Sistine Chapel?"

"I'm here by myself," I said.

"In Rome, by yourself?"

"Yes."

"How old are you?"

"Eighteen."

"What are you running from?"

"Nothing anymore," I said.

"What are you looking for?"

"What makes you think I'm looking for something?"

"I've been watching you."

"All this beautiful art and you're watching me? That's a mistake."

"No such thing as mistakes," she said directly into me.

My high cheekbones suddenly felt warm. To cool them off I looked back up toward the ceiling and broke our connection. "I'm not sure what I'm looking for," I said.

"Did your guide tell you Michelangelo hated the whole project?"

"He didn't use the word 'hate' but mentioned Michelangelo saw himself as more of a sculptor than a painter," I said.

"The best fresco painters of the time were brought in to paint the walls, but Michelangelo was given the ceiling, despite the fact he had never done fresco painting in his life."

"Why not turn it down?" I asked.

"You didn't say no to Pope Julius II. His nickname was *le terrible*. If you wanted to live, you painted. So, that's what Michelangelo did, except he left clues to let the rest of the world know how he felt about it."

"Where?" I asked.

She pointed up. "The most obvious is in the third panel, where God creates the sun and moon. Afterward, God flies away but Michelangelo decides to leave the backside of his robe open with his ass hanging out pointing to the papal ceremony area down here."

As I looked at the bare bottom of God above, she said, "God is mooning the pope in his own chapel."

"Could be just a bare ass," I said.

"On its own, maybe. But Michelangelo wasn't finished." She did a one-eighty, spun around on the floor, and faced in the opposite direction.

I followed her lead.

"Above the entrance, he was supposed to paint Jesus but instead painted Pope Julius II with two small angels looking on from behind. You'll notice the angel on the left has his right arm flung over the shoulders of the other angel and the back of his hand is pointed to Julius. You'll also notice there's a separation between the angel's fingers. Now, look at the panel with the Cumaean Sibyl." She pointed to a panel up on our left. "Behind the Sibyl, he also painted two small angels looking on. And again the right arm of one angel is flung over the shoulders of the other, and the back of his hand with the separation between the fingers is also pointed to Julius over there.

"Okay," I said.

"But what you can't see, because of the distance and size, is that in both, the angels have their thumbs sticking out between that separation, between their middle and index fingers like this," she said while giving me a close-up demonstration with her fingers. "During the Middle Ages that was by far the most obscene gesture a person could make."

I looked at the angels behind the Sibyl and then turned and again looked at the ones behind Pope Julius II.

"Are you saying Michelangelo was giving the finger to the pope?" I said.

"Yes, that's exactly what he was doing. Not only from two different angels but two different angles."

"How did he get away with it?"

"From here it's impossible to make out, but up close it's obvious. And no one back then other than Michelangelo ever got up close," she said as she looked into me a few inches from my face.

"How do you know this?" I asked, looking directly back at her and not pulling away.

"Unbalanced," she said.

"Might be," I said.

"And I might be an art history major at the Sorbonne in Paris."

"Impressive."

"Not really. Just my day job."

"You have a night job?"

"Not yet," she whispered as her perfume held me in place.

I was clearly in over my head. She pulled away and began talking again. "But the real insult, the real middle finger was telling the world you don't need the church to speak to God."

"Where did he do that?"

"In the first panel where God is separating light from darkness. It's impossible to see from here, but researchers recently found something strange with the way he painted God's throat."

I looked up at it. "It looks like a throat."

"Exactly. It's supposed to, but it's anatomically incorrect."

"Maybe it was a mistake."

She gave me a long look.

"No such thing as mistakes," I said.

"Michelangelo, like Da Vinci, was an expert on the human form, internal as well as external. It wasn't a mistake. Also, look at the angle he painted God. The neck, the throat area is pointing down at us. He wanted us to see it. He put it right in front of our noses for a reason. He wanted future generations to discover it, to know the truth."

"That we can communicate with God directly," I said.

"Yes. And in Michelangelo fashion, he hung it right over the altar, above the head of every pope from then till now."

"But he wanted to stay alive so he hid the message?"

"Yes. It wasn't an uncommon trick for artists of his time to hide messages in their paintings. They achieved this by combining different layers of meaning. You might say a double meaning."

"An illusion," I said.

"Yes. An illusion."

"So what is the other meaning?" I asked.

"The researchers looked closely at his version of the throat and discovered it was the exact shape and dimension as a human brain stem."

"Michelangelo put a brain stem in God's throat."

"Yes."

"Why?"

"All signals coming into and out of our brains must pass through the brain stem."

"Including the voice of God," I said.

"Including the voice of God. Or to put it another way, our connection to him isn't through the church but through ourselves," she said.

I looked back up to the first panel. "Maybe it's just a throat."

"Maybe. But why would he show us how?"

"How to what?" I asked.

"Connect to him," she said.

"God?"

"God, Yahweh, Jehovah, Allah, Shiva, Cujo, Father, intelligence, the light, the it."

"The it?" I asked.

"Lie down," she said.

"Now?"

"Yes now."

I followed instructions and we both lay back and were directly under the Creation of Adam.

"What do you see?" she asked.

"I see an outstretched God trying to touch the finger of what looks like a not-too-interested Adam."

"You know why Adam looks like that?" she asked.

"Because God hasn't given him life yet."

"Adam's eyes are already open, so he's already alive."

"Good point." I thought about it more. "God isn't giving him life, he's giving him energy, intelligence," I said.

"Yes. Intelligence. But God isn't just giving him intelligence, he's transferring intelligence."

"Transferring?"

"Yes. It wasn't a one-time thing. Anytime man wants to touch that energy, anytime he needs the intelligence of the universe, anytime he needs a spark from God, he just needs to tune in for it to be transferred."

Intelligence transfer. The it. The energy transferred from God, the universe, the Divine, the big-ass library in the sky, from Frank to us.

"How do we tune in?" I asked.

"Look. It's right in front of you."

I studied the panel for the hidden meaning yet couldn't see it.

"Look at the angels surrounding God, look at the shroud that covers them. What does it look like?"

I took another look. There it was. "It's a brain! It's a cross-section of a human brain," I said.

"A physician discovered it about twenty years ago, and unlike God's throat in the first panel, it is anatomically correct," she said.

Once you saw it, it was obvious. The brain, the noggin, the noodle, the computer, *el cerebro*. My sweet, sweet coconut.

"Also notice the right hand of God is transferring that intelligence through the left hand of Adam," she said.

"He's left-handed," I said.

"Yes."

"Adam is an artist. Everyone is an artist. And the brain is our pen, our brush, our instrument," I said.

"We just have to know how to use it, know how to play it."

That sounded like something Konka would say. I looked back up at the panel. "And Michelangelo showed us how?" I asked.

"It's hard to say for sure, but it's quite interesting"—she looked back up at the fresco—"where he placed God's right arm."

I stared at his right arm stretched out through the forehead of the surrounding brain.

"That is the position of our prefrontal cortex, our frontal lobes." She took her finger and placed it on my forehead between my eyebrows in the exact position as Reverend Willie had. "That is where we have the power to focus, concentrate, where we have the greatest sense of self, where we think and problem solve."

"Our consciousness. Our ego," I said.

"Yes."

"Art history major?"

"And pre-med."

"Pre-med?"

"Something to fall back on."

"Being a doctor is your fallback?"

She smiled and tapped my forehead with her finger. "When that area is still, quiet, or shuts down, artists are at their best. Energy, vibrations, electricity flows."

"Movement and stillness. Man can communicate with the universe. We can receive its message," I said.

"And it ours."

"With what?" I asked.

"The medulla," she said.

"Say again, doctor."

"The medulla. The part of our brain that doesn't use conscious thought—that part that controls our breathing, our heart rate." She moved her finger from my forehead and placed it over my heart. "The part that's automatic. The part where the soul speaks."

"Where's that located?"

"In God's throat," she said.

At which point we heard someone clearing his. It wasn't God. Just Nicole's father.

"*J'arrive* (I'm coming)," she said as we both pulled ourselves up from the floor.

As her father walked away, I took another look at God's throat in the first panel. I believe the medulla is part of the brain stem. If correct, was that our antenna to the universe: our eyes, ears, nose, hands, tongue to that universal energy? Is that how our mind and heart communicate? How they connect? How the heart can see, hear, smell, feel, taste? Is that how we can properly invoke Frank?

"Anyway, that's my theory," she said, breaking my concentration.

"But is it correct?"

"I don't know. Only Michelangelo knows for sure."

"Maybe it's delusions from an unbalanced mind," I said.

"Might be."

There was a slight pause in the conversation as we looked at each other.

"So, what are you and your unbalanced mind doing later?" I asked.

"Flying home."

"That's a mistake."

"No such thing," she said.

"Might be."

Another pause.

"Did you find what you were looking for?" she asked.

"I think so," I said into her as the raspberries returned.

"So, what's next on your travels?" she asked.

"Don't know."

"When will you know?"

"When the universe tells me," I said.

"Are you sure it hasn't already?" She grabbed my pen and with her left hand wrote her number down in the Big Chief Tablet. "In case your medulla isn't working," she said.

As she finished writing her number she noticed the words *La danse de l'esprit*.

"*La danse de l'esprit*?" she asked.

"The spirit dance," I said.

"It could also mean soul dance or even mind dance," she said.

"Mind dance?" I asked.

"*Esprit* in French can also mean mind."

"The Mind Dance. The Soul Dance," I said.

"Double meaning?" She pulled me down and kissed me on both cheekbones. "*Au revoir*," she said.

"*Au revoir*, Nicole," I said.

"It's Nicky," she said and walked away.

"Nicky," I said.

She stopped and turned back.

"You don't know my name," I said.

"But I know who you are."

With that, she walked toward Michelangelo's largest fresco, *The Last Judgment*. Jesus in the middle of the painting as the sinners and the saved swirled around him on their path to either heaven or hell. She looked up at it and stopped cold.

"What?" I asked.

She turned back toward me. "Son of man," she said.

"Who?"

"Jesus. The son of man. That's what he called himself."

"Okay."

"In sanskrit, man means mind. Son of mind."

"So?"

She smiled, turned, and disappeared through a door beneath the west wall.

I now stood in the Sistine Chapel alone.

I looked at my Big Chief Tablet. La danse de l'esprit. The Mind Dance. The Soul Dance. It was a double meaning. Konka had given me the answer to the problem. It was with me my whole journey. Three simple words. Right in front of my nose. The answer, hidden in the riddle. That's how he was able to disappear, how he was able to contact the universe at will. Konka was in total control of his mind. The left and right, logic and intuition, ego and soul, doing and being, the scientist and artist, were in total balance. They didn't fight. They danced.

I looked back up to the ceiling to where God was separating light from darkness.

That's what the white wolf was doing in my great-great-grandfather's cave. He was looking deeply into himself, to the dark side of the moon, to the dark wolf. He was separating the darkness from within himself so he could see him, so he could shine a light on him, so he could tame him. Once he did and the dark wolf was no longer in charge, peace was restored, the brothers could dance, and the Indian chief received intelligence from the universe. Frank ignited him with energy. He gave him a spark that radiated through his being.

La danse de l'esprit. That was the path. The way. A permanent road to freedom. It wasn't the white road. It wasn't the red road. It was a new road. A new path. One where ego serves Soul Brother instead of controlling him. And a way for technology to care for nature instead of destroying it.

Looking down, I stared at what was left of the bracelet that Sama had given me. I could barely make out the letters that spelled DANCE.

I looked back up to Jesus in *The Last Judgment*. I don't know how I'd missed it before, but Michelangelo had painted a light around Jesus that illuminated from his soul. His body was twisting, and both arms swung in movement - the left, the right, in perfect balance, in perfect unison.

The son of man was dancing.

The mind was dancing.

All heaven. No hell.

CHAPTER SIXTY

"Lady with the grin at two p.m.," it read.

I looked up from the technology and would soon head toward the Louvre. Every Friday afternoon I got a decoded text from Nicky where to meet her. It usually had something to do with art or history and involved a museum. It was a game she loved to play and it forced me to do two things. Bone up on my historical art and purchase a phone. I had done both.

I was still a touch wary of the phone, but when a smart, sexy, fun young lady insists on it, you make sacrifices. I don't know if you would call us together. Neither of us had yet the need to define it, but we were spending more time with each other and having a blast. While she was in school I wandered around Paris, writing daily in my Big Chief Tablet. It was getting full, and Nicky suggested it was time to get another, perhaps one with a keyboard. I'm sure that made more sense, but I loved the texture of the paper and the connection to the hand—the left hand. More technology would have to wait.

It had been over two months since I'd arrived, and springtime had finally cracked its door open. I didn't know how long I would stay or what my next move was, and so far the universe had kept quiet. I guess until it spoke I wouldn't leave and I'd continue to write. I suppose there are worse places.

I put the phone in my backpack and looked out over the Luxembourg Gardens. It had become one of my favorite spots to not only meditate but to write, especially now the weather was becoming more cooperative. I looked back down and flipped through the filled pages of the Big Chief Tablet, stopping when I got back to the first page. After leaving the Sistine Chapel, I had scribbled a paragraph under where Konka had written *La danse de l'esprit.* It read,

The Mind Dance.

A beautifully orchestrated dance between the two sides that brings out the best in each. Instead of fighting each other, they know when to lead and when to follow. Both know their roles. Their responsibilities. The brothers become best friends and work as one, each relying on the other's strengths to fill the hole in their own deficiencies. Eventually, it becomes a self-fulfilling prophecy. The more they dance in this fashion, the stronger they become. The stronger they become, the more they dance. The dance becomes automatic and the swing perfectly balanced. The dance becomes one. Doing and being at the same time. The Me becoming the We.

Was this what Konka wanted me to do? To share the wisdom in these pages, to spread this knowledge to other young people, to show them that dance? The Mind Dance.

I'm sure the universe would toss another coconut to let me know for sure.

While I was lost in thought, a ray of sunshine broke through the cloud layer and landed on my Big Chief Tablet at the spot where I'd been reading. I put my hand out so the ray had a place to sit. I followed that beam from my hand through the naked space in the tree branches and back up to its source. Nearly ninety-three million miles away, yet closer than my thoughts. Movement and stillness. Intelligence transfer on perfect display for all to see.

I stared at the beam as it rested in my palm.

Woodstock was wrong.
You can catch the sun.

ACKNOWLEDGMENTS

I want to thank my friend and editor Rhonda Hayter for keeping the ship sailing in the right direction. If not for your insights, honesty, and big brain I would still be drowning in a maze of my design. The truth is sometimes hard to swallow when one can't see it. I can't thank you enough for helping me see it in the nicest and most encouraging way possible.

I am a better writer because of you.

I would also like to thank Lois Friedman for being that extra set of eyes that pulled out the unwanted weeds in the garden. A slow and tedious process I am ill-equipped to handle. Thanks for being part of the process.

A big thanks to Brooks Becker for the final proofread and for correcting the Spanish and French translations. You went above and beyond to help make this thing shine. You are a credit to your profession.

A special thanks to Laura Duffy, who somehow came up with the perfect cover despite all of the wrong roads I led her down. Your patience, professionalism, and creativity are beyond appreciated.

I want to thank Bodie for the unconditional love, licks, and forcing me out of the cave after a long day to play fetch. You saved my sanity.

I want to thank my better half, Beth. I could not have done this without you. Thanks for listening, reading, re-reading, again and again, for being that sounding board I could bounce off of, for giving me the alone time needed to get through this, for still speaking to me whenever I abruptly left the room in mid-conversation to write down a sudden thought, and for not calling the authorities as the walls of our second bedroom began to resemble an FBI sting operation.

Most importantly, thank you for understanding. I know it's not easy watching your man spend several years of his life on a project with zero promises.

Thanks for being a true partner and for taking care of me when I needed it most.

Lastly, I'd like to thank my parents for always letting me follow the beat of my drum.

Also,

ABOUT THE AUTHOR

After twenty years pursuing other goals, Joseph Clinton found himself without a passion or direction.

A year later while visiting his father in South Texas, they found him.

It was a 100-degree day in a small bar with no air conditioning in an old country town the size of a bus stop.

Four roosters, two dogs, and one truck patrolled the outside - the mayor, the bartender, a bull, a rattlesnake, a bobcat, a hawk, him, his dad, a photo of Willie Nelson and a jukebox full of Hank Williams melodies, the inside.

Several hours and many beers later he had an idea. That night he sat his butt down and wrote the beginning of what he believed to be a short story.

After three years, his butt finally arose out of the chair with his first novel.

You can visit him online at josephclinton.com

Made in the USA
Las Vegas, NV
12 April 2023